Starworld

Starworld

AUDREY COULTHURST

and

PAULA GARNER

CANDLEWICK PRESS

Copyright © 2019 by Audrey Coulthurst and Paula Garner

First edition 2019

Library of Congress Catalog Card Number pending
ISBN 978-0-7636-9756-3

19 20 21 22 23 24 LSC 10 9 8 7 6 5 4 3 2 1

Printed in Crawfordsville, IN, U.S.A.

This book was typeset in ITC Giovanni.

Candlewick Press
99 Dover Street
Somerville, Massachusetts 02144

visit us at www.candlewick.com

For Shy and Maud

Sam

If I have a superpower, it's invisibility.

Like the perpetually overcast skies of Portland in winter, I'm part of the background — a robot with a disappearance drive, the dullness against which everyone else shines. My nondescript jeans and hoodies, along with the absence of any observable personality, allow me to slip through entire days with negligible human interaction.

With the power of invisibility comes the freedom to day-dream, which is useful because I've never been a fan of reality.

Reality overflows with unanswerable questions:

How many colors does it take to properly render a nebula?

Why do people like having televisions on in the background?

Would my mom be more or less tolerable in a gravity-free environment?

Thinking of the world in terms of fantasy is sometimes the only thing that helps me survive. Homework is the paperwork that keeps my kingdom running. Puddles that soak my shoes could be portals to other dimensions. The legions of people who overlook me in this hellpit, better known as high school, are trolls to be dodged or ghosts to slip between.

It's barely a month into senior year and I've already built a fortress of enormous canvases in the back of the art classroom, staking out a corner that makes the most of the weakening natural light as fall edges toward winter. There isn't much of a view through the windows — just the greenway that hugs the south side of the school heading back toward the football fields. I have the perfect vantage from which to see the occasional stoner or handsy couple heading into the woods when they're supposed to be in class. Sometimes I spin stories in my head of what their lives might be like, knowing only that they're nothing like mine.

As usual, the art room is populated with a mix of dedicated artists and people just looking for easy As, all of whom are happy to treat me like a piece of furniture. I swirl oil paints together on my palette, waiting for just the right shade of indigo to develop as I mull over some equations I'm certain will be on the AP Physics quiz later. Lost in a mix of math and pigments, I nearly crap a clutch of flaming dragon eggs when an unfamiliar voice behind me softly says, "Oh god, this is perfect!"

I swivel around on my stool only to be shocked immobile by the girl standing in front of me. Her wavy dark-brown hair cascades over a sweater the color of seafoam, and a little star pendant rests between her collarbones.

Zoe Miller spoke to me. I've clearly entered a parallel dimension.

Unfortunately, there are no nearby supply closets in which to hide from the inevitable shame I'm about to bring upon myself if I try to respond. With my brain short-circuiting as I try to determine why she's talking to me, my eyes drift slowly down until I'm staring her right in the high beams. And when I realize what I'm doing, heat rises into my cheeks until I'm sure they're a shade best used to paint the ass of a fire truck.

"This is amazing, Sam!"

I force myself to meet her gaze, staring back with the poleaxed expression of a dead fish. Her eyes are an impossible shade between green and blue, dark around the edges and fading into a hint of unexpected bronze near the pupils.

It seems highly unlikely that Zoe would know my name. This is the girl with a transcendent voice who made half the assembly cry with a song from *Les Mis* in middle school, the girl pretty enough to coast on her looks but whose name regularly appears on the high honor roll, the girl at least half the school worships from afar. Thankfully, unlike those dickhats, I'm immune to the senseless adulation of beautiful people—largely because, with the exception of my best friend, Will, I mostly like to pretend other humans don't exist.

"This landscape is so surreal," she says, pointing to a

finished canvas, seemingly not bothered by my corpselike response. "And the light! It's amazing."

I turn to the painting she's talking about. It's one of my smaller ones, about three feet by four, a landscape that kind of looks like the deranged product of a mind meld between Paul Nash and Bob Ross.

She gestures to another painting of a dragon playfully rolling on the grass in front of a castle, the background bedazzled with enough color and glitter to outfit ten marching bands. "This is yours, too? It's so different. It reminds me of a fairy tale I loved when I was little." She smiles at me.

Even though I continue to respond to her compliments with silence and twitchy blinking, she soldiers on.

"Is there any chance you'd consider letting me borrow the landscape? I'm helping with the set design for STOTS, and it's perfect for this year's play." She tosses her dark hair over her shoulder, and a wave of subtle perfume hits me. It may be a rainy fall day in Portland, but the girl smells like pure summer — sunshine and citrus and verdant things.

"What's STOTS?" I finally manage. They must be putting on an awfully strange play for one of my paintings to make sense as part of the set.

She tilts her head at me, as if she's surprised that this isn't common knowledge, which, for all I know, it might be. "Student theater? It stands for Students Take Over the Stage. In the fall we do a show that's completely written, designed, and directed by students, with no teacher supervision. Well, theoretically, anyway." Her expression confuses me. It's warm and kind of conspiratorial — as if she knows me or likes me or something. I feel vaguely hypnotized, which makes me think it'd be wise to flee this situation at Mach 10.

"I don't know," I mumble. Something on display means visibility — the last thing I want this close to freedom. It's finally senior year, and I'm certain my goal of never gracing the pages of the yearbook is within reach.

"We'd be super careful with it," she says. "Everything gets locked up at night." She turns to look at the landscape again, her expression filled with something that looks strangely like admiration or wonder. "It's just so perfect for this play." She raises her graceful eyebrows in a hopeful expression.

The stool squeaks as I shift my weight uneasily. I'm not sure how to respond but am increasingly uncomfortable with the intensity in her eyes. No animal, vegetable, or mineral has ever looked at me like this in the history of my entire life.

"I'm not sure," I say, which is at least marginally better than *wow you smell good please go away but maybe let me sniff your hair first.*

She nods, but I can tell she's disappointed. "Would you at least think about it?" She gives me a smile that makes me feel like my stomach is full of rocket fuel and I just swallowed a match. "Can I give you my number, and you can let me know if you change your mind?"

I pull my phone out of my messenger bag and hand it to Zoe, wondering how I fell into this alternate reality. Five minutes ago, this girl giving me her phone number was as improbable as Pegasus flying me to the moon. I peer around the canvas I was working on until Zoe interrupted me. The rest of the class is somehow completely oblivious to the rupture in the space-time continuum that made this exchange possible.

"Okay if I text myself from your phone so I have your number, too?" she says. "Not that I'm going to keep bugging you." But she glances up as she says the last part, a tiny mischievous smile on her face that fries my few remaining circuits. I nod weakly.

"Thanks," I manage to say as she gives my phone back.

"See you later," she says, and walks off, leaving me gawking after her.

Will is going to lose his mind when I tell him about this. His mom made him take choir freshman year, and Zoe was one of the star singers — he had a hopeless crush on her that he wouldn't shut up about all of fall semester. Thankfully he came to his senses by Christmas, because no one in our social cesspool could ever hope to get a date with her.

In my haste to clean up and get to AP Physics in time to text him before class, I drop my dirty paintbrushes on the floor, ensuring my lateness unless I run. I make a mad dash through the crowded halls and text Will as soon as I take my seat in class.

You are not going to believe who just gave me her phone number.

He immediately responds: Jyn Erso? Princess Peach? Diana Prince?

I roll my eyes. Granted, any of those is about as realistic.

Me: Zoe Miller.

Will: Are you ducking with me?

I keep telling him to fix his phone so autocorrect won't

make him constantly talk about ducks, but he thinks it's funny. Now *quack* has become our code word for times when profanity is best avoided.

Me: **Nope. No quackery.**

The bell rings and I shove my phone into my messenger bag. He's going to have to live with the suspense of not finding out the details until physics is over.

I try to focus on the problems in front of me, but my mind keeps dredging up Zoe Miller: arching eyebrows, seafoam sweater, my humaning failure, her perfect hair. Now that she's gotten within a few feet of me, I can see (or smell) why Will was smitten with her. Instead of launching into my explanation of Newtonian mechanics, I sketch a rocket propulsion system in the margin of my paper to try to get my head back in the game.

"Miss Jones," Mr. Sherman barks as he paces past my desk.

I startle, then hunch lower over my desk. His tolerance of anything resembling daydreaming is on par with the hospitality Satan would offer a snowman.

I abandon the shading on my combustion chamber and start filling in the answers to the questions. I can't afford to get any negative attention from teachers. Flying under the radar with the highest possible GPA is my one-way ticket to an aerospace engineering program at a decent college somewhere — anywhere — that isn't here.

After class I pull out my phone as I let the flow of foot traffic guide me toward my locker and ultimately the hellpit's exit. Will's texted me half a dozen times.

Zoe Miller???? For real?

How the duck did you get her attention?

You better not be making this up.

WTF is going on?

WHY CAN'T YOU TEXT ME BACK IN CLASS LIKE A NORMAL PERSON?

He gave up about halfway through last period, but I'm sure he still checked his phone under his desk every five seconds.

I type: I'm not a normal person. I'm a robot.

He writes: EXPLAIN YOURSELF, ANDROID.

Everyone is grabbing coats from their lockers and pulling their hoods up before they head out into the afternoon. I glance out the window. The pickup area out front is a blur of yellow school buses against the tall evergreens thanks to the raindrops collecting on the glass. I forgot my raincoat this morning, and the walk home will be just long enough to drench me completely. The bus isn't an option — spending ten minutes in an equally enclosed space full of space cockroaches would be preferable to enduring a bus mostly full of freshmen.

Me: Can you give me a ride home? I'll explain on the way there.

Will: What's in it for me?

I lean against my locker and roll my eyes. Our usual bargaining has taken a turn for the hardcore in the past two weeks thanks to his repeated attempts to get me to part with some paladin armor he's been lusting after and can't beat the side quest for in our current favorite game. No doubt he either wants that or for me to play meat shield in some stupid first-person shooter.

Me: First-person shooters this weekend. 2 hours without complaints.

Will: **DEAL.**

I open my locker, revealing a collage of rockets, shuttles, satellites, probes, and rovers designed all over the world. By the time I'm done shoveling books from my locker into my bag, it weighs as much as an adolescent hippo. I slam the locker shut, then look at my phone again.

Will: Is it cool with you if we stop by the comics store on the way?

Why? I text back.

Will: Kitty got a part-time job there . . .

If I were still sitting at a desk, I'd bang my head against it. Kitty always regards Will with the hungry gaze of a velociraptor, and he looks back at her with bloaty heart-eyes, yet he still can't seem to ask her out. Personally, I think she smells kind of like canned green beans, but to each his own.

Me: I guess so. But I have to be home before 5, and I'm docking half an hour from the first-person shooter deal.

If he's going to spend my time trying to grow big enough cojones to ask Kitty out, I'm setting a time limit on it.

Will: Cool. I'm in the car now.

I scurry out the front doors of the school and make a dash for the senior parking lot, where Will's ancient Subaru hatchback is idling with the subtlety of a jackhammer. It's a miracle the thing still runs.

"Your chariot, my lady," Will says as he opens the passenger door from the driver's side with one of his freakishly long arms. The hinges creak ominously, just as one would expect for a vehicle that's twice our age and looks like something salvaged from the set of a horror movie.

"Debrief me on Zoe Miller," he says before I even find the sweet spot in the seat where there aren't any springs digging into my butt.

I explain what happened in art class as he pulls out of the parking lot.

"I wonder why she's working behind the scenes instead of in the show," Will says. "She usually has a leading role."

I shrug. "All I know is what she told me." I don't really pay attention to anything happening at school other than what's necessary to get good grades.

"So why don't you just do it?" he asks. "They'll probably put your name in the play program. That'd be cool. And maybe you could put it on your college applications to make you look more well-rounded. Schools love that stuff."

"It's not like I'd be in the play."

He shrugs. "It's even better. You get credit for involvement without ever having to show your face. You should text her now."

"Ugh," I say, my stomach churning at the thought. But Will has a good point about college applications, which I've already been working on. My grades are good, but the essays are more challenging. What am I supposed to say when I have no life outside of school and gaming with Will? I have about as much interest in extracurriculars as I do in licking the inside of a trash can.

I pull out my phone and scroll down to the bottom of my paltry list of contacts, half expecting Zoe not to be there.

My stomach flutters in an unfamiliar way as I reach her name and remember her eyes. It makes my head hurt thinking about all the colors I'd need to paint them. Even her eyebrows have the kind of long, sweeping arch that begs to be drawn. I'm not sure I'm ready to agree to my painting being put on display in such a public place, but I sort of want to talk to her for some masochistic reason. People sometimes notice my paintings, sure. But they don't look at me the way she did this afternoon. Even though it scared me, I want it to happen again.

"I don't know what to say to her," I say.

"Might I suggest, 'Sure, you can use my painting for the play if you go to coffee with my adorable friend Will'?" He grins impishly. "Even ten minutes with one of the most unattainable girls at school would certainly up my social standing."

"No way. She has a boyfriend," I say. I've often seen her holding hands with Hunter, a basketball player who is part of a social echelon neither Will nor I could ever hope to reach unless gravity underwent a sudden reversal. And even if Hunter were out of the picture, Zoe probably has no shortage of willing suitors. Competition for a girl like her is undoubtedly stiff—in every sense of the word.

"Alas, my princess must be in another castle," Will quips.

"Yeah, the comics shop," I mutter, chucking my phone back in my bag. I can't do it.

I'm spared from having to think about Zoe further as Will launches into a list of Kitty's virtues that he's clearly spent far too many hours developing.

"Why don't you just ask her out already?" I say when he finally takes a breath.

"I'm not sure she likes me as more than a friend."

I snort. "Get your eyes checked — she wants to climb you like a utility pole. You should go for it." Just because I don't see the appeal doesn't mean he shouldn't be happy.

"You think so?" He's all smiles now.

"It makes more sense than stalking her like a creeper," I say. We've had this conversation approximately five hundred times since the beginning of our junior year when she moved from California to Oregon and immediately fell in with his group of friends. I don't understand how his optimism and boneheaded recalcitrance to actually do anything go together so comfortably.

"Maybe," he says, running a hand through his tousled brown hair.

When we arrive at the comics shop, all six and a half feet of Will goes flying out of the car with the eagerness of a gawky puppy. I leave my messenger bag in the car and follow him, manually locking the passenger door since the electric door locks died sometime in the Mesozoic era. The sign above the comic book store reads AWESOMESAUCE COMICS in a neon-green typeface. The smell of freshly baked cookies wafts over me from the place next door, Karen's Kookies. I grimace at the sign. Why businesses feel the need to abuse the English language in order to stand out has never made any sense to me. It's the marketing equivalent of a taxidermist stapling a dead squirrel to his face to advertise his services: a unique idea, but not one that's likely to give customers faith in anything besides the proprietor's stupidity.

We walk into the shop and hardly anyone is in the place. A couple of middle school boys are trying to get their dad to buy them plastic light sabers, and a bored, stoned-looking dude with ragged facial hair and gauged ears watches them from behind the counter.

I scan the place for Kitty so we can get this over with. The mother lode herself is ass-up in the fourth aisle shelving issues of *Squirrel Girl*, wearing a crop top that's wildly out of season, suspenders, and a cat ear headband. Her tiny butt is emphatically swaying to whatever is streaming through her hot-pink earbuds.

"Over here," I say to Will, pointing.

He grabs the sleeve of my hoodie and tugs me in the opposite direction. "Don't let her see us!" he says, his eyes wide as he looks for a place to hide.

"Isn't seeing her the point?" I ask, amused by the panicked expression he's wearing.

"But how do I approach her without it being weird?" he whispers.

"Just go buy the latest issue of *Squirrel Girl*," I say. It's hilarious that he's asking *me* for advice about how not to be weird.

"But what should I say?" He runs his fingers through his hair again, making an even bigger mess of it.

"Ask her if she wants to study together or something. Don't you both have Cass for history?" I can't believe I'm having to coach him through this given that I've got the social skills of a potted plant and would communicate entirely in integrals, surrealist paintings, and spaceship blueprints if I could get away with it.

"You're a genius," he says, and bounces on his toes before heading back to the aisle where Kitty is. I flop down into one of the beanbag chairs at the front of the shop and stare at a mobile of the solar system hanging overhead. The planets move slowly, pushed by air coming through a vent in the ceiling. It bothers me that the model isn't to scale, even though that's impossible: if Earth were the size of a dime, proportionally Jupiter would be half a mile away. I hope someday I'll be one of the people who helps figure out how to cross those unfathomable distances. Maybe I'll even engineer machines capable of exploring new planets. I love finding the intersection between math and art where designs are born, whether it's a miniature rocket my dad helped me build or the pinecone catapult I got in trouble for testing on the mailman's truck when I was ten.

Will's face looms over me a few minutes later, his grin so wide I can practically see his molars. "She said yes!"

"Achievement unlocked." I smile, and then a little wave of sadness follows. I may have talked him into being brave, but it brings my own shortcomings into sharp relief. After more than three years at the same school, I haven't managed to be absorbed into Will's wider circle of friends. I can't even come up with something to text to Zoe, in spite of the fact that "Sure, you can use my stupid painting" is all she needs to hear. How am I going to survive college when I can barely function in the place I've spent my whole life?

Will pulls me off the beanbag, and we head back out to his car. On the way home, he rehashes his interaction with Kitty no fewer than three times. I make vague noises of interest while composing and deleting messages to Zoe until I give up in frustration and check my email.

There I find something I would never have expected: a message from my dad.

He doesn't write very often outside of birthday and holiday cards, probably because I was so upset when he moved to London five years ago that my response rate to his emails has remained close to zero. A familiar surge of anger briefly consumes me, and then I shove it in the black hole where I put all my feelings.

It never occurred to me that I'd be left alone with my mother. Even though my parents divorced when I was six, my dad stayed nearby until he took a job in England. Before he left, his Lake Oswego townhome was one of my favorite places to be. We spent weekend afternoons exploring the tangled woods behind it, and that forest remained an endless source of discovery and magic.

When I was a kid, Dad and I had family traditions for every holiday. Ice cream at Cannon Beach on New Year's no matter how absurdly cold it was outside. Going up to Mount Hood to build a snowman on Presidents' Day. Finding a restaurant where we could eat rabbit on Easter. Alpine slides for the Fourth of July. Labor Day camping. Early dinner at an absurdly fancy restaurant before trick-or-treating on Halloween. Now, any missive from him is a crushing reminder of his absence, what I lost, and what he left me with.

My stomach lurches, and I'm not sure if it's Will's driving or my dad's email. I read the message, hearing every word in his lilting British accent.

Sammy,

How is your autumn so far? The trees are changing here and it always makes me think of you crashing through piles of leaves like a tiny sozzled bulldozer when you were little. I can hardly believe you're eighteen, or that almost three years have passed since I last saw you. It's been far too long, and I miss you so much. Your mother hasn't been keen on you making a trip to the UK in the past, but I feel you've reached the age at which it's your decision. I have a spare bedroom in my flat with your name on it and there's a Doctor Who museum in Upton Park which I've held off visiting because I'd rather go with you. Won't you please consider visiting London?

Love,
Dad

What does he mean Mom hasn't been keen on me visiting? He's never even invited me. Not that I blame him — I haven't exactly rolled out the welcome mat for him in the past few years, given how he ditched me. But in spite of that, alongside the usual churning vortex of anger, a tiny spark of hope blooms in my chest.

He wants to see me.

Then I think of Mom, and the spark winks out.

When Will drops me off, I pull up my hood and dash to my front door, drips slapping onto my head. I fumble with the lock until the door creaks open. As usual, the silent interior of my house holds all the warmth and cheer of a mausoleum. I peer into the kitchen. The clock on the stove reads 4:13 in bright-blue numbers that stand out in the dark. It's four minutes fast, just like every other piece of timekeeping in our house other than our phones, which refuse to obey Mom's need to be ahead of everyone else. My shoes go into the coat closet beside the door, perfectly lined up, and I flip on the porch light and lock the door before flying up the stairs to my room.

My phone dings with a text notification as I drop my bag, which knocks over a haphazard pile of yellowed paperback sci-fi and fantasy novels next to my bed. The text message can't be from Will since he's still driving, so it must be Mom. My stomach drops. If she got stuck late at work or something else threw off her schedule, there's no telling what the rest of my night will hold. Mom plans her life carefully around routines that are comfortable for her. I plan mine around hers. When those plans go awry, both of us fall apart.

I pull out my phone and nearly drop it in surprise when I see who messaged.

Zoe: Still hoping you'll change your mind about the painting . . . ☺

Before I can even process the first text, a second one comes through.

It's like it was made for this show! It evokes the main character's longing for the home he can't remember (another planet). Also, it's incredibly professional-looking. You're really talented.

My stomach does a weird little flip.

I put my phone down on my nightstand for a minute and then pick it up again. The words are still there. She's given me the opening I spent all afternoon trying to figure out how to create. If Will can ask Kitty out without quacking it up, surely I can compose one text message.

Me: *opens databank and activates thinking.exe*

Microseconds after I hit send, I curse my stupidity. Zoe can't possibly even know what I'm talking about. I'm babbling the kind of ridiculous gobbledygook only Will would make sense of, and he probably only understands me because of his obsessive interest in robotics and vintage computers. Attempting to be human is a waste of time. I should do my homework or think about how I'm going to respond to my dad — or if I should even bother. After all, if he wanted to see me, maybe he should have thought about that before he put an ocean between us.

Zoe's response comes through faster than I expected.

admires processing capacity

Instead of flipping, this time it feels like my stomach is trying to exit through a random hole. She's playing my game. I can't resist responding.

Me: *completes processing; concludes that painting may be used*

Quack me.

My immunity to Zoe Miller has been compromised.

Zoe

The October trees sing with crimson and rust and amber
outside the library's great bank of windows. I'm trying to
focus on trigonometry, but the shimmer of the Willamette
River in the late afternoon sun hypnotizes me. It reminds
me of Sam Jones's painting, even though hers had an unreal
quality. I don't understand her reluctance to display her work.
The idea of creating something that extraordinary and not
caring if anyone sees it is something I can't quite fathom.
Approval and admiration are like oxygen to me. What does
Sam survive on?

The ruffling of pages brings me back to the task at hand.
Hunter sits across from me, trying to help me study for the
math quiz I'm anxious about. He knows me well enough to
know we're not going to escape the library and make out in
his car until my work is done. An essay completed or a quiz

well prepared for means a tangle of tongues, the shiver of warm breath in an ear, a large hand gently tracing a small breast . . . Business before pleasure.

"Trig identities: go!" Hunter has my book open, his finger poised over the definition I'm meant to recite.

"Um . . . Sine squared u plus cosine squared u equals one."

"Good! Okay, all done." He smiles at me, all dimples and deep-blue eyes and black-framed nerd glasses. He's at his charming best, and I know it's because there are things he wants from me, most of which hinge on Homecoming, which is fast approaching. He's not a bad person. But if he had a trig identity, it would be uncomplicated and easy to memorize. Like A = B. Boy = horny. Homecoming night = score.

As if to prove my theory, he leans over and brushes my hair out of my face and says, "Hey. Have you thought about Homecoming night?"

I lean away from him and move my hair back so it covers the birthmark on my forehead, which I've always been self-conscious about. The sweep of hair from my side part keeps it covered nicely.

"We'll talk about it later, okay?" I say, the irritation in my voice coming through loud and clear. I feel a small stab of guilt for being so prickly about Homecoming, but the pressure of his expectations is getting to me — especially attached as they are to this particular event. I don't know that there's anything magical about Homecoming that makes it the night to have sex for the first time. The more I think about it, the more it seems like *not* the right time. The focus is on friends and partying, obviously. Adding sex to the mix is maybe fine for people who do it all the time or have a casual attitude about it, neither of which describes me. Unsurprisingly, Hunter seems kind of oblivious to this sort of idea. I guess to him sex is the icing on the Homecoming cake.

To be fair, I know it's not just the "after" on his mind; it's the "before," too. He wants to pick me up and greet my family and take photos — the whole formal dance ritual.

I'm happy to go to the football game and the dance with him, but with everything that's happened in my family in the last year or two, my house has become a no-fly zone — even among my best friends. If Cammie, Syd, and Erin can accept that, then shouldn't Hunter be able to as well?

"It's senior year, Zoe." He turns wounded eyes to me. "We've been together a long time. I want to get to know your family better. Your parents must think I'm an asshole."

"No! They understand," I say quietly. And they do. Mostly, they do. "And it's not like they've never met you." My father insisted on "giving the young man the once-over," to my mortification, when Hunter picked me up for our first date in September of our junior year. My dad was friendly enough, even when he interrogated Hunter about where we were going and what time Hunter would have me back. Hunter was so nervous, so eager to pass muster . . . I remember thinking it was kind of adorable, despite my embarrassment at my dad's 1950s behavior.

He also met my mom — at the studio theater play in April, when I played Petra in *An Enemy of the People* (during which, on the night they attended, there was a prop malfunction that ended with a belated dump of an entire crate of fake snow at once, to unfortunate comical effect in a tense and somber scene).

"Maybe if they knew me better, they'd trust me and feel better about the overnighter." He sighs. "Also, I feel like I should ask your mom how she's doing. What if she thinks I'm avoiding her because she's sick? And I've never even met your little brother. Whatever you're worried about, I promise, it would be fine."

He has no business making such promises — he has no idea what he might be met with in my house.

"My mom isn't feeling up for company right now," I say, avoiding his eyes.

"Oh, gosh," he says, wincing. "Okay. I'm sorry. I don't know how long it takes to recover from . . ." He gestures. "Chemo and the surgery and stuff."

I feel like a rat. My mom's illness has been rough, but I know perfectly well she'd be happy for Hunter to come in and say hello. I'm the one who can't handle it. It's been a struggle to see her so thin and frail, let alone the still-jarring aspect of the double mastectomy. I couldn't bear to see someone else's reaction to what she looks like now. It would make it that much more real, and it's real enough already.

And then there's Jonah.

"I don't mean to be pushy," Hunter says. "I just feel like I should be doing something. You know?" He shrugs, and I can see how lost and confused he feels. Part of me feels compassion for him because he's sincere and kind of vulnerable, but another part of me chafes that, by his own admission, he has motives.

Even if I were sure I wanted to have sex with Hunter, I can't imagine my parents' reaction if I asked to go away overnight with my boyfriend to a rager at a house on Lake Oswego. Deep wrinkles would appear on my mom's brow as she started asking questions: *Who will be there? Will there be parent chaperones? Will there be drinking? What will the sleeping arrangements be?* And all the honest answers would be the wrong answers, but that's probably moot, because I'm pretty sure my dad would preempt all that with a quick *HA-HA-HA NOPE.* Whether I go to the party or not, ask my parents or not, sleep with Hunter or not, I am doomed to be a disappointment to someone. And I hate disappointing anyone.

I reach over to take the textbook. "We can talk about this stuff later, okay?"

"Promise?"

I nod.

"Okay. I'll be quiet." He mimes locking his lips and throwing away the key. But then he opens his mouth, which sort of defeats the whole *lock* thing, and says, "When we're finished, you wanna go to Noodle Kingdom? Come on, you know you can't resist Bangkok noodles with extra sriracha."

My mouth waters at the thought. "I can't." I would kill for some spicy noodles, but I have to get home. It takes a lot to keep our household running smoothly these days, and my parents depend on me. And he should know this: if my time were still my own, I'd be at rehearsal right now instead of studying at the library. Giving up being in the plays and musicals was heartbreaking, but it's more important to be the daughter my parents need me to be. Helping with set design at least lets me stay involved in theater, and it's really the only thing I can do and still be home to help with the Jonah-getting-home-from-school/pre-dinner crush.

"Dinner duty or brother duty?" he asks.

"It's all one thing," I say, trying not to let my annoyance show. I know he's just trying to be nice, trying to get close in the ways he thinks are correct. But where my brother is concerned, I don't want anyone close. People always stare at him pityingly or even disgustedly. And I can't bear it. It hurts me for Jonah and fills me with anger and resentment. That's part of why I'd rather just keep people away from us: I'm not really comfortable with the part of me that wants to tell people off. I only know how to be nice.

It's nearly five when I finish studying and we head for his car. It's Thursday, which means my dad can be at home in time to intercept Jonah's bus. This buys me a little free time after school.

It's misting out, and the smell of pine and moss hangs heavy in the air. "Look how pretty," I say to Hunter, pointing at the evening sun filtering gold through the trees.

"It's beautiful," he says, glancing over. He unlocks the car but then slips around in front of the door to block me. "But not as beautiful as you." He's kissing me before I even realize what's happening. That's his style. It's not rough or terrible. It's just that he doesn't like to waste time. And it's possible that I am the biggest time waste of all. He probably deserves credit for patience, because after a year of abstinence, I'm still not sure I'm ready.

He pulls back for a moment and runs a finger along my collarbone, giving me goose bumps, but I pull away and get into the car—I'm getting stressed about the time. He gets in and sets his hand on mine. It's a nice hand. Warm, long fingers. Fingers that can be alarming tools of persuasion, especially when he lightly skims them over my jeans when we're kissing. So far, though, I have resisted. I always thought I'd want to do it by now, but for some reason, it still doesn't seem right. Maybe I've watched too many movies, but I always imagined having sex as being something important and amazing, and being so in love with the guy I could barely tell where I left off and he began. I guess I've been waiting to feel sure it would be like that with Hunter, but for some reason, I don't. And I don't know what the problem is.

When he drops me off at my house minutes later, he kisses me slower. Softer. He trails his fingers lightly over my breast, and for a moment I might be starting to see things his way. But then I see the light flick on in my brother's bedroom and I come to my senses. Five o'clock: toileting time.

"See you tomorrow," I tell Hunter, giving him one more kiss before I get out of the car.

Inside, the house smells of cinnamon oatmeal, one of Jonah's approved low-calorie snacks. I get out of my shoes and jacket and bring my backpack up to my room. I hear my dad in the bedroom next to mine, struggling to get Jonah cleaned up and changed. He keeps telling him to hold still, and at least once I am almost certain I hear a *dammit* emit from under his breath.

I poke my head in when I hear they're finished. "Hey, guys."

"There's my girl," my dad says. He gives me an air kiss instead of a hug, which I appreciate—he's headed to the bathroom to wash up. "Can you clean up the kitchen from Jonah's snack? He got his hands into the oatmeal, and I wanted to get him washed up first."

"Sure." I step into Jonah's room to say hello. It doesn't smell, apart from the powdery whiff of wipes: that means no poop. Always a relief. He's usually a late-morning pooper, which means during the week someone else is getting Jonah cleaned up, and despite the years he's been in school, it never stops feeling strange and worrisome to me, someone I don't know providing such intimate care to my brother. I hope they are patient with him. I've been to his school a couple of times, and everyone seems nice, but . . . That doesn't mean that no one gets frustrated with Jonah when no one else is looking. And if anything happens that hurts him, he has no way of telling us.

"Hey, sweetie." I reach up and give him a quick hug, catching sight of the spray of whiskers on his chin and upper lip. He doesn't tolerate the shaver very well. I tighten the clasp of his helmet, surprised my dad didn't notice it was loose. Jonah is perfectly capable of getting injured when he falls from a seizure, even with the helmet on—he's had more stitches than a baseball (literally—my dad has kept count).

So a loose strap is a nonstarter. Even if the friction against his chin bothers him.

"Bao Bao," he says. My name. He leans down to me until the front of his helmet rests on the top of my head. That's just for me — he has never done that with anyone else. I hold his hands and sing to him — "Greensleeves" — a song that my madrigal group does each winter, and one of his favorites. He listens, silent except for the squeak of one of the floorboards as he rocks back and forth. I rock with him.

When I finish, I stand there, enjoying our stillness, until he deems the moment over. Then we make our way down the stairs to the living room and pick out one of his nature videos. He reaches for one of his favorites — *Majestic Birds.* He noises happily, making the sign for *bird.* I praise his signing with a pang in my chest. It's so easy to make Jonah happy: nature shows and birds and potato chips and cookies . . . That's all he needs. But he can't spend his life staring at screens, and he can't eat just junk food all day. I wish he could. I wish he could be happy all the time.

"Question," my dad says, ambling down the stairs, looking like a parallel-universe version of Jonah, from his close-set brown eyes to his towering height and large frame. He gestures toward the fireplace. "Too self-aggrandizing?"

Centered on the mantel is the framed cover art to his book, *Black Robe, Black Soil: The Jesuit Mission and Agriculture in the American West.* "No, that's great," I say. "It looks good with the matting."

"Yeah, they did a nice job at the frame shop."

"You sure it's safe there?" I ask. Our house is carefully

undecorated, a zone free of valuables and breakables. Mom affectionately calls Jonah a bull in a china shop, and the comparison is apt. It's not his fault — he can't help his size or his lack of coordination or carefulness. Maybe he can't help the fits of temper, either. But everyone — and everything — is safer with the minimalist approach. And even though I miss acting, there is an aspect I really enjoy about helping design sets, which is being able to fill a world with all kinds of neat objects — and they don't get broken unless they're supposed to.

My dad reaches to touch the frame and glances at Jonah. "He could reach it, but it's not that flashy. It should be safe."

I nod hopefully.

It's the only item on the mantel.

I follow Dad into the kitchen. Half the table is smeared with oatmeal, and the other half is covered with students' assignments from Dad's senior seminar course at Reed College: Saints and Sustainability in Environmental Practice. I barely understand his area of study, but he says I'll understand it better when I take his 200-level course — something about nomads and the renaissance in the American West or something equally glaze-worthy. It's inevitable, though: Reed, being free to children of faculty, is my destiny. And I'm lucky, I know, to have an education waiting and paid for. Cammie says I'm also lucky I don't have to deal with the exhausting task of choosing a college, but it's not as if I'm oblivious to my friends' excitement as they plan school visits and come back full of stories about cross-country flights and sprawling campuses and fraternity parties. What can I contribute to these conversations? *Oh, I met my dad for lunch at Reed and had a surprisingly serviceable turkey burger in the commons.* Yeah, no.

"I'll move those," he says, gathering the papers into a pile. "Sorry. Behind on grading. So what'd you learn in history today?"

I smile and shake my head at my dad's standard version of *how was your day* as I wipe up the oatmeal. "I learned about the fantastic relationship between Pope Innocent IV and Güyük Khan, and all the great things they did to dissolve the hatred between the Christians and the Mongols."

When I dare to glance up, I collapse into giggles at his expression.

He squints and shakes a fist at me. "Why I oughta . . ."

"Couldn't resist," I say, rinsing the rag in the sink. "What time will Mom be home?"

"Soon, I hope. The appointment was supposed to be short."

I hope it's good news, because if it's not, she shouldn't be alone for it. But it's hard for one of us to be available to go with her, with work, school, and caring for Jonah. Anyway, her appointments have all been similar: okay but not great (i.e., the cancer is not entirely gone, but not growing or worsening) since she finished her second round of chemo in June, but I never stop waiting for the other shoe to drop. How can I not, when the cancer is still there? They call it "partial remission," which to me almost seems like an oxymoron.

I peer into the fridge. There's a container of meatballs and tomato sauce from the store. I'll make spaghetti — easy, and

Jonah loves it, although afterward he'll look like a silly string factory exploded on him.

My dad pours himself some red wine, mumbling something in Latin like he always does, and takes his work into the living room to grade while he sits with Jonah.

I'm putting a pot of water on to boil when my phone dings with a text message, *bong-bong*, a perfect fourth that always gets "Here Comes the Bride" stuck in my head. I pick it up, guessing it's my mom, and then worrying it's bad news. But it's not Mom. It's Sam Jones.

Curious, I open it, hoping she hasn't changed her mind about lending me her painting. Her message says: Bring me back another slice of pizza or I'm gonna mess up your Temporal Omnibox with my Fission Pole.

I stare at her words. The only noun I understand is "pizza." This message clearly came to me by mistake. I consider what to do about it.

Sam is . . . different. Prior to yesterday, my primary memory of her was from seventh-grade art, when she used to hide under a table in the back of the room, drawing. Even in middle school she never wore anything but jeans and hoodies, her dark-blond hair in its ever-present ponytail. She was the best artist in the grade by miles, and I don't know if she was just trying to isolate herself from the rest of us or if she somehow felt unsafe in the world. Whatever it was seems to have held true, if her personal fortress of giant canvases in the art room is any indication. I can relate to that; I know a thing or two about the need for walls.

Before I can respond, another text comes through.

Sorry . . . that was for Will. *unplugs self and implodes into mortification vortex*

I grin despite myself—the way she narrates her actions cracks me up. I write back: Don't be mortified. I once accidentally texted my dad a message meant for my boyfriend. It might have contained the phrase "bulge in your pants."

The response that comes says: *peers out of vortex* You win. *gives you a trophy and also a medal* Luckily, my dad might as well live on another planet. And actually be an alien life-form. Without the abductions or probes.

I laugh. I'm surprised somehow—I had no idea she's so funny. I guess you never know what lies under the surface. Still, I'm not sure how much she's joking. Maybe there is something really weird about her dad.

I write: *is not sure what to make of that*

Unlike before, she takes several seconds to respond. Finally, she says: He moved away a long time ago.

A sudden cold ache spreads through my chest. I'm starting to see why she might need walls.

Before I can respond, another message flies in: At least nobody makes me eat beans on toast anymore.

Beans on toast? Why would anyone make someone eat beans on toast? While I'm trying to think of a response, I become aware of the sound of Jonah's slow, shuffling footsteps. He stands in the doorway of the kitchen, rocking back and forth, avoiding my eyes.

"Dinner's soon, sweetie," I tell him. "Not yet. Later." I make the sign for *later*, a swift downward motion with the letter *L*.

He makes a noise and takes another step into the kitchen,

angling toward the pantry. He wants to sneak food, and I'm foiling his plan.

"No, Jonah," I say, stepping toward him. Then I hesitate.

Handling Jonah isn't as easy as it once was — not since he hit an early puberty, eclipsed two hundred pounds, and his outbursts of temper got harder to manage. Three years ago, when he was twelve, he broke my mother's finger when she tried to take a bag of cookies from him. I remember running downstairs to see what the commotion was, how my heart hammered in my chest as she screamed at Jonah to let go, how my father came flying up from the basement — he's always been the best at calming Jonah down. When they left for the emergency room, nervously leaving me to watch Jonah, it was like the world started over. I was beginning to process that it wasn't just Jonah's body that was growing and changing as he was going through puberty. He was changing emotionally, and his outbursts were changing and growing, too. As my mother headed out with my father, her hand packed in ice, she pulled me aside and said, "If he tries to take food or whatever . . ." She closed her eyes, shaking her head. "Just let it go."

Jonah continued to act out, and with increasing frequency, and none of his medication adjustments or behavior modification programs through his school seemed to make much difference. And it was during this time that my mother found a lump in her breast.

The diagnosis, the surgery, the chemo . . . It is impossible to adequately express the devastation — the shock, the fear, the horrors of treatment, the ongoing question of whether or not my mom would be okay. It would have been overwhelming enough just on its own, but the combination of that and the increasing difficulty of taking care of Jonah and meeting all his needs with my mom out of commission . . . Our struggle to hold it all together became hopeless. That's when Jonah went on the waiting list for placement at a residential facility for people with disabilities.

My parents had avoided this step for years. Whenever it came up — either between themselves or in conversations with friends they've made through state organizations — one or the other of them would always say, "But he's so young!" There were certainly aspects in which such a move might even be good for Jonah — a richer social life, more activities, easy access to therapies and programming and doctors — but weighing that against tearing up our family made for some dubious math. And as things grew more unmanageable, Jonah's age no longer seemed like the determining factor. Suddenly the path veered into this new and terrible direction, steered by the realities of bodies, of mortality, of things we cannot control.

It was the hardest decision my parents ever made, although it's probably moot — one of the first things we learned is that people spend years on waiting lists. The idea of continuing to manage Jonah on our own forever is almost as worrisome as the idea of him being far away from us, cared for by strangers. It makes it hard to even know what to hope for.

I watch Jonah, cautious. He's about to make a move for the pantry — I can feel it. I gently try to turn him back to the living room.

He strikes out an arm, which fortunately I anticipated. Normally, he's slow as molasses in January, my mom likes to say, but when he's mad, he's *fast*. When he's mad, he is not to be underestimated.

But then the front door opens, and Jonah is distracted. My mom slips off her jacket and shakes the rain out of her closely cropped hair, which is finally starting to grow out post-chemo. "Hi, baby," she calls to Jonah, who has turned in her direction. She comes over and gives him a long hug, which he leans into, making one of his happy sounds. *Meeee*, it sounds like. "Hey, honey," she says to me over his shoulder. "How was your day?"

"Good." I point at Jonah and then the pantry, mouthing a warning. "How was the appointment?" I ask her.

"It was good," she says lightly. She lets go of Jonah and gives me a hug. "No changes."

But my heart drops. That means the cancer is still there. I hate that the new standard is that such a thing can be considered "good." I hate the freedom cancer seems to have to do what it wants. I hate that we can't fully outsmart it. I hate everything about it. But I have to be positive for my mom. Being positive, being good — that's my role. "That's great, Mom! I'm so glad."

"Yes, me too."

I gesture at the stove. "Water's on for pasta."

"Oh, thank you. You're such a good girl." She lays a hand

on my cheek, and I jump because it's so cold. She laughs. "Sorry — it's freezing out."

"It's okay. Do you need more help with dinner?" I still have Sam on my mind. I want to respond to what she said, maybe ask her about her dad, but since she only texted me by accident, I'm not sure where the line is between prying and responding to something personal that she chose to share.

My mom says, "No, you go ahead. Thanks for getting it started."

I head up to my room, where I review the messages I've exchanged with Sam. After some thought, I write: That sounds pretty rough.

While I wait for her response, I send a quick message to Elliot Levine, the writer and director of the play: Found the perfect painting for the dream sequence set. Can't wait for you to see it!

He writes back: Ah, you're the best! I wish you could have auditioned — everyone misses you. But I'm so glad you're still involved.

I smile sadly. I'm glad to be missed, but god, I wish I were in this show. Even Syd, a sometimes-theater person when it's not volleyball season, has a small part. I would have killed to play Fiona, the main character's loving, long-suffering wife who is always trying — often in vain — to help, to fix things, to make people happy. It's a perfect role for me. Instead, Serena Alvarez has the part. I force myself to wish her well, to hope she'll be great. But it would be a lie to say I hope she'll be better than I would have been.

I go back to watching my phone for Sam's reply. Minutes more pass before it comes. It says only: **Sorry for the misfire.**

Her unexpectedly terse response stings. I intruded, and now I feel stupid. And weirdly hurt that she didn't want to talk, that she rejected me.

A chord resonates in me — the adoptee chord, as in tune as ever. I will probably never know why my birth mother didn't want me, but the pain of it never abates. Even the smallest slight reminds me of my first life experience and forever legacy: rejection. My parents don't understand this at all — *But of course you were wanted! We wanted you! You were everything we'd ever dreamed of!* I have long since stopped trying to explain, because no one understands, and because it hurts my parents to hear, since they can't fix it. I wish having been unwanted didn't hurt so much, but it does.

So I do what I do best, which is to be helpful. I help serve dinner, help feed Jonah, help clean up. As an accidental and unwanted addition to the earth's problematically vast population, I feel an obligation to justify my existence. So I try to be useful, to walk a straight path, no detours allowed.

And as much as I love my family and as fortunate as I am, there is a dark little place inside me that envies my brother. Unlike me, he has nothing to justify — he was called into the world intentionally, a joyous surprise that arrived years after my parents gave up on conceiving and adopted me. Unlike me, he was never unwanted. He has been loved and cherished since he was conceived.

Jonah was a miracle.

I was a mistake.

Sam

School on Monday morning sucks with the ferocity of a black hole.

In English Mr. Tatlow announces we'll be spending the week doing collaborative analyses of *Hamlet*. Of course I get assigned to work with someone I'd rather set on fire — Connor Armstrong, a guy I've somehow been stuck in English with every year. He only reads Shakespeare for the dick jokes and thinks he's clever for repeating them at every opportunity. At least it's only an in-class project and we won't have to meet up outside of that.

As if that weren't bad enough, five steps after I leave the English classroom, some oblivious clod of a jock knocks my messenger bag off my shoulder. I spend the next three minutes playing a frantic game of pick-up-shit as the clueless masses trample my stuff. This unfortunate exercise makes me late to gym, which means I have to run laps — something I'm only motivated to do when being chased by a *T. rex* made of chain saws (i.e., never). By the time class ends, all I want is five minutes of humanless peace.

I duck into the bathroom closest to the gym to avoid the flood of people heading for the cafeteria. With everyone making a run for the lunch lines, it's empty and quiet other than the slow drip of a leaking faucet. I enter the least befouled stall and slump against a wall to check my texts.

I'm tempted to flush my phone when I read Will's latest message.

Hey robot. You. Me. The rest of the gang. HOMECOMING.

There's no decision time required for my response.

No quacking way. Would rather eat fewmets.

Of course he replies in an instant even though he's got a different lunch period than me and is probably supposed to be calculating derivatives right now.

COME ON. We're SENIORS. It's our civic duty. The dance is Gatsby-themed. We can do awesome costumes!!!

As if I could have missed the 1920s-style signs plastered all over school.

I reply: **No. Squared. Ask Kitty.** Gross as it is, they'd be cute together, and it would save me the awkwardness of spending an evening with Will's friends. It's not that I don't like them, it's just that even though they sometimes try to include me, I never feel like I belong. They have so many inside jokes, stories of things they've done together, and a universal obsession with *Planet Quest*. All I have is Will, but I'm okay with that. I don't need anyone else—not now, anyway. I can make new friends after I put a few thousand miles between myself and the hipster lumberjack capital of the USA.

Will writes back: Can't. She already said she'd go with Carlos as friends. You should eat lunch with her. She can tell you all about the after-party!

I roll my eyes even though there's no one here to see.

He writes: You're coming to Homecoming. Even Caroline is coming and she hates everyone. PLEASE. For your best friend.

Me: No.

Will: I'll free you from the rest of your first-person shooter obligations.

I weigh the options, trying to decide whether attending a loud, stupid dance full of vacuous half-drunk morons is preferable to an hour and a half serving as Will's meat shield in whichever game he chooses as my punishment.

I'll think about it, I say. He'll know it's a lie, but he also shouldn't expect to get more out of me.

As I fire off the text, two giggling girls burst into the bathroom. I freeze like a prey animal, then tiptoe forward to peer through the crack in the stall door. Syd and Erin, two of the vapid harpies Zoe hangs out with, zip over to the mirror to reapply makeup for reasons I can't fathom; nothing looks wrong with what they've already got on. I retreat, hoping it won't take too long to wait them out.

I wonder why Zoe is friends with Syd and Erin. I've worked hard to avoid Syd since sixth grade when she made fun of me in the locker room for not wearing (or needing) a bra. And rumor has it that in eighth grade Erin smuggled in a flask of her dad's vodka when we took our week-long Outdoor School trip and then she made out with one of the counselors. I don't know if there is any truth to the story, but at the time I was thankful for any gossip that drew attention away from the drama my mom caused. That was the week I learned that leaving Mom on her own, even for a few days, is impossible.

I open a game app on my phone and blow up some pandas, letting Syd and Erin's conversation fade into the background until I hear them mention something of actual interest to me: Zoe.

"Is it weird, being in the play without Zoe?" Erin asks.

"Totally," Syd replies. "Elliot had always planned for her to play Fiona, and everybody knows it."

"It sucks she had to quit," Erin says. "Is her mom doing any better, do you know? Zoe never talks about it."

"Cammie says she's doing well, but you know Cammie. Ever the optimist."

"Yeah," Erin says. "But Zoe hasn't had us over in ages. Actually, it might have been sophomore year, the last time I was there. That doesn't seem to bode well."

"That might be more about her brother, though," Syd says. Her voice drops. "Did you know that he broke her mom's finger once? Can you imagine? Not being safe with your own brother?"

"Jesus," Erin says. "They're about as opposite as two people could possibly be."

"Right?" Syd says. "Well, it makes sense, since they're not even related."

My mind reels. Zoe's life is apparently nothing like the perfect universe I imagined her in. I don't know what's going on with her brother, but the way her friends talk about him is pretty cold. And if her mother is having problems, too . . . That all sounds like a lot.

I pull out my phone as Syd and Erin's conversation devolves into a discussion about some guy in Erin's gym class whose abs she wants to bathe with her tongue. All I have is a giant pile of texts from Will, still hammering on at me about Homecoming. I try to think of something to say to Zoe, to maybe let her know someone understands what it's like to have a messed-up home life, but my heart feels like a hamster doing crack-addled laps in my rib cage. It's not like I can offer sympathy about her family situation when she hasn't told me anything about it herself.

Questions. I should ask a question. I read in a book once that it's a good way to get people to talk to you.

How come you're doing set design this year instead of acting? No, too loaded.

What kind of shampoo do you use that smells so good? Ugh, too creepy.

CAN YOU PLEASE TEACH ME HOW TO BE A NORMAL HUMAN? Yeah, right. That's too Herculean a task for any mere mortal.

When do you need my painting? I finally text. So stupid, but it's the only thing that might warrant a response. A couple of butterflies try to eject themselves from my stomach, but I talk myself down before it becomes a full-on chunderfest of the lepidopterous variety.

She answers quickly — she must have the same lunch period as me. I'm so glad you didn't change your mind! The play opens the week after Halloween. It would be great to have it before tech week, if you'd be okay with that. Maybe the week of 10/19?

Me: *salutes* Brilliant. I'm back at a loss for real words even though our two-text conversation had all the substance of a boiled cabbage.

Zoe: *rejoices*

Despair fills me as I realize our conversation is over unless I do something to keep it going. I scroll through our previous exchanges, desperately looking for something to reference.

Me: *hopes your weekend didn't involve any more misfires*

Zoe: Just the usual fires ☺ How was yours?

My heart leaps at her quick response, and at the fact that she asked about my weekend.

I write back: *hopes my next one's better* *isn't optimistic* Last weekend was a study in silence — and me lacking the brass ovaries needed to ask my mom about a trip to London, or whether or not she had any role in keeping Dad from suggesting it in the past. His email hangs over my head. I wonder if he still wears the Ravenclaw scarf I gave him when I was twelve, or if his graying hair is still as badly in need of a trim as it always seemed to be when he lived here, or if his eyes are really the same shade of brown I remember. The longer he's away, the more I forget. I used to tell myself that's how I wanted it, but I don't really know anymore.

Part of me wants to tell him to sod off, but I'd be lying if I didn't admit the thought of going to that dumb *Doctor Who* museum with him dredges up all the best memories of my childhood. We loved that show in every incarnation.

As for this weekend, all I have to look forward to are first-person shooters or Homecoming, both of which sound about as appealing as brushing my teeth with a sandy pinecone.

Outside the bathroom stall, Syd and Erin finally pack up and walk out.

I exit as soon as it's safe and blaze my way to the library at top speed. My usual lunch spot will provide me with a quiet place to try to continue my conversation with Zoe. The library is familiar. It's safe. And if Zoe doesn't respond, I can lose myself in a few pages of a book that will take me somewhere far, far away — preferably a different solar system where the problems are big enough to make mine seem small.

I settle in the back of the SF/F section in the library and pull out my peanut butter and jelly sandwich. Strawberry jam, quartered radishes, barbecue-flavored chips, and Twizzlers: Mom chose a red theme today. I dig in and pull out my phone. My heart lifts at the sight of another message from Zoe in response to my gloomy weekend prognostications.

Zoe: **What would make it better?**

Really, a whole other world might be the only thing that would make things better.

Me: **An alternate reality.**

Zoe: **Ah. Is that why you paint such fantastical worlds?**

She's not wrong. Painting helps me feel like I'm somewhere else — like the places I create could maybe be real.

I'm not sure what to say when the truth is way too much.

Zoe: It would be nice to spend a weekend in that fairy-tale castle.

After hearing what Erin and Syd said, I have a tiny sense of why she might also want to escape.

Me: *books tickets*

Zoe: Who needs tickets? We have something much better than planes! *points to dragon in your painting*

Me: *gathers sparkly treasures into a pile, hoping to lure him*

Zoe: *sets off a flare to draw his attention*

Me: *ducks behind nest as he careens in*

Zoe: *admires his magical shades of green*

Me: *scrambles around and puts a bow tie on him*

Zoe: SO HANDSOME! He needs a name. Sheldon? No, too mama's boy . . . Dexter? No, too bespectacled and lab-ratty. HUMPHREY.

She has me laughing, and the exhausting weight of my entire life is temporarily lifted.

Me: *lassos a spike on Humphrey's back and climbs up*

Zoe: *scrambles aboard, climbing up his shimmering scales* *clings to your hoodie* TO INFINITY AND BEYOND!

The notion of her wanting to come with me, of her holding on to me, is so absurd that my breath catches. How is this even happening?

Me: *pilots Humphrey toward a distant star*

Zoe: *gazes at the shrinking Earth and into the great dark beyond, wondering if there are Taco Bells in space*

Me: *hopes you don't like beef burritos because they're Humphrey's favorite and he'll fight you for them*

Zoe: *buys Humphrey bunches of beef burritos to keep him

fueled* *adds extra hot sauce to enhance combustion*

She's fallen into the story with me so easily, it's like she was always meant to tell the other half of it. My hamster heart is in its death throes now. Why is she talking to me beyond what's required to get my painting? Why does she seem to care about this story we're making up? Something doesn't compute. She's an unexpected side quest on the quacktacular odyssey that is my life.

Before I write back to Zoe, I send a text to Will.

Fine, we can go to stupidfuckinghomecoming.

Zoe is sure to be at the dance.

I spend the rest of the afternoon thinking about the texts Zoe and I exchanged during lunch. She went quiet during the period after that, but part of me is still wandering around up in the stars. I want to know where Humphrey's story goes and where it might take us. Even more, I want to know how and why she ended up in it with me.

When I get home from school, I toss the mail on the kitchen counter for my mom and then head straight upstairs to get started on my homework. Time alone in the house is precious and must be optimized for any tasks that are better done without interruptions. Once Mom arrives, my time will no longer be mine. I manage to type up a shitty first draft of a history essay and am halfway through my calculus homework when my phone vibrates on my nightstand. I jump up from my papasan chair, shivering as I leave the soft nest of afghans knitted by Mom.

Will's with Kitty tonight on his long-awaited study date,

so I'm not expecting to hear from him until afterward. The rest of my minuscule contact list is made up of unfortunate souls who had to collaborate with me on group projects for school or online pen pals I stopped talking to years ago. Who would text me?

Then a stupid hopeful feeling rises out of nowhere that I want to kick back into whichever of Tartarus's fiery armpits it came from.

Maybe it's *her*.

I pick up the phone to see a message from Mom and curse the fleeting pang that it's not Zoe.

Mom: I'm on my way!

I look at the clock and a bolt of panic lances through me. I should have started dinner half an hour ago. I scramble downstairs to get the prep work done before Mom gets home, already at a disadvantage because I don't even know what I'm going to make. There isn't much to work with, but we have some leftover roast beef from the weekend. Stroganoff, or whatever bastardized version I can create out of what's in our fridge, will have to do.

I try to cut the beef into even cubes, but working in haste makes me sloppy. Meat juice runs off the cutting board and onto the counter, which is the last thing I need my mom to see when she walks in. I spill egg noodles on the floor when I go to pour them into a measuring cup, and when it comes to the sour cream . . . well, I decide measuring isn't worth it.

My phone buzzes again.

Will: Help what the duck do girls like to talk about??

As if a robot would know, I joke. Then I decide to throw him a bone and give him the same advice that worked for me earlier. Ask her questions.

Will: About what???

Me: TV, comics, Planet Quest . . . LITERALLY ANYTHING.

Kitty will talk enough for both of them if he gets her started. She's always one of the first to jump into class discussions, usually while I'm still pondering what one obligatory thing to say to make sure I get my participation points.

I barely have the onions chopped when my phone sounds again. I huff in irritation. Of course the busiest night in my entire history of text messaging is the night I don't have my shit together and am running behind. I already have half a snarky text to Will mentally composed before I pick up the phone, but the message isn't from him.

Zoe: *wonders where Humphrey is now*

My heart sings.

Me: *points to him sleeping in his nest* *warns you away from the little flames that shoot out when he snores*

I throw the onions in the pan to sauté, watching my phone with bated breath.

Zoe: *peers curiously around his cave*

Me: *admires the glittering of all his treasure*

I hear the garage door rumbling open on the other side of the wall. The cutting board is still covered with roast beef and meat juice, and the dishwasher is only half unloaded with the door hanging wide open. I snatch up the mail, bolt down the hallway to the living room, and set the pile of credit card offers and advertisements on the coffee table as an attempt to divert Mom.

"Hi, honey!" Mom says as I zoom into view. Even at the end of a long work day, she looks so put together in her gray suit and silk blouse. Her hair is the same ash blond as mine, but she mostly wears hers in an elegant twist as opposed to my haphazard ponytail.

"Hi!" I try for enthusiasm, but it comes out sounding more panicked. "I started dinner if you want to go ahead and relax. The mail is on the coffee table," I say, gesturing to the living room.

"That's so sweet of you." She sets her keys in the dish and slides her purse into its cubby beside the door. "How was school? And was your lunch okay?"

"Same as always, and yes," I say, because it's how I always answer. Today, neither was quite true — the first because of Zoe, and the second because honestly I think Twizzlers taste kind of like vinyl and suffering. I sidestep, hoping I can push her into the living room with the force of my body language alone.

"Kerry asked if you'd started applying for college yet, and I told her how well you're doing in your AP classes," Mom says, smiling as she slips off her shoes. "Her son goes to MIT — I'm sure he'd be willing to talk to you about it if you're interested."

I barely manage to resist rolling my eyes. Even if MIT were a reasonable option for me, how on earth can she advocate for that when my being a long flight away would surely give her a fit of distress?

"MIT is out of my league," I say, following her as she pads into the living room. Mom tries to be supportive, but she doesn't have a clue. Unless I crack the secret to FTL travel or cure cancer before the end of this semester, there's no way I'm getting into MIT. Perfect grades and the slew of extra summer school classes I took to get out of the house only count for so much at schools like that. I hate that great things are expected of me no matter how unrealistic they are. Maybe it's the curse of all only children, that all their parents' hopes and dreams are pinned on them.

"Nothing is impossible, honey. You should reach for what you want." She sits down and starts thumbing through the mail.

I fume silently. She's oblivious to the fact that what I want doesn't matter. If and when I leave for college, her routine is going to be quacked half dead, and if she does fall apart, no one will be here to pick up the pieces. If I want to go, I have to figure out how to help her survive, but I don't have any idea where to begin.

"So the vice president nominations go in tomorrow, right?" I ask.

"Yes," she says, and the brevity of her response tells me that she's nervous about it.

"I'm sure you'll get it," I say. She's the head of her division. The promotion is only a matter of time now that the douchecanoe CFO who kept cockblocking her moved on to another company full of like-minded pricks.

"Kerry says it's a sure thing, but I don't know . . ." She bites her lower lip.

"You're the best accountant they have," I remind her. Meticulousness is a good thing when one is employed as an accountant at a financial company. Even if she isn't the fastest of her colleagues, feeling compelled to quadruple-check everything means she almost never misses an error. She also always sees around the corners, always anticipates anything that could go wrong. I push aside the familiar prickling resentment that she manages to excel at work while our life at home feels like a train wreck about to happen.

"Thanks, honey. Let me go change and I'll help you with dinner."

"That's okay," I say hastily. If she does, we might not eat until ten. "It sounds like you had a hard day. Why don't you go unwind with a book or work on your knitting?" I have to admit the latter is a self-serving suggestion — knitting always calms her.

"It's been a while since I started a new project, hasn't it?"

"It's been a really long time since you went to your Stitch and Bitch group, too," I say. She used to love those nights at the library, and so did I — they meant two extra hours of freedom.

A flicker of unease dances over her face. "There's just always so much to do around the house."

But there isn't.

"I should check on the food," I say.

"Okay, honey. I'll go change." She pulls me in for a hug.

I hold my breath, afraid she's somehow going to spot a problem in the kitchen from all the way down the hallway — a sauce splatter or an odd number of dishes remaining in the dishwasher, or any of a thousand other ways I might have broken her unspoken rules. Still, it feels nice to have her arms around me. It's comforting. She's always been there, and she's all I have now that Dad is gone.

She smiles when she pulls away, and I exhale. Safe. For now.

Mom sniffs the air. "Is something burning?" Not so safe after all.

"I'll go check you can go sit down no need to follow me," I say in a rush.

But of course she does.

I fly through the kitchen ahead of her at the speed of light, chucking the roast beef into the onion pan. A quick flip of the cutting board puts it clean-side up, creating the illusion that I already washed it. I whirl around to face her and body-shield the other counter detritus from view, stirring the onions and beef with my arm at an angle that's positively absurd.

My phone buzzes again, and I jump.

"Oh my god! What's that on the counter?" Mom asks.

The smallest amount of roast beef juice has escaped from beneath the cutting board.

"Is that meat?" The pitch of her voice rises, and my tension along with it.

"Sorry, I was in a hurry. I lost track of time doing homework," I say. "I'll clean it up."

"Your studies are important, but you need to structure your time so you can do things the right way. You know what kinds of bacteria grow in meat sitting out at room temperature—horrible things that could make you very sick." Mom glances around the kitchen, her breathing getting shallower. She taps the thumb of her right hand sequentially against the tips of her other fingers. Even though she's not counting, I can still hear it in my head: one-two-three-four, one-two-three-four.

"I was careful," I say. A lie. "I'll bleach the counters right away." Not a lie. "Please don't worry. I only just started, and the beef has only been out of the fridge for a few minutes . . ."

"Did I close the garage?" She suddenly looks stricken, like she hasn't asked me this question nearly every day, like she doesn't always close the door on her way in from work. But anxiety has its own logic, like a spark that leaps from one stressor to the next until even the smallest thing is swallowed in flames of worry and fear.

She hurries out of the room, and I exhale a long, rattling breath.

I check my phone to find a text from Will and another from Zoe. I go straight to hers. It's a whole series, and my heart grows ten sizes with each one.

tiptoes over skulls

approaches giant chest

lifts creaky lid, jumping when Humphrey snorts in his sleep

ogles mountain of sparkling gemstones and gleaming bricks of gold

sifts longingly through rubies and sapphires

unearths the occasional bottle of Dragon Fire sauce XXX hot

I love how the place we are building expands with every text she sends. I feel like I'm floating as I write my responses:

hands you a tiara that sparkles with jewels

picks up a sword and tries to sneak off with it

face-plants into a pile of rugs and tapestries

It's like I'm five years old again and playing pretend, but so much better.

I flip over to Will's message. **OMG YOU ARE A GENIUS.** He goes on to tell me at length about his date with Kitty. As far as I can tell, it mostly consisted of them preparing for a quiz in AP History and talking about Kitty's obsession with *Yuri on Ice*. Apparently he now thinks I'm some sort of girl whisperer, since asking her questions got him a detailed description of the entire plot of the aforementioned homoerotic sports anime.

I can't say I follow his logic.

Unfortunately, right now I'm out of time to respond. I rush around the kitchen, unloading dishes and tidying the mess. My brain needs to shut up, but it's caught in an infinite loop of everything Zoe has written to me — shimmering words of imaginary places, and friendliness and kindness I doubt I deserve. I think back to her response when I told her about my dad: *That sounds pretty rough.* I don't know why I spilled about my boring personal tragedies, even as a joke. It was stupid — why would she care? But then her response was sympathetic. She made me stop and realize maybe my life is kind of rough — not just because Dad left, but because Mom is still here.

When Mom cooks, everything has to be in even numbers, certain foods have to be cut into exact cubes, and anything involving raw meat requires complete sterilization of the kitchen after it goes into the pan or oven.

I don't remember it being this bad when Dad was here.

Her anxiety never seemed as bad back when he was local,

but maybe that was because I had breaks from her then. Now she has me all the time, and my need to be fed and driven places, my unkempt bedroom — they're challenges to her. I try to make life easier for her, to play along with her rules outside of my own room, but somehow it's never enough.

On the other side of the wall, the garage door goes up and then down. Checking to see if it's closed won't be sufficient — she has to open it and then close it again to make it feel right. I briefly feel bad about bringing up VP nominations since that's probably a big part of what has her on edge.

I turn the Stroganoff down as low as the burner will go and pray it doesn't congeal into a brick while I scrub the cutting board and load the dishwasher.

Then I hear the garage door go up again.

As always, I'm going to have to intervene. People on the street might see her standing there opening and closing the door. What would they think? I don't want their judgment or their pity, and I especially don't want Mom to have to face that. Mom tries so hard to do everything right — it's just that her version of right is different from the rest of the world's.

My pulse pounds dully in my ears as I walk to the garage. Maybe I'm an idiot to be texting with Zoe Miller when trying to make new friends is pointless. I'd either have to train them on all the rules, which would be ridiculous, or I'd risk my mom melting down when someone doesn't accommodate her needs, which would be horrifying. And then how could I protect my mom from being judged, maybe even being the subject of gossip and ridicule? This is why the sum total of my friends is likely to remain Will, who obeys the invisible barrier surrounding my house and my need for schedules because he's one of those people who is totally unfazed by people's quirks. But even he doesn't know what this is like—being here, right now, with Mom. Being the one who makes sure she's okay, and that we get through, and that sometimes I get almost enough sleep.

Mom stands by the button to the garage door, her finger hovering over the button to close it again, but she's also counting under her breath. There's no telling how many times she's going to open and close the door if I don't stop her. The only guarantee is that it'll be some multiple of four.

"Dinner's ready," I say, keeping my tone light.

"I'm not sure it's closing all the way," she says. "It doesn't feel right."

"I know," I say, but I really don't.

I don't know why a door can be closed the same way but either be right or wrong.

I don't know why things are easier for her when they involve even numbers, preferably fours.

I don't know why she has to go up and down the stairs a certain number of times a certain way before it "feels right."

I don't know why she has to check the windows every night to make sure they're latched, even though we never open them except in summer.

I don't know why she is reluctant to start a new task if the clock isn't on a number that ends in zero.

"How about I'll close it while you put dinner on the table?" I suggest.

She looks at me, and then back at the door.

"You opened it twice and closed it once, so closing it this time will be the fourth time you pushed the button," I say. Mom logic.

"Okay," she says, hesitating.

"I've got this. It's fine," I say.

"I love you," she says, and squeezes my shoulder before heading back into the house.

I wait a few moments to make sure she isn't coming back, then close the garage door a final time.

Dad is fucking fahrbot for inviting me to England. He lived with Mom. He must know what she's like—even if the divorce made it a thousand times worse. How on earth can I ever take a trip when she's like this? Moreover, what is going to happen when I leave for college? Who is going to extricate her from her rituals, interrupt her when she compulsively recloses doors and checks windows, and make sure she doesn't get too distracted to eat? Who is going to help her finish what she starts when it's the only way to calm her down?

We're like two cogs in a machine that need each other to keep the system in motion. She's the train and I'm the railroad switch keeping her from going down a bad set of tracks. What will she do without me?

How can I ever leave?

Zoe

On Wednesday I linger after class while Miss Delegatti grades the math quizzes, not minding being late for lunch. At this point, Homecoming is all anyone can talk about — mostly the after-party. I'm not in the mood for the questions and the pressure.

Miss Delegatti turns to me with her toothy smile and says, "Ninety. Good job, Zoe." I'm disappointed. A ninety is not enough to raise my grade from the B+ it's hovering around. And I'm firmly at a B in physics, too, so this feels like a bit much. My life was once a B-free zone. My dad will probably ask what happened, like he has the few times I haven't gotten all As. Sometimes I kind of resent it — I mean, a B is not even that bad. Still, I hate disappointing him, so I'll just have to try harder.

There are no retakes, so I ask her if I can have an extra-credit assignment, which she gives me because she's kind and decent. "Thank you *so* much," I tell her as I'm heading out. I only mean to be polite, but even to my own ears I sound like a suck-up.

Between there and lunch, I head to the library to pick up the book I ordered on interlibrary loan — something to help me with design ideas for the English country estate set. Elliot's play, *The World Over,* is about an alien engineered to look exactly like a human, only he's programmed to forget he was ever an alien when he's sent to Earth, and so for decades he searches the planet for a place where he feels comfortable, a place to call home. It's actually a really cool story, but it's a pain for set design. Too many different places, countries, and times. And, of course, no budget. My mom will be useful, though. She's a curator at the Pittock Mansion, so she knows a lot about period design (and sometimes is a lifesaver at sourcing props from estate sales and her various connections — she found us some great dusty old books and a beautiful chess set for *Enemy*). She'll probably be happy to help find something for that English country scene. I sometimes wonder if part of why she loves her work is for the same reason I love set design: it's the canvas our house can never be for beautiful and treasured possessions. But does she ever feel the way I sometimes do, that choosing all these nice pieces is like window-shopping at expensive stores, where you can look with longing but you can't *have*?

My thoughts go to Sam's painting, which will be pivotal. I can't wait to show it to Elliot and to share the set ideas it gave me for the dream-sequence scene.

I wish I could use the one with the castle and the dragon,

even though it's wrong for the play. It reminds me so much of *Princess Safirina and Her Dragon,* my favorite story when I was little. A princess runs away from her father, a tyrannical king, and is rescued by the dragon the king had ordered his knights to slay. The dragon, Murgatroid, turns out to be very elegant and refined, and he makes her delicious stews and cakes and teaches her Latin. The princess sends a message to her father that she is holding herself hostage, and the cost of her return will be a home for Murgatroid at the castle. Her father agrees, and Murgatroid becomes the castle's greatest protector while continuing to tutor Princess Safirina — and supervise the castle chef's cooking.

Looking at Sam's painting brings all that back in one great, intense, nostalgic rush.

While I'm at the library picking up my book, a message comes from my mom: Sweetie, can you call me when you have a minute?

My stomach drops. She's never asked me to call her from school. Maybe her test results got mixed up — maybe she's *not* actually okay. Fear surges up in me like a geyser, and I'm desperate to know things aren't as bad as what I'm imagining.

I glance around. The library is as good a place as any to make a call; the halls and certainly the cafeteria will be too loud. When I get my book checked out, I head to the stacks in search of a quiet spot and dial my mom.

"What is it?" I ask as soon as she picks up.

She starts with a great rush, and as she talks, I slide to the floor, utterly unprepared for the bomb she drops.

A bed has opened up at Little Lambs Village.

A bed. It sounds so small and simple. A bed! A piece of furniture. But what "a bed" actually means is the end of life as we all know it. It means shipping Jonah off to a "home," to be cared for by strangers. A place where he doesn't know anyone.

Where no one knows him.

Where no one loves him.

My mother sounds borderline hysterical — maybe because it's such devastating news or maybe because it's such great news. Maybe both. This is something people wait years, even decades for! Little Lambs Village is one of the best facilities in the state of Oregon! He will have professionals caring for him! He will have activities and friends!

I struggle for words. Jonah had a weekend visit at Little Lambs Village in the spring so they could evaluate him or whatever, but I didn't expect anything to come of it. "I thought there was a long waiting list," I finally manage.

My mom says, "There is, but it's not that simple. They factor things in. My cancer diagnosis . . . We were moved up on the priority list because of that, and the vacancy is in a unit that has kids like Jonah. You know — very high staff ratio. So it's not right for everyone on the waiting list."

Yes, it would have to be a high staff ratio. Sometimes three-to-one hasn't been enough at home.

I hold myself together as my mother finishes explaining about all the things they have to do before he's admitted a week from Friday. There is really nothing to decide: they might not get an opportunity like this again for years, perhaps many years — even into Jonah's adulthood. And if something happened to my mom before then . . .

It's as good as done.

I wish I could say what I'm really feeling: *Please don't give Jonah away. You can't. You just can't.*

The legacy of being thrown away . . . It's more terrible than my parents know — or will ever know, because I have never been able to tell them.

To my parents, my story is a fairy tale. When I was growing up, they had all sorts of romanticized ways to frame it: it was a charming stork story, or a lucky twist of fate, or proof of guardian angels, or a tale of the department of cosmic fulfillment finally getting an order right.

There were newspaper stories, too. The clipping my dad loves most: "Safe Haven Brings Happy Ending for Texas Family." A "happy ending" story . . . What kind of paradigm is it where a new life is an "ending"? I mean, yes, it was happy news for my parents and an incredible stroke of luck for me. But it was a beginning, not an ending. For me, it was the beginning of life as a "safe haven" baby — i.e., a throwaway.

My parents do not understand my feelings about this — my dad especially. Any efforts I ever made to express my sadness about being abandoned, my curiosity about my birth mother or my other family, have been met with anxious, tense reactions. Why would I focus on that? This is my family now, and it was meant to be, and there is no point in ruminating over unknowables. I have never known how to make them understand that wishing I knew more about my biological family does not mean I'm not grateful for the family I have, not glad for the outcome. But it's moot, because the subject is best left alone, which means all of my guilty and fretful worries and longings reside tidily within the walls of my own heart.

But now there is another reason not to tell them how I feel about placing Jonah, and why I feel that way: if they are forced to think of this as what it is, as relinquishing their child, it will decimate them.

And since I can't speak my truth about that, I just listen. I know the sound of my mom's voice — I know how hard she's trying to be enthusiastic because there is no other viable option. I also know that she's dying inside.

I am, too.

I try to say some encouraging things before telling her I have to go or I'll be late for class. It's not true, but I don't want her to hear me crack.

Little Lambs Village is an amazing place — I know that. When Jonah had his visit there, we were given a tour and a chance to see activities and meet some of the staff, and I totally get why my parents were impressed by it. It's a cheerful, modern place with great facilities and programs, and the grounds are beautiful. But despite the impressive tour, a lot of important questions remain unanswered in my mind. Like, how will they handle it if he has one of his rages and hurts someone? Will they kick him out if he's too difficult? How will they get him to cooperate with bathing and shaving and tooth-brushing? Will they overmedicate him? How will he understand what we've done, sending him away?

Who will hug him? Who will stroke his back the way he likes?

I try to stifle my sobs, glad to be hidden in the towering bookshelves of the library. I go farther back, almost to the end of the row where no one could possibly wander by, and slump to the floor. A barrage of questions rolls through my mind, and there is no answer for any of them. Jonah, without us? Jonah, far away? With no way to tell us if things are okay there? To tell us if he's sad and confused and misses us?

Will someone sing to him? Will they let him watch his nature videos?

Oh my god — my dad. How will my dad cope with this? My dad's devotion to Jonah is complete. Imagining him separated from Jonah, not being able to see him every day and know he's okay, is unbearable.

I dig in my backpack for tissues, but I can't find any. I fling the bag aside.

"Um," a voice says.

I glance up, alarmed. It was so completely silent that I thought I was alone. But peeking around the shelf, looking indescribably awkward, is Sam Jones, holding out a napkin.

I'm mortified. I scramble to my feet, wiping my eyes. "Sorry," I say. "I didn't know anyone was here."

"Do you need this?" she asks, her gaze skittering around like it's not sure where to land.

My nose is running like a faucet. I take the napkin she's offering. "Thanks," I say, embarrassed by what a mess I am.

Sam looks so confused and uncertain that I feel like I should offer some explanation for my presence and emotional state.

"I was just picking up a book on English country manors. For STOTS," I begin. She nods, and then in a rush I add: "And then my mom called and said we're sending my brother away!" I blink, alarmed that I actually said it. I'm always very careful about what I say out loud — the version of me I show the world sometimes bears little resemblance to the person I am inside.

"Sending him away?" she says, her expression baffled.

I could kick myself. "I'm sorry," I say. "I'm just babbling." I glance at my phone to check the time. Fifteen more minutes before this period ends. Fifteen long minutes. What am I going to do until then?

"Do you . . . do you want to sit?" Sam gestures behind her.

"Oh! Um, sure. Thanks." I'm pretty sure I'm going to be lousy company right now, but I don't know how to say no without risking hurting her feelings.

I follow her around the shelf. Her messenger bag and unopened sack lunch sit near the wall at the end of the row. Outside, the sun has broken through the clouds, illuminating the bright-red leaves of the maple tree on the school's front lawn.

As we settle in, my phone dings with a message. It's Hunter. Where are you? I got you tater tots — the line was long. And Cammie is doing gross things to them that she says you'd approve of. Ranch dressing mixed with hot sauce. He sends a horrified-looking emoji.

There's no way I'm going back to the caf in the shape I'm in, but his message reminds me that Sam hasn't touched her lunch. "I'm sorry — I interrupted your lunch," I say.

"No, that's okay," Sam says quickly. She looks at her lunch bag, then back at me, then back to her lunch bag. Four paper clips are holding the folded top in place.

"Please, go ahead," I say. "Don't mind me."

She pulls the paper clips off her lunch bag and fiddles with them, linking them together in a chain before setting them aside. She heaves a loud sigh, then opens the sack. "Um," she says. It's like she's talking to the bag, because she sure isn't looking at me. "Do you want to share my lunch? I'm happy to share it with you, but it's . . . weird."

My stomach growls with embarrassing volume at the thought of food, answering on my behalf. "Weird how? Is it, like, a liverwurst and jelly sandwich?"

"No. It's just . . ." She sighs again and opens the bag. A lingering dash of periwinkle paint colors the very edge of her thumbnail. She removes four items in Ziploc bags and then flattens the paper bag, laying the food out on top.

There are four squares of sandwich with the crust cut off. A stack of some kind of orange-dusted Pringles. Some baby carrots cut into skinny little sticks, as if they're not small enough to begin with. And a snack-size bag of what look to be M&M's, but they're all orange.

"That's not so weird," I say. "Standard lunch: sandwich, chips, vegetable, and dessert."

"Kind of," she says, opening the sandwich bag. She offers me a square. "It's American cheese. Is that okay?"

I accept it, nodding. "Are you sure you'll have enough?"

"Yeah, it's fine." She takes out another square and nibbles on it. She glances over at me, chewing, and then sets her sandwich down. "You will notice," she says, "that everything in my lunch has something orange in it. And I can guarantee you that those Pringles number some multiple of four — looks like either twelve or sixteen. And the carrots were also cut into fours. And I think the M&M's speak for themselves."

I swallow my bite of sandwich. "So, you like orange and you like fours?"

She shakes her head. "It doesn't have to be orange. It can be any color, as long as it's in all four things. But it always has to be fours." She looks down and picks at the paint on her thumb. "And it's not me. It's my mom."

"Does she . . ." I speak softly. "Does she have, like, OCD or something?"

Sam doesn't move for a moment, and then she nods — just barely. "Don't tell anyone," she says, still avoiding my eyes. "Okay?"

My heart aches for her. I know what it feels like to say those words, to plead like that, terrified that people will find out your secrets. To be ashamed of something you can't control and the way people might judge you and your family. "I won't," I tell her. "I would never. I promise."

She's as still as a statue. I look for some way to defuse the seriousness, because it's heavy. I gesture at her lunch. "This is actually very useful for splitting lunches fifty-fifty."

She cracks a smile, but it's like she's still afraid to look at me. I lean over and peer into her face, and she smiles a little more, then laughs. She divides the chips and M&M's into two equal piles and hands me my halves of things.

I open my sandwich square and stick a few Pringles inside, then mash it back together.

"Oh, Jesus," she whispers, staring. "My mom would shit an entire litter of kittens if she saw that." And then she laughs kind of hysterically and copies me. She looks nervously at her creation before biting into it.

"Is she okay with going out to eat? I'd die without my Ace's burrito fix," I say.

"Actually, my mom loves Taco Bell. Because . . ."

I chew some carrot slivers, watching her. "Because why?"

"Because. *T* and *B* are even. And *taco* and *bell* have even numbers of letters. And they're even more perfect because both words have four letters."

She takes a deep breath and keeps going.

"Other fast-food places are kind of a mixed bag. Burger King is sometimes okay. *B* is even and both words have even numbers of letters. McDonald's is the ultimate fail: nine letters plus the asymmetry created by the apostrophe, so . . ." She makes a buzzer noise. "Don't even get me started on Burgerville." She sighs. "If I want my Walla Walla onion ring fix, I have to bribe Will to take me."

I don't want her to feel uncomfortable, so I try to keep it light. "Wow, you must eat a lot of Taco Bell," I say. "No wonder Humphrey is so well fueled."

"Yeah. Hopefully enough to get me out of here," she says.

"College is my only hope to break free. Or ever getting to try Dairy Queen." Her tone fails to match the lightness of the words.

"Has your mom always had all those rules?" I ask, reeling at the impossibility of what Sam is saying, about the tight parameters she apparently has to steer her life around.

"I don't remember," she says. "It was definitely bad after she and my dad split up. And then it got worse when he moved to London."

"I guess all those changes might have been hard on her," I say. I don't know much about OCD, but I can certainly imagine that changes a person can't control could be a struggle.

Sam nods. "Yeah."

"My house is the opposite of yours," I say, wanting to make her feel less alone about her problems at home. "Maintaining control over things is a lost cause."

"That sounds like heaven."

"Hardly!" I hesitate, and then for some reason I let a thought tumble out. "Do you ever just imagine your life if it had taken a detour at some point and you ended up somewhere totally different?" She watches me, not answering, so I continue. "I'm adopted, and sometimes I think about my life and how I ended up here, and I can't help imagining: What if my birth mother had decided to keep me? Or even if she didn't want me, what if my birth father did? Or what if I had been adopted into another family? Where would I be? What would my life be like?" I don't know what is making me tell her this. It's like I pulled a few little twigs from the dam when I admitted what's going on with Jonah and now it's collapsing. I've never said any of this out loud before, and I'm seized with guilt. The memory of the time I met Cammie's great-grandmother nudges at me. When she learned I was adopted, she pointed a gnarled finger at me and told me I should be very grateful, that not all unwanted children were so lucky.

It stung. She seemed to assume I *wasn't* grateful, which was unfair, and she also seemed to assume my life was some kind of fairy tale, like adoptees' lives are all rainbows and unicorns. *Happy endings*. But her words — *unwanted children* — echo in my head to this day. And of course there is the guilt whenever I feel anything besides gratitude. There is also at times resentment of my friends — they are not obligated to be grateful. They can just *be*.

I'm suddenly self-conscious of my babbling to Sam, about how I must look to her. I rush to say, "Not that I would trade! My family is amazing. I just . . . sometimes I wonder what the other forks in the road looked like." I chance a peek at her. "Terrible, right?"

But her expression is kind, understanding. "I don't think it's terrible to think about if things were different."

"It feels terrible," I say. "Especially now that my mom . . ." I hesitate. It's hard to talk about my mom. It's real enough, and yet somehow talking about it makes it seem even realer. "She has cancer," I finally say. When I see Sam's concerned expression, I rush on to say, "She's okay. She had treatment and surgery, and she's in what's called a 'partial remission.' Meaning she's better and it seems to be stable, but there's still cancer there."

"That doesn't sound very reassuring," Sam says gently. The calm, utterly transparent compassion on her face makes me feel so completely understood, and it's such a relief. It feels so much better than the usual responses, which range from the uncomfortable-backing-away-slowly to the over-dramatic show of sympathy.

"Exactly! That's exactly it. Like, I don't want this reality." I gesture in frustration. "We did everything, so why is it still there? I just want to stop worrying."

She nods.

"So, anyway. That's another reason I feel bad for wishing I knew about my birth mother."

"What do you mean?"

I struggle to articulate it. "It feels disloyal somehow. Like, how can I be thinking about finding another mother when my own mother might be . . . ?"

Her brow crinkles with concern. "I understand why you'd feel that way," she says. "But I don't think wondering about where you came from means you don't love your mom, or aren't grateful, or whatever. It's hard to live with unanswerable questions." She looks down for a minute, then scoops up her M&M's. "To be honest, sometimes I wish I were adopted."

I've heard people say that before, and it always makes me bristle. *You have no idea what you're talking about,* I usually find myself thinking. But with Sam, I know there's something more than ignorance behind it, so I ask her why she feels that way.

"I worry about the genetic thing," she says.

"Is OCD hereditary?" I'm afraid to hear the answer.

"Anxiety disorders do tend to run in families. And my mom . . ." She shakes her head. "She has so many routines — you can't even believe how many. And if I mess with any of them or do something wrong, it's a disaster. I can't have someone over to the house. Like, ever."

I stare at her. "Oh my god — same. Nobody comes to my house. Not anymore." I shudder, remembering the last time. The event that put a wall between Cammie and me that has never fully come down.

She stares back, then looks down. "I never would have thought I had anything in common with Zoe Miller."

She says my name like I'm famous or something. "Why?" I ask.

She shakes her head. "You're just . . . You're kind of a prominent figure at West Hills."

I scoff. "I am not."

"You are," she says seriously, glancing up. "You're beautiful and talented, and everyone admires you. And you have the best singing voice I've ever heard."

My cheeks warm, and I wonder when she's heard me sing. Probably my solo at eighth-grade graduation. I never see her at high school shows, or really anywhere, for that matter.

"I never knew you were so nice," she says. She looks down again.

I'm a little jarred at first, because I would have thought everybody thinks I'm nice — I certainly always try to be. But then I look at this from Sam's point of view. It sounds like she's not accustomed to kindness, and the thought makes my heart hurt for her.

She looks at me, then hesitates. "What did you mean about your brother being sent away?"

My chest aches even more with the reminder of what's happening, and she sees it right away — I can tell by her panicked expression.

"I'm sorry," she says.

"No, it's okay." I want to tell her about it, for some incomprehensible reason. The thing I never want to talk about to anyone, I maybe want to share with Sam Jones. "He's disabled. Like, super disabled. And I just found out we're sending him away to live in a facility." The thought of hugging Jonah goodbye and walking away from him makes my eyes well up again, and this poor girl looks like a deer in headlights.

"Oh," she says, so softly I barely hear it.

"I don't usually talk about him," I say, wiping my eyes. "People tend to react badly to Jonah. And it really hurts when people think my brother is weird or gross." What I need to do is shut up, because I'm upsetting myself even more. Memories creep up on me that I would give anything to erase . . . Middle school kids following us and mocking Jonah at the grocery store. A couple with a perfectly behaved toddler glaring at us in an ice cream shop when Jonah bellowed in anger because my mother tried to stop him from eating ice cream with his hands. The little boy at the barbershop who pointed at Jonah and asked his mother, *Mommy, what is wrong with that boy?* I wish we never had to take him anywhere. People can be so awful. My parents have always told me to try not to get upset about it, that people can seem unkind out of ignorance, but that never made it easier for me.

"I know what it's like to feel that way about someone you love." Sam gives me a small, sad smile. "You just want to build a wall around them to protect them. And sometimes it feels like it would be easier to just run away from it all."

"God, exactly," I say. "That's part of why I love the startalk so much."

"Startalk?" She tilts her head.

"You know, with the stars? The asterisks. And Humphrey. It's like being swept away to a whole other world."

"Starworld," she says, a corner of her mouth quirking upward.

"Starworld," I repeat, a small smile finding its way to my face. "I like it."

The bell rings. She jumps and gathers up her things, and I do, too — I have choir, and the music department is clear on the other end of the school.

"Thanks for lunch and everything," I tell her.

"You're welcome," she says. "Actually, thank *you*."

I realize we've both trusted each other with the most tender thing we have. I touch her arm. "I guess our secrets are safe with each other."

Sam

My circuits won't stop malfunctioning after my unexpected lunch hour with Zoe. I keep waiting for people to look at me differently, like they know my secrets, but it doesn't happen. She's as good as her word. By AP Calculus on Thursday, I'm so obsessed with unraveling why Zoe kept a promise to someone as insignificant as me that I barely manage to take notes. Instead, the margins of my notebook fill with doodles that encroach on the neatly penned formulas.

I sketch a graceful hand, then try to conjure eyes of blue and green and bronze despite the monochromatic capabilities of my mechanical pencil. Next a dragon takes shape, his wings sweeping across the page. Wisps of smoke curl from his nostrils as he looks eagerly upon a trough of Taco Bell hot sauce. I add a sprig of cilantro poking out of one side because it seems like the sort of detail Zoe would appreciate.

I am losing my quacking mind.

Tonight's homework is going to be a real problem, and destroying the perfect grades I spent all of high school maintaining isn't an option. Thank the USS *Enterprise* I have Will, who got a head start on AP Calculus this past summer "for fun."

I text Will before the bell rings to signal the start of last period.

Study tonight? Willing to trade pb barfs for calc help.

As the sticky patina on his video game controllers can attest, Will is powerless in the face of my "peanut butter barfs," which are basically just cereal blobs held together with a candied mix of peanut butter and corn syrup. They're messy and asymmetrical, aka kryptonite to my mom, but fast enough to make that I can be in and out of the kitchen before she gets home. However, Will doesn't respond until school is out and I've walked most of the way home.

Sorry, I can't. Kitty and I are getting hot dogs tonight.

Wow, another date already? I push aside the tingle of worry trying to rise. He wouldn't give up our standing game time on Sundays, even for Kitty . . . would he? Sometimes it's the only thing I have to look forward to.

Me: **Is that a euphemism?**

Ha ha ha, perv, he says.

I text: **Have fun, but don't stick your USB into her slot on the second date.**

STOP NOW OMG! he replies.

I laugh a little because I know I made him blush, but something aches in me too. After eight years of friendship,

I've seen him through a lot of hopeless crushes. He usually pines after girls who look like the real-life incarnations of elves and princesses from our video games minus the impractical fantasy armor and swords held in suggestive ways. Or girls like Zoe — completely unattainable. But now that he's got a real date that's going somewhere, and all I've got to do tonight is a huge pile of math homework, my solitude has dimensions much larger than I'm used to. Still, I want him to be happy.

When I get home and open the front door to the house, I don't even get my shoes off before a thump from upstairs makes me jump half a mile. I drop my bag in surprise, and it hits the floor with earth-shaking force more appropriate to Mjolnir.

"Mom?" I call tentatively.

Footsteps sound, and then she appears on the stairs carrying a basket of laundry, a cross expression on her face. She's already in yoga pants and her favorite of the thick wool sweaters she knitted herself.

"Did something happen at work?" I can't fathom why she's home, or why she looks so scary.

"We had a team meeting all morning, and Kerry let us go early," Mom says. "So I decided to get a head start on this weekend's laundry."

That's when I notice the sleeve of one of my hoodies dangling from the basket.

I swallow hard. She must have gone in my room.

"I need you to clean your room tonight," she says, confirming my hypothesis. "I went in there to get your laundry, and I couldn't even tell what was clean and what was dirty because clothes are scattered everywhere."

"I can do my own laundry," I say defensively.

She goes on, undeterred. "I picked up this sweatshirt and found a dirty cereal bowl crusted with old milk from who knows how long ago. And the missing spoon I've been looking for! I don't ask much of you, Samantha —"

"What? You don't ask much of me?" I say incredulously. Memories of my lunch with Zoe flood back, of trying to explain the parameters and codes that govern my life. "It's not enough that I help cook dinner? That I waste time I could be spending on homework rinsing and re-rinsing the same vegetables over and over and wiping down the counters four times?"

Emotions cross my mom's face in rapid succession. Confusion. Hurt. Frustration. Anger.

"Living in this house means following a thousand rules that don't make sense!" I rant. "What do you even think is going to happen if a dirty bowl sits in my room? News flash: nothing!"

"You need to clean your room," she says firmly. "While you are under my roof, you live by my rules, and I will not allow you to endanger yourself by living in that disaster zone. It will take five minutes to pick up your clothes, and five more to make sure there aren't any more dirty dishes in there. This is not a complicated or unreasonable request."

"My room is *mine*! You didn't even have to go in there to get my laundry. I can do it myself — some other night when I don't have a ton of homework!"

"Samantha, I was only trying to help, and now I need you to do the same. We are a family, and you need to do your part around this house." Mom's voice shakes, her movements becoming jerky.

Anger surges in me. "Maybe if you do my homework for me." My voice rises. "How are you at parametric, polar, and vector functions? Do you know how to analyze planar curves? I spend so much time doing a bunch of crap that doesn't even need doing! And the one time I actually need to put homework first, you're telling me I don't help enough? That's bullshit!"

"Watch your language!" Mom snaps. She doesn't move toward me but looks like she wants to. Her body is tight as a piano wire.

Now that I've started ranting, I can't seem to stop. "What's more important to you? My room being clean, or my grades and my future? If you need help around the house so badly, maybe you shouldn't have driven Dad off. Or at least you should have had more kids first. Then you'd have a whole army of minions to clean all day long!" My voice rises like a tsunami until it's no longer under my control.

All the color vanishes from Mom's face. Guilt and anger tug me in opposite directions, but anger is stronger. "Has Dad ever talked to you about me visiting him? Or him coming here?" I ask.

She blinks at me like she can't decode the question.

"He says you're not keen on it," I continue. "What does that mean? What did you say to him?"

She comes the rest of the way down the stairs and turns away from me, headed for the laundry room.

I follow.

"He's been upsetting you from the start." She loads the laundry aggressively, like every item of clothing wronged her somehow. "You used to come back from those camping trips with your lower lip chewed half raw. He was always letting you watch those alien shows that gave you nightmares. And then he moved back to England after promising he wouldn't. Of course I try to protect you."

"Protect me? From knowing my own father wants to see me?" She won't look at me and it's making me livid. "Why didn't you tell me he wanted to see me? I thought he didn't even care!"

"We'll discuss it later," she says, still refusing to meet my eyes as she closes the washer.

There's no point.

"Forget it. I'm going to study at Coffeehole." I snatch my messenger bag from where I dropped it, hoping Coffeehole isn't too crowded. My anger with my mom smolders. If she'd let me drive the car, I could go somewhere farther away — somewhere I'd be less likely to see anyone I recognize.

I hoof it out the front door, letting it slam behind me, and stomp away in defiance of another one of my mom's rules: if a door is slammed on purpose or by accident, it must then be immediately closed again four times quietly.

Mom's texts start coming when I'm barely more than a block from home.

How dare you leave like that?

Your father has always upset you. How can you expect me to send you to England where I can't even look out for you?

The late afternoon sky pisses rain on me the entire half-hour walk, and my anger is the only thing that keeps me warm. In spite of the jagged feeling, I'm drunk on some strange power—the power to walk away from my mom. It's the first time I've ever done it. Until today, I'm not sure I knew that I could. What will the impact be? Our contract has always been that I'm good, that I'm quiet, that I help her or get out of the way.

I don't know if I can do that anymore.

Her texts keep coming.

We'll talk about this when you get home. What time will you be back?

Answer me right now, or you're in deep trouble.

SAMANTHA! ANSWER ME OR I'M GOING TO CALL.

I huff, frustrated at her ability to know exactly the threat that will get me to respond. Don't smartphones exist so that humans have plenty of ways to communicate without having to talk? I text her a halfhearted apology, telling her I'll head home later and let her know when I'm on my way.

By the time I arrive at the smallish strip-mall coffee shop, I'm soaked and freezing. My anger has faded, and I'm ready to drink plain hot water if it'll warm me up. I shove open Coffeehole's battered front door. About three-quarters of the tables are occupied with West Hills' usual mix of teenagers and gossipy suburban moms. A low hum of conversation fills the room, punctuated by an occasional burst of laughter that rises above the folksy music. From behind the counter, the fauxhawked barista raises an eyebrow at my drowned-cat chic, smiling as I approach. My discomfort with the situation dials up to eleven.

I skim the menu, picking the thing that sounds closest to hot chocolate without giving away that I'm a total wimp who would gladly drink chocolate milk with every meal given the opportunity.

"Mocha with extra whip, please," I say. Hopefully the milk will make up for the dinner I decided to forgo by running out on Mom.

"Did you go for a swim?" Fauxhawk gestures at my sodden sweatshirt.

"It's raining," I say.

"What? In Portland?" she teases.

I attempt to laugh, which comes out sounding more like a cat trying to cope with a hair ball of formidable dimensions. My verbal communication abilities apparently begin and end with stating the obvious. My skin crawls with discomfort until I feel like it's separating from my body. Is this what it'll be like when I go off to college? Every new place seeming like somewhere I don't belong? Every social interaction impossibly awkward?

The barista turns away to pull shots with practiced ease. She's more comfortable in her abundantly tattooed skin than I've ever felt my entire life. All I want is to hide, but I can't, so I go to the only safe place I have right now. Zoe is going to get the startalk she asked for. I dismiss a message from my mom acknowledging my apology and send Zoe a text.

Me: *peers out of window of ship orbiting Earth at top speed* *regards chaotic gauge indicators with alarm*

Zoe: Everything okay?

Me: *sends high-frequency transmission reading: MOSTLY*

Zoe's response comes right away. Uh oh. "Mostly"? What's going on?

With a stab of guilt, I remember the look on my mom's face when I turned to storm out the front door. It seems stupid now that I'm half an hour's walk from home with soaked shoes.

Me: *technically should not be at Coffeehole*

Zoe: You're at Coffeehole? Yum. Hunter and I just stopped for caramel lattes to help with the studying.

Ugh. Hunter. My stomach drops. She must be with him, which bothers me for reasons I can't quite identify. There's nothing wrong with that. He's her boyfriend.

Zoe: Are you AWOL?

Me: Affirmative.

Fauxhawk hands me my mocha. The whipped cream towers to a dizzying height, and she even dusted it with cocoa powder. I slink around to a booth on the far side of the coffee shop.

I sit down and write: *feels bad for crashing your study date with Hunter*

I don't actually feel bad, but for some reason it feels necessary to push at the edges of my discomfort over knowing she's with him when I just want her in Starworld with me.

Zoe: Study date with Hunter: answer to the question WHAT IS

AN OXYMORON? He had some creative ideas for trying to help me understand magnetism. NOT HELPFUL. Men!

I wouldn't know the first thing about men, but I do know some things about magnetism.

Me: Tell him you'd both have to eat a bunch of magnetized rocks. *points out that only ferromagnetism is strong enough to be felt by humans*

Zoe: Clearly I have the WRONG TUTOR. ☺ Anyway, are you all right? I'm glad you reached out.

Her gladness goes off in me like a firework.

Me: *drowns sorrows in mocha*

Zoe: *wishes for another caramel latte*

Me: *designs a drone to bring you coffee* *names first prototype BOY-FRND01*

Zoe: *clones him so you can have a BOY-FRND02*

I hesitate before writing back. In theory, I could tell her that maybe it's not a boyfriend I want. It's as simple as a few words, and Zoe doesn't seem like the judgmental type.

I still can't bring myself to do it.

And that's when I have to face why Zoe is a worse problem than any of the incomprehensible math in my homework tonight.

A normal girl would envy Zoe — and not just for her weatherproof hair, flawless skin, and perfect curves. She holds that extra spark that makes her stand out in any crowd. Even when her eyes fill with tears, like they did in the library, her red nose and blotchy cheeks only serve to make her eyes look greener and more radiant.

But it's not Zoe I envy. It's Hunter.

I could do his job better. Zoe wouldn't have to dodge my roving arms. She and I would bow our heads over the same page until all the problems came clear, until the books closed and I leaned over to bury my face in her neck, where I could smell the sweetness of her skin and the invisible flowers in her hair. And then maybe she'd touch me, too, like she did in the library, her hand setting off sparks that race through me to make me feel like I exist. Like I matter.

My heart races like a wild animal and it's not the caffeine.

It's also not the first time I've felt this way.

There was Ms. Greeling, my ninth-grade chemistry teacher, who might be half the reason I've done so well in every science class since. She had brown eyes warm enough to turn me to liquid, and I loved how by the last period of the school day she always had wisps of hair escaping from the bun she wore it in. She looked barely older than the seniors when she got a little unkempt like that, and as the term wore on, my curious eyes kept finding their way to the gap where her button-down shirt sometimes showed a flash of her bra. Most days I wanted to stay in her classroom for hours and learn all the mechanics of the universe. Some days I wanted other things, and I liked to think about her slender fingers laced with mine.

But that was a silly fantasy, and I recognized it as such. And while it's statistically unlikely that I'm the only girl at West Hills High who sometimes thinks about kissing girls, it is far more unlikely that a human of any gender would like me back, if they noticed me at all. But Zoe makes me want to revisit my no-dating policy, which is strong evidence that it might be best if I never speak to her again. Because she's not a fantasy — she's a person. She has a boyfriend and a life and problems of her own. I can't ever be anything more than the weirdo hanging around the fringes of her world.

So instead of writing back, I jam earbuds into my ears and open my AP Calculus textbook. I study until the world fades away, the dregs of my mocha grow cold, and I'm pages beyond the stupid drawings I did during class in the afternoon. I pause only to answer yet another text from my mom, asking for confirmation that I'm still at Coffeehole.

When I finally look up again, the whole place has cleared out. It's just me and Fauxhawk, whose tattooed biceps bulge as she wipes the counters with a stained rag and hums along to some indie band on the speakers that sounds like a bunch of melancholy goats bleating into a mandolin. It's almost nine p.m. Almost closing time. I pack up my stuff and slink out the door.

I'm barely two blocks from Coffeehole when Mom texts again.

Do you need a ride? she asks.

No, I'm already walking. I'm not sure I'm ready to face her yet. Even though I'm not mad anymore, I'm also not especially contrite, and I can't figure out if I should be. There are still a lot of thoughts in my head to untangle.

My sweatshirt still isn't completely dry, so the damp night air makes me shiver. Even through the rain, a hint of wood smoke hangs in the air, which makes me think of Dad again: of campfires and fishing trips and staring up into the impossible explosion of summer stars. He loved the outdoors in the Willamette Valley, saying that all the rain reminded him of England — his home.

He had a laugh that came easily, the contagious kind. He called me "Sammy" or "love" or "Smarzolian," which was some type of alien he made up. He thought it was funny if I accidentally knocked over the popcorn and never asked me to help him clean it up until our show was over. It was at his house every other weekend that I fell in love with old sci-fi TV shows we watched together: *Doctor Who*, *Star Trek*, *Firefly*, and *Farscape*. His friends from the engineering firm where he worked taught me to play poker and how to draw perfect circles. He was the one who signed me up for Imagineering as part of the Talented and Gifted program in elementary school and photographed the moment my eyes lit up when we launched the first rocket I designed myself. My times with him were the reason I'd started dreaming about the stars, wondering what I might be able to do to help humanity reach them.

But somehow, in spite of the good times we'd had, he left. When he was offered the job transfer to London, the pull of his homeland was stronger than any connection he felt to me. I understood some of his reasoning — he worried about my grandfather, who had been alone and in declining health since my grandmother passed away. I knew he missed his "mates" from Cambridge, most of whom chose to stay in the UK. He used to tell me all the time that he loved me, and nothing in the world was more important to him than I was.

Still, it wasn't enough to make him stay.

My parents asked me if I had any feelings about the custody arrangements, Mom with tears in her eyes and Dad with a worried crease in his forehead, but how was I supposed to feel anything but confusion and heartbreak? I loved them both. I needed them both. Middle school had been a horror of alternately being teased and ignored, and Dad's move was the shit frosting on a cake made of misery.

As it turns out, judges don't like to take children from their mothers, especially when they've had primary custody for seven years. Dad agreed it would be terrible to move me so far away, leaving Mom all alone, so Mom got full custody.

The day Dad came to say goodbye, he brought me a box filled with the last of my things from the town house: old toys and gadgets and books he'd turned up as the Craigslist buyers and movers and friends emptied his home. Dry late-August summer heat scorched us both as he told me he would miss me, that I could visit, that he'd never be more than an email or a phone call away. He hugged me so long, I thought maybe it was all a mistake, maybe he wouldn't leave, maybe he was just getting a new place in town and my life as I knew it wasn't really ending.

But it was.

And it did.

I had walked back into the house feeling like a hole had been blown through me, like my guts lay strewn on the patio and my heart was on its way to catch a plane to London. Up in my room, I shoved the box of memories under the bed. I wasn't ready to deal with it. Still, all around me there were reminders of him — things like the Wonder Woman poster he'd given me the prior Christmas; *Runaways, Paper Girls, Ms. Marvel,* and the rest of the shelf full of graphic novels he'd introduced me to; and a goofy-looking robot he helped me make out of an empty soda can when I was eight.

Staring at that stupid can, I knew exactly what I needed to do.

Be a robot.

Feel nothing.

How else would I ever survive?

My phone buzzes in my palm and breaks the bitter reverie just as I walk in the front door of my house. It's Zoe again.

Zoe: *looks up in search of Humphrey*

A thrill races through my body. She's asking me for an escape — for somewhere to go.

"I'm home!" I yell. The TV blares from the living room, and I fly up the stairs hoping Mom won't follow me. Once I'm safely shut in my room, I switch to my computer so I can type more easily.

Me: *throws a grappling hook into the stars* *tugs, popping open a door in the sky*

Zoe: *grabs you and jumps on a comet to follow*

Me: *conjures a palace out of stardust and paves the entryway with polished asteroid flagstones*

"Samantha, did I hear you come in?" Mom calls from downstairs.

I bristle at the interruption. I don't want to talk to Mom right now, and I especially don't want to rehash what happened earlier.

"Yes, but I still have work to finish!" I shout.

Zoe: *plants the comet we rode in on and grows a giant fractal tree to shelter the castle courtyard*

Me: *coaxes flowers out of the ground until they blossom with sparkling starlike hearts*

Zoe: *whistles for Humphrey to come pose for a topiary shaped in his likeness*

Downstairs the TV shuts off and I can hear Mom pacing around in the living room, but something is off about it. She keeps going in and out of the kitchen through the front hallway. The floor at the bottom of the stairs creaks every time she walks over it.

Me: *weaves a crown from the flowers and places it on your head* *twists a fractal tree branch into a scepter with a nebula for a jewel* *dubs you queen of Starworld*

Zoe: *knights you with the scepter*

Me: *pulls a sword out of a star in preparation for adventure*

Zoe: *packs spicy snacks for the journey*

I'm giddy. Starworld is starting to feel bigger and more real — like somewhere we could spend forever exploring.

Me: *activates the conversion mechanism to transform one of the castle turrets into a rocket ship*

Zoe: *sits in captain's chair, hoping you know how to navigate*

Me: *initializes launch sequence* *buckles up for entry into hyperspace* *guides ship into a wormhole to carry us across multiple galaxies*

Mom's pacing is driving me up a wall, somehow seeming to grow louder with each pass she makes. I resent the distraction from my conversation with Zoe, not to mention that if she doesn't knock it off, I'll never be able to finish the last of my homework later, much less sleep.

Me: *carefully lands on a new planet where the sun is just rising over the crimson hills*

Zoe: *marvels at Technicolor landscape*

Me: *points to a blue forest filled with tree houses that comprise a robot factory*

Zoe: *wonders if they are working on a new and improved BOY-FRND model*

Me: *heads for the closest ladder into the trees*

Zoe: *takes the pulley-operated elevator*

I laugh. I love that she always adds something new to whatever I create.

Mom creaks past again, then comes up the stairs. I brace myself for her knock on my door, but it doesn't come. She goes back down and makes her loop again.

It almost would have been better if she confronted me, because I'm the one who set her in this pattern. I know what's causing it.

Me: *must step away from treetop robot factory to untangle compulsion loop on the home front*

Zoe: *sends you good untangling vibes* *sighs sadly* *also returns to home front and homework*

I leave my phone on the bed and pad down the stairs, waiting until Mom is in the living room again — close enough to hear me, but just far enough away that she's unlikely to start a conversation.

I close the front door four times, softly. As much as I hate doing these pointless things, it's easier to finish the routine and placate her. I can't live with the guilt of being the reason she's anxious.

I go back upstairs to find one more unread message from Zoe: Good night, Sam. See you in Starworld tomorrow?

Me: *will always be on the other side of the door in the sky*

I set down my phone and open my window to let in a gust of chilly air, hoping it will bring me back to earth. Raindrops blow off a pine tree into my room, spattering the worn green cushion lining the bay window. I try to breathe like a normal person, but my head still swirls with stars.

Late Sunday morning, Cammie, Syd, Erin, and I are on our way to our weekly "appointment" at Ace's Famous Burritos.

Cammie has a Bach sonata playing on loop—a piece she's trying to learn for college auditions, since she hopes to play in the symphony wherever she goes. She will, of course; I don't know why she stresses about it. In senior superlatives, she'll be our class's Most Likely to Succeed, without a doubt. Erin will be Biggest Partier, which is funny, because when we became friends in middle school, she was even shyer than I was. Syd, I don't know. If anything, probably Biggest Gossip—she always has her thumb on the pulse of what's going on. Me, maybe Best Singer? But for Cammie, everything has always seemed clear and certain. If opposites attract, that would explain a lot about our friendship.

In the back seat, Syd is talking about who's hooking up with whom in STOTS.

"How's the play going, Syd?" I ask, craning around to look at her.

The briefest expression crosses her face before she responds. Guilt? Worry? I know she feels bad that I'm not in the show. She says, "It's okay — you know how it is with STOTS. It's a disaster until opening night, pretty much."

"Right," I say. It's true. But that was part of the thrill of it. The drama around the drama.

"The play sounds bizarre," Erin says, not looking up from her phone.

"*Elliot* is bizarre," Syd says. "I've known him since kinder-garten. He's always been strange. Nice, but strange."

"He is not," I argue. "He just has his own style." An understatement. He has had an incomprehensibly full beard since freshman year and is typically outfitted in some combination of graphic tees, resale shop blazers, and neon high-tops.

Cammie turns down the music. "What's the play about?" she asks.

"It's a really cool story," I tell her. "It's about the longing for home, basically." I think about Sam's painting, and how perfectly it calls to mind the main character's home on Gorxon, which he can't remember but is clearly imprinted in him somewhere. "This guy, Chris . . . He longs for something, he feels something missing, but he doesn't know what it is, and he spends his life unconsciously chasing the past he's been cut off from. And he never quite finds happiness." Again I have a pang thinking of what I might have brought to the show in the role of his wife, who would move mountains to make the world okay for him. Caring so deeply that the people you love are okay—there are few things I understand better than that.

"Sounds cheerful," Cammie jokes.

"I think it's kind of brilliant," I say.

"Really? Well, I can't wait to see it," she says. As she pulls into the parking lot at Ace's, it occurs to me to wonder if it's a place that would work for Sam's mom. *Ace's Famous Burritos.* I can see immediately it's a lost cause: A is odd, and it's probably a nonstarter anyway because of the apostrophe. I think about telling Sam she should try this place, but then I wonder—does she have friends, besides that tall guy she seems to hang out with? People to go out and have fun with? Maybe making restaurant suggestions would be kind of a jerk thing to do, if she's trapped in her mother's world of matching colors and even numbers.

We climb out of the car and duck through the light rain toward the door. "Are you wearing your hair up or down, Zo?" Syd asks me.

I mentally scroll back to the background noise in the car and realize they've been talking about Homecoming. "Down," I say. I don't have to think about it; I always keep my birthmark covered, except at home, where I sometimes wear a ponytail or twist my hair into a clip to get it out of my face. The mark isn't giant or unsightly—it's just a light brown random blob, about the size of a dime—but it's a mar, an imperfection. It bothers me a lot, and it bothers me that it bothers me. It's not that I think my birth mother would have kept me if I didn't have this flaw, but sometimes it's hard not to be overly critical of every little thing when you don't know *why* you were given up.

Cammie pulls the door open, and we enter a vapor cloud of spicy meat and fried things, causing me to salivate instantly. We grab our regular booth in the back. When we go to Ace's with Cammie — something we've done nearly weekly since Cammie got a bright shiny Ford Fusion on her birthday sophomore year — our whole bill is half price, since Ace is her cousin (and he's actually Uriel, but "Uri's Famous Burritos" seems a clear marketing fail).

"We have to get nachos," Cammie says. "Uri changed the cheese sauce and it's amazing." She's applying Dr Pepper lip balm and looking at something on her phone; she doesn't need to read the menu. "Guys, the final count from the instrument drive was forty-six! Damn. We do good work."

Cammie is president of Sister Symphonies, an organization at our high school that collects used instruments to donate to less fortunate schools. She may look like her father — dark hair and brows, olive skin, wide gleaming smile — but personality-wise, she's a carbon copy of her mother: confident, extroverted, and ambitious. Her mom is president of the PTO, and I would wager any amount of money that twenty-five years from now, Cammie will be, too. She can rope anyone into anything. Case in point: she got us all to join Sister Symphonies, and none of us even plays an instrument. Except Cammie, who of course is first chair violin in the symphony.

"It was the free cake you got the French bakery to donate,"

Syd says, not looking up from the menu. "People get kind of stupid about cake. It was brilliant to include that on the flyers."

"Oh my god," Erin says, glancing up with her nearly perfectly round blue eyes. "Did you try the one with the hazelnut buttercream? I hurt myself on that one."

"I was too busy mainlining the chocolate mousse cupcakes," Syd says, laying down her menu. "Does anyone want to get the chipotle chicken burrito and go halfsies with me on the chorizo-and-egg one?"

"I will," Cammie says, gathering the menus. "I'll go order. Zo, I'm guessing you want the usual?"

I always get the carnitas burrito, but today for some reason I'm eyeing the Inferno: *Chile de árbol-simmered pork, hot Hatch chiles, Chihuahua cheese, and a ghost chile and habanero sauce. Highly inadvisable.* "I'll have the Inferno," I tell Cammie, handing her the menu.

"No." She shakes her head. "You will die."

"I saw someone eat one of those once, Zoe," Syd tells me. "The man was *crying*."

"Well, maybe I feel like crying," I say. I kind of do, but I'm not ready to tell them why. Until I can talk about what's happening to Jonah without crying, it is not up for discussion.

"It's your funeral," Cammie says, striding off to the counter.

Cammie's been my best friend since sixth grade. But Jonah, through no fault of his own, has infiltrated every aspect of my life, and his reach is impressive. We became friends right around the time I was becoming more sensitive to people's responses to Jonah, and more guarded. But Cammie was a good person, kind, and easygoing, and I felt okay about her being around. But Jonah as a little boy was different. Yes, he was messy and sometimes loud and he could be stubborn, but those things look different on a cute, chubby kid than they do on a towering giant of a young man.

And of course, with puberty, other things changed, too. And something happened last year that put an end to my having people over. Even Cammie.

The memory floods back. Cammie and I were in my living room working on a joint biology project on the effects of microwave radiation on seed germination. Her house was under renovations and the library was closed, and my mom insisted it was fine that we work at our house, even though she was still recovering from her latest round of chemo. I was joking around, naming the seeds according to what shape or animal the sprouts looked like to me, when I realized Cammie wasn't laughing. She was staring across the room.

I followed her eyes to find Jonah making his way slowly down the stairs, buck naked.

I froze, horrified. Jonah stopped halfway down the stairs, and then I saw what he was doing, where his hand was, the way his penis pointed skyward. I wanted to scream at Cammie to stop looking, but instead I screamed for my mother, who was coming for Jonah as quickly as she could manage, which in her current condition wasn't nearly quickly enough. She hadn't even paused to grab the sky-blue stocking cap she'd taken to wearing as her hair fell out.

"Sorry about that," she said to us, clearly mortified,

presumably by Jonah's nakedness, but maybe also by someone outside of the four of us seeing her baldness. When she reached him and saw what he was doing, her ashen face flushed noticeably. "Oh dear," she said, turning him away from us. "Come on, Jonah, upstairs." Her eyes caught mine for just a moment, and her expression was so defeated, so apologetic, that it was almost too much. I wanted to run, but where would I go? Instead, pushing down tears and avoiding Cammie's eyes, I said to her softly, "Don't tell anyone."

"I won't, Zoe," she'd said, reaching for my hand. "You know I won't."

And it wasn't that I didn't trust her. It was that the possibility that she'd tell anyone, no matter how infinitesimal it was, and the way people might react or laugh or gossip if they knew filled me with panic.

I can't say I hadn't been embarrassed by Jonah before; you go somewhere with someone like him, someone who makes strange noises and gestures, and people are going to stare and whisper and look judgmental — or worse, pitying. But this was more than embarrassment. This was *shame.* And not just shame over Jonah. Shame that I felt shame. Sometimes the line between wanting to protect him and wanting to protect myself is uncomfortably blurry.

Cammie slides back into our booth, bringing a whiff of herbal shampoo with her, pulling me back into the present. "Apparently," she says, "Uri's mom had a boob job."

A chill runs through me at the thought of breast surgery, and immediately that familiar feeling hits me of being alone in a room full of people, of being on the outside looking in.

To me breast surgery means mastectomy, not jokes and cosmetics. It's hard to have a sense of humor about this subject.

Cammie slips the paper wrapper off a straw and sticks it into her water. "Uri says she will show them to literally anyone." She chortles. "I believe it."

"Is this the aunt who won the limbo contest at your bat mitzvah?" Erin asks. "Did she get boobs?"

"No," I say, forcing myself to participate before anyone remembers about my mom's cancer and the mood is killed. "That was her aunt Mo. She means her aunt Becca, and I'm guessing this was a reduction."

Cammie grins. "A major reduction. She's now a small C, Uri says. She was, like, a G cup or something before. Apparently she's obsessed with them."

"I would have taken the leftovers," Syd says, making a face.

Erin laughs and bumps Syd's shoulder. "Be glad you're so small. Less to travel south."

Syd glances down at herself and says, "I could be twice as big and still be small."

Cammie tells Syd, "Well, you come by it honestly." And everyone laughs, because Syd's mom is also flat-chested. They're built exactly the same, Syd and her mom, and now I can add "chest size" to the ten thousand things I wonder about my birth mother.

The server approaches with a tray of food, and I'm relieved for the distraction. I slide my water and phone aside as he hands us our orders.

"My eyes!" Cammie yells, passing my plate to me. "The

steam from your death burrito has singed my corneas! I'm blind!"

I can't help laughing at her drama. But she's right — it actually *smells* hot, and the plate is surrounded by a warning medley of hot chiles for garnish. *Humphrey*, I think. I pull out my phone and snap a picture, then, before I can overthink it, I send it to Sam Jones. I quickly type: *wonders how far this could get us*

I set my phone on my lap so I can feel it buzz if she replies. I feel everyone's eyes on me as I cut into the burrito. It spills with melted cheese and red-orange oils — it looks indescribably delicious. "Oh my god, stare at something else," I tell them, laughing. I take a bite.

It takes a long moment for the full impact. There are several kinds of heats: a fast, exciting one on my tongue and lips, and then a slower, burnier one in my throat. There is also a feeling of my sinuses being napalmed. And then, a flash of complete fire brings up the rear.

I give them a grin and *mmmmm* loudly. Syd passes me a napkin and I wipe my eyes. "More," I say, waving a hand at her. My nose is running, too.

"You never listen," Cammie says, petting my hair. "Silly foolish girl."

In response, I take another large bite. It hurts. But it's *so good*.

When my phone buzzes, I jump about a mile. When the others start to eat, I sneak a look.

Sam: *stares* *pulls out Scoville/dragon scale and calculates distance in excess of twenty billion light-years*

My friends' conversation turns to college visits, a subject to which I have little to contribute. I type a response to Sam.

EXCELLENT. I could use a few billion light-years away from here. How are things with you?

Sam: **I could also use some distance. And maybe a planet where odd numbers are allowed. *is trying not to interfere with certain people's routines***

Me: ☹ **Sorry things are rough. Things at my house are kind of a dumpster fire, too.**

Sam: **Blergh. Speaking of fires, are you actually eating that burrito or is that just some scary photo you found on the internet?**

Me: **I AM EATING IT. *breathes fire***

Sam: ***hides behind Humphrey in hopes that he's flameproof***

Suddenly Cammie is leaning in, trying to see my phone. "What are you grinning about? Is Hunter sending you pictures of the bulge in his pants?"

I jerk away, shielding my phone, and everyone laughs. They watch me expectantly.

"Maybe," I say, angling myself so Cammie can't see my screen. I feel bad, especially because lately it feels like I share less and less with my friends. But it's easier to let them think it's Hunter than to explain texting with Sam Jones.

It occurs to me with a stab of sadness that at one time, it *would* have been Hunter's messages that I couldn't resist, that made me happy. But that giddy, all-encompassing preoccupation with him has faded.

I go back to messaging Sam: ***pats Humphrey carefully* *wonders what else he can do***

Sam: ***sets him loose to rampage & burninate our enemies***

Me: *pretends to know what burninating is* *wonders if it's urinating with fire*

Sam: *pees fire and dies laughing*

I'm trying not to laugh, but I'm halfway through my burrito and pretty much crying, as warned, so it might be hard to tell the difference. I message Sam between bites, while trying to act interested in what my friends are saying.

Me: *urges Humphrey toward the castle now that the world is burned down*

Sam: *lands him atop a spire from which the smoking Earth can be seen in the distance*

Me: *adds a slide to the turret and rides it into a window*

Syd nudges me from across the booth with her foot. "Zoe! I was talking to you."

"Sorry," I say, setting my phone down. "What were you saying?"

"I was telling Erin about that time in sixth grade when you broke a beaker in science and you cried."

I laugh, although it certainly wasn't funny at the time. The sudden hush after the shatter, all the eyes on me. I was mortified.

"Oh my gosh," Erin says, making a sad face at me. "You poor thing. Did you get in trouble?"

Syd laughs. "No, Miss Grossman *hugged* her because she felt so bad for her."

My eyes sting stupidly, remembering. Miss Grossman's hug made me feel better, but it also embarrassed me and made me cry harder. "She was so nice."

"Yeah," Syd says. "Anyway, to get to my point . . . I saw her at Target — in the condom aisle!" She pauses to giggle, covering her mouth with her blue-manicured fingers. "And she's now Mrs. Flanigan, and she's moving to Costa Rica."

"Oh, wow," I say. It's interesting, but not as interesting as Sam. I glance back at my phone.

Sam: *swoops in after you only to crash headlong into a rusty suit of armor* *stumbles blindly through the castle with helmet on backward*

I barely stop myself from giggling.

Me: *pries helmet off your head with scepter*

She goes off on a goofy romp through the castle with silly actions and mishaps, and I am so entranced that I all but forget where I am until I notice the time on my phone.

"Hey, I need to get going," I tell Cammie. My dad wants to take us all to Bonney Butte for birding, hoping to catch some fall raptor migration for a last family hurrah. With luck, Jonah will see some hawks — maybe even an eagle or a merlin. I don't even know what a merlin is, but if there is one, my dad will point it out to Jonah and they will both be overjoyed, and so my mom and I will be, too.

"Okay," Cammie says, and she immediately takes over, as is her wont. She moves my burrito into a container and arranges the chile garnishes to rise vertically from the top like trees. Only in my mind's eye, they're not chiles on a burrito or trees in a forest. They're Humphrey's gleaming spikes.

I peek back at my phone to see what Sam's up to.

"I need a boyfriend," Cammie says, shaking her head at me. "Look how happy you are."

The irony doesn't escape me. Hunter has been more a

source of stress and pressure than comfort lately. On top of that, my mom's cancer won't go away, and Jonah is being relinquished to strangers. "Happy" is not how I'd describe myself.

And yet . . . I'm smiling.

"You don't have time for a boyfriend," I remind her, petting her knee.

"That's not true!" she says, an expression of mock outrage on her face. "I have twenty-five free minutes on Thursdays between my violin lesson and dinner."

Syd points out that's more than enough time for sex with every guy she's ever slept with, and we all crack up.

We head out to the car. As we make our way to my house, they talk again about the overnighter on Lake Oswego after Homecoming — what swimsuits they'll bring for the hot tub, what kind of booze they're getting, if there might be drugs and which ones they would try.

"Did your parents say you can go, Zoe?" Erin asks. "Connor said Hunter hasn't paid his share because he doesn't know if you can go."

I can't even imagine asking them now, with everything that's going on with Jonah. The idea of my dad's disappointed expression is more than I can bear.

"I can't go," I say, putting on what I hope is a regretful expression. "But I haven't told Hunter yet."

"Aww, no!" Cammie sticks her lower lip out in a mock pout. "Do you want my mom to talk to your mom?"

I almost laugh because that would totally work, if my mom were the problem.

Erin says, "Sneak out! I do it all the time."

All three of them crack up, which I guess goes to show how absurd the idea of my sneaking out is.

Cammie pats my arm. "I understand, Zo. We'll miss you."

Gratitude rushes through me — not just for knowing she'll miss me, but for her easy acceptance. "Thanks, Cam. Take lots of pictures!" I pull out my phone and pick up where Sam left off our adventure in the castle gardens.

Me: *pulls you out of the space briar patch* *finds you an emerald-adorned suit of armor to bring out the green in your eyes* *has the castle seamstress add on a hoodie*

I smile, anticipating her response. While I wait, I stare out at the rain and sing along quietly with the radio, putting on a harmony, annoyed as always that the wipers refuse to obey the music's rhythm.

Sam: *draws hoodie strings tight and accidentally twirls into a pillar*

I crack up again, just as we pull into my driveway.

"What's so hilarious anyway?"

Erin's voice in my ear makes me jump. She's leaning over my shoulder from the back seat.

"Sam Jones?" She says it in the same tone one might say *day-old sushi?* She tells the others, "She's messaging with Sam Jones."

"Why?" Syd asks, sounding as baffled as Erin. "That girl's weird as shit."

I glance up at Cammie, who is looking at me with a confused expression, although she doesn't contribute to the stream of insults.

I want to defend Sam, but the idea of explaining my relationship with her seems complicated. "She's lending me her painting for the show," I say, typing out a last message to Sam: Almost home – gotta go for now. My face feels hot. "See you," I mumble to Cammie as I climb out of the car.

When I walk in the door, I hear a commotion upstairs. Mom is shouting at Jonah to give her something. He's bellowing back at her. My heart pounds, because I know the sound of Jonah's anger escalating. I run to the kitchen to put away my burrito. As I close the fridge, I hear my mother shriek, "Jonah! Let go!" and then there's a loud bang.

I race up the stairs, where I find my mom in the hallway, holding the back of her head. "He pushed me into the wall," she says.

Jonah is facing away from us both, clutching something that's making crumbs everywhere. Potato chips, maybe.

"Are you okay?" I ask my mom, who's still holding the back of her head. I shoot a frustrated look at Jonah. I'm angry with him, even if I shouldn't be. He hurt Mom, and she's already weak. And right now she looks like she might cry.

"Where's Dad?" I ask.

"Out getting Jonah's prescriptions. He wants to be on the road ASAP, but I'm going to need to get Jonah showered first."

That's when the smell hits me: excrement.

Jonah turns slightly, rocking back and forth on his feet the way he does, and he sort of side-eyes my mom as he lifts a handful of chips to his mouth. She sighs. She waits for him to finish the chips, then softly says, "Come on, Jonah. Bathroom."

"I'll clean up the chips," I tell my mom, gesturing at the floor.

"Thank you."

She doesn't have to thank me. I'm getting the easy job here and we both know it.

I sweep up the crumbs and also clean the kitchen; detritus from Jonah's lunch is everywhere. In five days, there won't be any more of Jonah's messes to clean up. It should be a bright spot in this whole thing, but it's not remotely bright. My anger dissipates as I worry that we're making a terrible mistake, but then I think about my parents' worst fear, which my mother's cancer brings into sharp relief: what happens to Jonah if and when something happens to them? And I know that this is necessary and sensible and also kind of a stroke of good fortune.

I never imagined a stroke of good fortune could hurt so much.

Upstairs, Mom is giving Jonah a shower. I can tell by the dueling voices that my mom is washing his hair—the only part of showers Jonah doesn't like. My dad usually showers Jonah because he's tall enough to keep shampoo from getting in Jonah's eyes. I wonder how showers will go at Little Lambs Village. Will they get soap in his eyes? I disappear into my room, closing the door softly behind me. I flop down on my bed and let myself cry.

How is this all going to work? What if they can't handle him? What if they don't like him? What if he hurts them? Worse, what if they are too rough with him? I can't bear the thought of anybody hurting him. I lie with my face in my pillow and let my tears soak in. The worries in my head spin into infinity. My whole family seems to be falling apart, one by one. Who's next? My dad has high blood pressure. What if he has a stroke? I can't bear the thought of a single thing getting worse.

I wish there were something, anything, I could do. It's not as if I can move in with Jonah and spend a week helping him transition, explaining all his quirks and preferences and noises to the staff. In a way, it's probably a good thing his first day at Little Lambs Village is a school day and I'm not going with my parents to drop him off. I'm sure I'd cry and make everything worse for everyone. And I know my parents are perfectly capable of advocating for Jonah. I just wish I felt confident that the staff there will understand him, and that they'll be kind to him.

After fretting about it a while, it occurs to me that maybe there *is* something I can do.

I go to my computer and open a document.

ABOUT JONAH MILLER

1. He loves birds and nature. He will sit very still and quiet when nature videos are playing.

2. He very much likes to be petted on his arm or his back. He likes to be soothed this way, and he will make humming or cooing noises sometimes. That means he's happy.

3. He loves being sung to.

I pause, considering naming some of his favorite songs, but then I worry: Will it confuse him, someone else singing him the songs I sing to him? Will it remind him of me and make him sad? Unable to bear the thought, I leave number three as is.

4. He sometimes gets upset if he wants food and can't have it. Things that help are distracting him with songs or videos, or . . .

I sigh. Sometimes the only fix is letting him have what he wants. I don't imagine that's going to go over well in a professional setting, whatever that is. I decide to come back to number four. I type a 5 and stare at the screen, wishing for some way to tell them everything I want them to know about Jonah. I type:

5. He is really a sweet kid. You might have to be patient with him sometimes, but if you give him a chance

I break off because I'm crying again. After a while, I type:

6. I love him with my whole heart.

I close my computer, feeling beaten. I can't make strangers be loving and kind to Jonah with a stupid list.

I lie back down on the bed. Mom is getting Jonah dressed next door. He is still making noise but softer now. I hear my dad go in and try to get them to hurry up. He's worried about how much daylight will be left by the time we get to Bonney Butte. Moments later, my mom comes and knocks on my door.

"Ready to go?" she asks, poking her head in. I sit up as she enters, and her face falls when she sees mine. She sits next to me and puts her arms around me. "Oh, Zoe," she whispers. "What are we going to do?"

I lean on her quietly as she rocks us back and forth, my eyes falling on the pink lump of her chemo port scar, visible in the open neck of her collar. I hate seeing it, hate thinking about that port, that frail and hopeful tether to life — an endless, taunting reminder of how capricious and arbitrary it all is. Every day I worry that the cancer is growing, and I don't understand how the doctors think it is okay to go so many weeks without checking. Cancer calls the shots, not us — that much is clear.

"I wish it weren't so soon," she murmurs. "I'm not ready."

"We'll never be ready," I point out.

"But he's only fifteen," she says, her voice breaking, along with my heart.

I pull back, suddenly gripped with a thought. "What about his school?" He's used to his school — his bus, his teachers and aides. How hard will new people and routines be?

She brushes my hair out of my face. "He'll go to a new one in Eugene. There's a big meeting about that on Wednesday — transfer papers, his IEP, all that. The Baxters went through the same thing — you remember, the family we met at the fundraiser?"

I nod.

"Moira says that Little Lambs Village was really great about helping with the school transition."

I don't say what I'm thinking, because there's no point. Changing his school at the same time as we move him into a strange place . . . That's not fair. That's not reasonable. Really, it's kind of unthinkable. And I'm about 100 percent sure my mother doesn't need me to point that out.

The afternoon is good to us. Jonah is treated to an amazing thing at Bonney Butte: a whole bunch of broad-winged hawks coasting above on the thermals. A "kettle," it's called, according to a man we meet in the parking lot. He and his wife must be eighty at least, both with hats and binoculars. They are just returning from the lookout point, which is only reachable on foot, and given the shortage of time, we'll be looking out from the parking lot in the lawn chairs my dad packed.

As the midafternoon stretches on, we spot a merlin, which, it turns out, is a kind of falcon. I scoot my chair close to Jonah's and wrap my hands around his warm arm. He never takes his eyes off the sky, and he makes a happy noise and signs *bird* anytime a new bird comes into view. When that happens, my dad identifies the bird and my mom looks it up in her Audubon book and reads aloud to us. We sit in our folding chairs gazing at the sky and eating the apple slices and homemade oatmeal cookies my mom packed, and it's about as grand a final outing as Jonah could have had. Finally, when the wind picks up and brings rain with it, we pack up and turn back.

The drive home is quiet. I pull out my phone and look up birding in Eugene and discover there is an Audubon society and several good birding sites. Maybe we can take Jonah sometimes on weekends after he moves to Little Lambs Village. The thought brings a little surge of hopeful, good feelings where there so far have been none.

It's early evening by the time we get home, and my parents cap off the day by ordering pizza — one of Jonah's favorite meals.

I retreat to my room and curl up on my bed. I try to imagine the house without Jonah. I can't. Everything revolves around Jonah — it has to. If he's gone, do we even know how to carry on? But the truth is, how we'll carry on without Jonah is a minor concern compared to how Jonah will carry on without us.

Still, there's no denying how empty the house will seem. So much time goes into his care — how will we fill it? I won't even need to be home to help after school, to clean up and help with dinner. As the reality of it sinks in, I realize I could do theater again. Not in time for this show, of course, but the next one. And the spring musical, which is going to be *Rent*. I was pretty devastated at the idea of not being in the musical my senior year. And yet, somehow, the idea of being able to do it fails to lift my spirits. All I can think of is sending Jonah away. *Throwing him away,* a little voice in my head says. Nothing feels larger than that. Not even close.

When my phone dings, I reach for it quickly, hoping it might be Sam with more Starworld, which is just what I need. But it's not Sam. It's Hunter. Update: Janowski is bringing an espresso machine to the house. You could have a caramel latte in the morning (plus cider donuts courtesy of the Cavanaughs). Come? Please? Pretty please? Pretty please with a jalapeño on top? ;-)

Ha. My increasing obsession with spicy food has not escaped him. My amusement is short-lived, though, because I have to face telling him I'm not going, and I know how disappointed he's going to be. But I can't put it off any longer. I'm really sorry, I write. I can't go. I tried, but . . . You know how my dad is.

I feel a stab of guilt for the lie.

He writes: I was afraid of that. Maybe he'd have felt differently if you'd let him get to know me.

Trust me, it wouldn't have mattered! I write. He wouldn't let me go to an overnighter if it were chaperoned by nuns!

I guess we'll never know, he writes. Man. That sucks.

Guilt and resentment simmer in equal measure, until it hits me: Saturday is my family's first Jonah-less day.

How can I leave my parents alone on their first day without Jonah? And how can I have fun and pretend like everything is okay when it's not? I glance up at the shimmery aquamarine dress hanging in plastic from the top of my closet door, its tags still attached, wishing it were a simple choice to just bag on the dance and return the dress.

But I can't. Hunter's disappointed enough. No way can I back out on the dance now, too.

I stare at his last line, struggling to know what to say that won't make things worse. Finally I just write: I'm sorry.

I go back to my screen of startalk with Sam. I want more. I write: UGH BOYFRIENDS.

Long minutes pass. She must be busy. Or, possibly, *UGH BOYFRIENDS* is about the stupidest text anyone ever sent. I lie back down and listen to the sounds from downstairs. Dad has a video on for Jonah—*Animals of Madagascar*. I know the music by heart. To all of them. I'm fretting again about whether they'll let Jonah watch his videos at Little Lambs Village when the doorbell rings. Pizza.

I've just finished eating and am cleaning up the table when my phone finally dings. It's Sam! She says: *Runs BOYFRIEND through database* *no results found*

I excuse myself and run upstairs. In my room, I write: That tall guy you hang out with isn't your boyfriend?

Sam: Nope. Robots don't date.

Me: He's a robot?

Sam: No, I am. It's how to survive when people suck or you keep losing at the same stupid level of the same stupid game. Coast. Autopilot. Be a robot. Beep beep!

I'm not sure how serious she is, but if her MO is to try to avoid having emotions, then she and I are about as opposite as two people could be. I'm basically a walking sack of feelings. I cry at commercials. I worry about stray cats. I hyperventilate watching Olympic skating, peering out through my fingers. Sam would think I'm the world's biggest sap.

I write: What do robots do when other people cry?

Sam: Apply Rust-Oleum. And if it's a friend, launch missiles at their enemies.

She's sweet, in her own strange way. I want to be kind to her in return. I write: *launches missiles at lunches of matching colors and symmetry* *launches missiles at absentee dads*

Sam: *rolls through the post-apocalyptic landscape with immense satisfaction*

And before I know it, we're lost in Starworld again, taking Humphrey on some sort of magical snipe hunt. Sam stalks through an extraterrestrial jungle with the subtlety and grace of a drunken elephant, and her antics soon have me laughing so hard that the real world disappears.

Later, though, I realize at some point I'm going to have to deal with reality. I have to tell Cammie about Jonah, and Erin and Syd, although Cammie will tell them if I ask her to.

I send a message to Sam. Starworld saved my life today. It's been really rough lately, as you know. So thank you.

She writes: *bows* At your service, Your Majesty.

But I want to say something real to her. So I try again: Seriously. I don't know how I never realized how awesome you are. Apart from your art, anyway.

After a minute, there's no response, so I add: I'm glad I know you better now.

After a pause, the response comes: *searching database for appropriate responses to compliments from humans* *coughs up piece of paper that reads ERROR*

I have to smile. You're no robot. Robots don't care as deeply about people as you do, and they certainly don't make the kind of beautiful, expressive art that you do.

She writes: *dissolves into the data stream and crafts an invisibility cloak out of ones and zeros*

I write: *shakes head* Okay, good night, robot girl. Talk to you tomorrow?

She responds: *runs odds report* *calculates high probability*

I send her a smiley.

It is a comfort to know she'll be there with her kindness and wacky sense of humor and startalk through the days that lead up to Friday, when my parents pack up Jonah, drive him to Eugene, and leave him there.

A wave of pain crashes through me at the thought, making me go weak.

I don't want my brother to know what it feels like to be abandoned.

Sam

On Thursday I eat lunch with Kitty, Carlos, and Caroline, and only because Will swindles me into it with an evening invitation to play a new co-op RPG that I've been dying to try. Or rather, the three of them eat while I nervously fiddle with the paper clips securing the top of my lunch bag. Hanging out with Will's friends without him is weird. I hate that he has a different lunch period, especially today. The other problem is that even surrounded by other people, all I can think about is Zoe. Jonah moves out tomorrow.

It's a sunny fall day, warm for mid-October. Most of the school seems to be eating outside in spite of the stiff breeze shaking hidden raindrops free of the bright fall leaves. I'm perched awkwardly at one end of the picnic table, hoodie snug, ass slightly damp from the places where water lurked under the peeling green paint before I sat down. Across from me, Caroline and Kitty have laid out all their food on the table and are engaging in a complicated food swap that leaves Kitty with items that I swear are all phallic.

"Are you guys doing both days of Planet Quest Con?" Kitty asks. She finishes the question by unhinging her jaw and ramming half a banana into her tiny gullet, defying multiple laws of physics. With her tawny complexion and the splash of freckles over her petite nose, she's annoyingly cute, as is the thermal she's wearing that says SELF-RESCUING PRINCESS on the front.

"I'm going both days—if I survive Homecoming," Caroline says, adjusting her glasses. "At least they don't conflict this year."

"I have tickets for a couple of the VIP panels on Sunday," Carlos says without even looking up from his tablet. The day he doesn't have his face in some kind of device will be the day comic book movies start reliably passing the Bechdel test.

"Lucky," Caroline says.

"Whatever," Kitty says to Caroline, smacking on her banana. "You just have a crush on Adam Alvarado. You can see him at his signing booth later anyway. Probably closer up than at the panel."

Caroline shrugs and her face gets a little splotchy. "I just like the character he plays on *Planet Quest*," she says.

"Oh, trust me, anyone who has read your slash fics about General Garcia and Officer Cheng knows that," Kitty says with a smirk.

Caroline gets even splotchier and mumbles something indiscernible.

Planet Quest is not really my bag of eels, so I sneak a glance at my phone. My heart races when I see a message from Zoe.

Zoe: *could use an anti-worry robot in short order*

Me: *requests specs for said robot*

Zoe:

1. Drones to bring Jonah his favorite treats
2. Recording system so I can sing to Jonah remotely
3. Ability to manufacture colorful bird bots with GPS coordinates set to Jonah

Me: *warps to the robot factory planet and sets to work* *disassembles BOY-FRND02 to initialize new project* *hits mute button on BOY-FRND01 so he can't mansplain the best way to do this*

I look up. Across the quad Zoe's at a table with her friends, bent over her phone, shoulders shaking with laughter, typing something that is probably meant for me. The sight fills me with sparks that burst and hum through every circuit in my body. If I were human, I might try to catch her eye and smile, but instead I duck my head and grin into my phone so no one can see.

"So, Sam," Kitty says. "Who is your favorite character on *Planet Quest*?"

Even though she said my name, it still takes a second to register that Kitty is talking to me and expects a response.

"Um," I say. I can't decide if it would be seen as more loser-y to say that I don't watch much TV or that I don't like *Planet Quest*. I definitely can't explain that the reason I hate it is because the pilot aired less than a month after my dad moved to London. We'd spent most of that summer anticipating it right down to planning our themed snack menu. Then, in a span of only a few weeks came Dad's job transfer, the custody renegotiations, and the sale of his town house. Before I could even get used to the idea, he disappeared — leaving behind only a shiny new laptop as a consolation prize that was in no way a substitute for camping trips or poker nights or falling asleep on the couch with his arm around me.

When the Friday night premiere of *Planet Quest* arrived, my mom tried to help. She let me have dinner in front of the TV, which was usually forbidden, and didn't even chide me for ignoring my vegetables and eating only mac and cheese. But after my plate was empty, as the clock crept closer to seven o'clock, the absence of Dad burst in my chest like a supernova. When Mom left to do the dishes, I fled upstairs before the show even started. I waited for her to come comfort me, but she never did. There were too many things left to do, too many things left to clean, count, organize.

"Earth to Sam," Caroline says, waving a cheese cracker in front of my nose.

I snap back to rejoin the living. "Sorry," I say. "Just thinking."

"Is there anyone you're excited to see at the con?" Kitty continues. She's trying so hard.

"I'm not going," I say. It irks me that she makes so many assumptions: That I give a planet's ass about her favorite show. That I'm going to the con. I wish she'd ignore me like everyone else does. I fall back into my phone, to another message from Zoe.

Zoe: *dispatches BOY-FRND01 with coffee and silent moral support* *wolf-whistles at him and commands him to smile*

I smile at her antics. Zoe doesn't realize that in some ways, she's become all the moral support I need.

"Will and I are going to get our picture taken with Amanda Melillo during her signing on Sunday," Kitty says.

I desperately search for some fucks to give, but my reserves are empty. Also, now I'm worried. Does this mean Will made Sunday plans even though Sundays are supposed to be our gaming days now and forever?

"Great," I mutter, and go back to my phone to find a text from my mom.

Did you eat your lunch? How is everything?

This isn't an entirely new thing, her texting me while I'm at school, but there's been an uptick since the pre-Coffeehole meltdown. She's checked on me every day this week. I eyeball the untouched paper sack containing my lunch and squeeze the paper clips in my fist until I can feel them leaving imprints in my palm.

Lunch was good. Everything is fine. I don't know what to do other than to try to reassure her.

Do you know where you want to go for Halloween dinner?

I bristle. It used to be one of the family traditions I looked forward to most, so she kept it up after Dad left. However, with the increasing intensity of her focus on numbers, rightness, and food-borne illness, it's become more chore than celebration for both of us.

Still thinking about it. I send the message while the anger is still building so that I won't think it through long enough to send something I might regret. Between Will not telling me about his plans for next Sunday, the nosy banana masticator he's sent as his messenger, and my mom being my mom, I'm running out of ability to deal. Inside my head, I try out honest responses that I would never dare send to Mom:

We both know your OCD will make the final call, so why waste my time making me pretend I'm choosing?

I'd rather eat tuna out of a can in front of the TV than watch you try to turn your meal into an acceptable pattern of fours while you fret about the restaurant's sanitation practices.

Halloween is on a Saturday this year, so I plan to spend it partying with my friends. OH WAIT — I've never made any thanks to the impossibility of navigating them around your routines.

Maybe I'll save the cash for spending money in London, which by the way I'm going to visit whether you want me to or not.

The inside of my chest feels white-hot. I start doing multiplication tables in my head, beginning with sixes, a trick I've used for years to robot my way through upsetting moments. I flip back to Zoe's message and go back to Starworld, hoping my emotions won't follow me there.

Me: *adds functionality to dispense Kleenex out of one of its earholes when you are sad* *dubs it the Fairy Godbot*

Zoe: *dies*

Me: *promises to make him look less like a flying spaghetti monster after beta testing is completed*

Zoe doesn't respond, so I peek over at her table. Her phone is still clutched in her hand, but she's turned away now, talking to her friends. They're laughing about something, and she's shaking her head, protesting. But then she falls back into her phone, and two messages fly in:

*Thinks you should keep design and make him dispense

spaghetti* *is grateful to have laughed today when it didn't seem possible*

A thrill races through me that even when they're around her, she's still thinking of me. And suddenly I want to be alone with the way my heart is soaring, lost in Starworld, far away from reality and Kitty's annoying questions and the reek of Caroline's cheese-cracker breath. I manage to sit there fidgeting for maybe another five minutes before I can't take it anymore.

"I gotta go," I say, and jump up from the table.

I snatch up my bag and lunch and bolt for the closest entrance to the hellpit, which isn't far from Zoe's table. I keep my head down and my eyes averted as I pass, but just as I'm nearly to the doors and almost feel safe, Ethan, one of the guys at her table, jumps up on the bench and starts moving all jerky and weird.

"I AM SAM JONES, YOUR FAIRY GODBOT. WOULD YOU LIKE CHEESE ON YOUR SPAGHETTI?" he asks in a mechanical monotone.

I stop in my tracks.

Everyone at the table cracks up like Ethan is the funniest thing since cats on the internet. Connor Grigsby is practically convulsing. And suddenly, my invisibility has failed: even the people at surrounding tables who aren't laughing are staring at me, seeing me. But not like Zoe does. Not like I thought she did. She wrestles her phone back from Connor, and when she turns and sees me, her hand goes to her mouth. Clearly I was not meant to know that she was sharing my idiot antics with her friends for a laugh.

·123·

I bolt for the doors and don't look back, screaming through multiplication tables in my head at top mental volume, trying to drown out the chaos of feelings with numbers. But my stupid, broken brain keeps interjecting the same three words: *She told them.*

As it turns out, Will's new co-op RPG is a button masher, and consequently an excellent outlet for rage. I manage to mostly push aside my feelings about him ditching me next Sunday and channel the rest into pounding fuzzy blue squirrel monsters into pulp. To avoid thinking about Zoe, I muted all my message notifications except for Mom's and haven't looked at my phone since lunch. I can't. I won't. Everything I thought about Zoe is wrong. I shouldn't have been stupid enough to trust her — if she'd tell her friends about Starworld and let them mock the stories we made up together, the secrets I told her about my mother can't possibly be safe.

"Damn, woman!" Will says after the fourth time I massacre a pack of squirrel monsters with far more violence than is necessary. They make sad, pathetic squeaky sounds when they die, popping into little tufts of fur that get blown away in the wind. It's oddly satisfying.

"Don't call me 'woman,'" I say. My character in the game sheathes her sword and shakes open a treasure box left behind by the monsters. A dialogue box pops up that says "TRAP!"

Will groans as a second round of squirrel monsters explodes out of the treasure chest. These ones look like cute little robots, with little glowing antennae protruding from their adorable foreheads. It makes me think of Zoe and of Ethan and the spectacle in the quad. The burst of fury in my chest is instant and all-consuming.

"Fuckadoodledoo, shithooks," I say to the robosquirrels. Will scrambles to keep up, casting cure spells over and over as I throw myself into the fray with little regard for my character's hit points.

"Dude. Is everything okay?" Will asks.

His question tugs a little at something that could undo me.

"I guess things suck slightly more than usual," I finally say as I mass murder more woodland creatures.

"What happened?" he asks.

I'm surprised Kitty or Carlos didn't already tell him about lunch. Surely they saw what went down — Ethan wasn't exactly subtle.

"Some jerks reminded me today why I don't eat lunch in the quad," I say. Of course there's more, but I don't really want to talk about Kitty, or Planet Quest Con, or how scared I am of my best friend slipping away.

"Who said something? I told Kitty to be nice." Will's character gets chomped as he turns to look at me.

"No one at that table. Just some other assholes," I say. "Sometimes I really hate school. I don't know how I'm going to survive the rest of this year."

"You have enough credits to graduate early," Will says. "Why don't you just do that? You'd be done in, like, a month."

"The only thing worse than school is home," I say. "Where would I go?"

"You could always move in with me. My parents would be totally cool with that. They love you."

"Ha," I say. Mostly I think they probably just appreciate my neuroses, which made me a strong contrast with Will's overenthusiastic and less cautious nature when they taught us both to drive. I also appreciate the hell out of Will's parents. If not for them, I wouldn't have my license. Every time I bugged Mom to take me out to practice driving, it set her off into a routine spiral and there would be some excuse why she couldn't.

"'Why can't you be polite, like Sam?'" Will mocks his mother's voice. "'Why can't you remember to check your blind spots, like Sam?' She always wanted a daughter. Besides, even if my parents weren't okay with you moving in, Dylan makes so much noise, they probably wouldn't even notice."

As if on cue, his little brother goes galloping and screaming through the room upstairs, making the ceiling tremble. Will rolls his eyes.

I laugh. "Kitty would love it if I moved in with you, I'm sure."

"Yeah, she is a little jealous of you," he says.

I snort so loudly that it's a minor miracle that the mess of papers and candy wrappers and other junk doesn't get blown off the coffee table.

"How can she possibly be jealous of me?" I ask. Kitty might as well be jealous of one of Will's old T-shirts or the ratty brown couch he and I are sitting on that's got popcorn buried in it old enough to carbon-date. If anyone should be jealous, it's me, if Will starts bagging on our Sunday afternoons.

"She doesn't get why I wouldn't want to go out with you," he says. "Or maybe why you wouldn't want to date me. I told her we've never liked each other as more than friends, but she wasn't totally convinced."

"Speaking of Kitty, when were you going to tell me about next Sunday?" I ask. I try to keep the bitterness I feel out of my voice.

"Oh, you mean Planet Quest Con? That should be fun." He slurps some soda out of his Dr Pepper can. "But I told Kitty we could only go in the morning because I had to be back after lunch so I could meet you by two for gaming."

"Oh," I say. I should have known better than to think Will would ditch me. He's never been like that. Suddenly I feel guilty that my friendship with him might be creating problems for him and Kitty before their relationship is even serious. "Maybe Kitty won't be jealous if you tell her I'm a lesbo or something," I say. My tone starts out sarcastic but falters a little at the end.

Will pauses the game. "Whoa," he says, looking at me all brown eyes and floppy hair and curiosity tinged with concern. "Are you feeling more sure about that?" he asks.

I sigh and knead a hand into the lumpy couch cushion. Will and I talked about these things before, only in the most general terms — enough to establish that I knew I might be interested in dating a girl someday and that neither of us cared if the other was gay, bi, pan, ace, or anything else. I never had to have a firm answer to the question of my sexuality, because people never interested me all that much. And until Kitty, no one was ever threatened by my friendship with Will.

"Maybe," I finally say. "I don't know."

But how can I not know when something is so different about the way that Zoe makes me feel? When I get lost in Starworld with her, it's like I'm wearing my ass on my face and my heart inside out. In Starworld, she has the power to make me feel a thousand feet tall with a single message. In the real world, she can cut me off at the knees by letting people know I exist.

"Well, it's no big deal to me either way," Will says. "I'll only tell Kitty what you want me to."

"Thanks," I say. And his kind response makes me feel like I can tell him a little more. "The other thing is that my dad invited me to visit him in London."

Will's eyes widen. "I hope you said yes."

"I haven't answered him yet. I don't know if I want to go." It's not the whole truth, but I don't particularly want to explain why telling my mom about this invitation is virtually impossible. I've never told Will about her OCD.

"How can you not? You haven't seen him in forever. Besides, it's a free trip to London! You guys would have so much fun."

I discard the idea before hope can rise. "My mom wouldn't survive it," I say.

Will ponders this as we take out another batch of fuzz-balls in the video game.

"I guess Outdoor School was a bit of a disaster," he says carefully.

My heart sinks. Of course he remembers. He was right behind me on the log when I slipped and took a nosedive into the creek and got a deep scratch on the palm of my hand on the way down. It shouldn't have been a big deal—wouldn't have been, if my mom hadn't found out. The camp nurse got the bleeding stopped and closed it up with a butterfly bandage. Everything was fine until a photograph of me and Will doing crafts showed up on the Outdoor School website. In the photo I was laughing at Will's dip candle, a lumpy, melty-looking affair upon which he'd drawn a screaming face so it looked like a dying snowman. But god forbid my mother notice that I was having the time of my life—not when the bandage on my hand was in full view.

"I'm still bummed I missed archery," I say, trying to joke. But really, missing archery was the least of my problems. The problem was Mom driving to camp to take me to the ER, Mom melting down at the hospital in Nowheresville, Oregon and having to get a doctor to treat her for a panic attack, Mom upset to tears that the Outdoor School hadn't called her about my minor injury, Mom insisting I couldn't go back to camp because all it would take is one strain of flesh-eating bacteria to enter my wound and kill me, Mom taking the rest of the week off so she could make sure I didn't die of an inconsequential cut that didn't even leave a scar.

All of that without what I came home to, which was the smell of bleach so strong it nearly knocked me over when I entered the house, and Mom having gone through my room and thrown out a bunch of old blankets and stuffed animals in my absence because they were "contaminated" and might infect my hand. Later that week I overheard her on the phone with one of her Stitch & Bitch friends telling them how glad she was that I'd come home because she couldn't sleep while I was gone, even before I got hurt. Guilt rises up fresh. How can I ever leave when that's what happens in only two days?

"Have you thought about talking to your dad about her?" Will asks.

"We haven't really talked much since he left," I say. It seems unlikely that he doesn't know how bad things are with Mom, but I can't remember if she was different before he left. Sometimes I wish I had a sibling—someone to compare notes with to build a more complete picture of my family history. A person to lean on and share the burden with when things with Mom get hard.

"That sucks," Will says. "Those camping trips we went on were the best. Remember how he'd try to teach us to fly-fish even though he was terrible at it, and we'd all end up with our lines caught in the trees? And then there was that one time he finally got his line in the water and a bat took off with the fly? And then he had all these hilarious British swears, like 'oh blimey, we've got quite a cock-up on our hands' or 'keep your hands out of the fire, you gormless knobs.'"

I almost smile, but then I remember myself and tighten the armor around my mechanical heart.

"Yeah, but then he left and stopped giving a shit, so I've done my best to do the same."

"He's a jackass for leaving," Will says.

"You have to say *arse* because he's British," I point out.

"Arsewit."

"Fuckhead," I say.

"Chowderhole."

"Cuntbiscuit."

"Twatwaffle."

"Shitspider."

Soon we're laughing so hard we can't breathe, and, for a moment, it almost makes everything else stop hurting.

Zoe

Friday morning, I'm awakened by the sound of Jonah bellowing. It's barely five thirty, but my parents are trying to get him up. On top of the extra early hour, Jonah had a seizure last night. He didn't get hurt, thank god, but they always wipe him out, so I'm not surprised he doesn't want to get up. They're supposed to be at Little Lambs Village at ten. Two hours to get Jonah changed and fed and cleaned up and dressed, two hours to drive to Eugene, and a half hour for "padding," as my dad calls it. You never know when there might be a traffic accident or construction or any number of unforeseen delays, so he likes to preemptively outfox them. My mom's tendency to run behind schedule drives him completely bonkers — it's the number one thing they end up in tense arguments about. But today, they are both up and at it early.

I pull my pillow over my head. Everything about this day is terrible. When I come home from school, Jonah will be gone. He'll be a kid who doesn't live with his family. He'll be in a strange place, in a strange bed, with strange people. Our family at home will be three and not four. And even though I finally confided in Cammie and she hugged me and sympathized, for some reason it's still Sam whose understanding I want most. And she's not speaking to me.

I scroll through the texts I've sent Sam since lunch yesterday. I've apologized ninety ways to Tuesday for the jerks at my lunch table, but she won't respond. And it feels so unfair — I couldn't help it that Connor grabbed my phone and passed it down the table! I snatched it back as fast as I could, and I told them off for being jerks. But even when I told her that I explained to them that she's my friend, she ignored me. Even when I said I loved the Fairy Godbot, no response. Even when I tried startalk, nothing.

Even when I messaged her in tears, upset about Jonah's last night at home, crickets.

It hurts so much that she can so easily turn away from me, especially when she knows how hard this weekend is. That familiar chord resonates in me again. What is it that makes me so easy to throw away? Sam's disappearance adds further credence to the belief that there must be something fundamentally wrong with me — something I think of as the Theory of Original Defectiveness. Why else would my birth mother have thrown me away? The only thing she knew about me was that she didn't want me.

But unlike my birth mother, Sam actually knew me.

Which only makes it worse.

I stay in bed as long as I can, listening to the sounds of my parents getting Jonah ready to go. Finally, with about twenty minutes remaining before Cammie picks me up, I crawl out, get ready, and go downstairs. I don't want to say goodbye to Jonah. What I want is to call the whole thing off.

I find Jonah standing stock-still in the living room. My mom is whirling about trying to make sure she doesn't forget anything, and my dad is loading Jonah's things into the car.

I take Jonah's hands and gaze up at him. I can't find any words, so I sing to him. Because I don't know how long it will be before I can sing to him again. When my dad comes back inside, I ask, "Did you pack his parrot?" I gave Jonah a parrot for his twelfth birthday, and even though it only has one eye and one wing now, he still loves it.

"Yeah," he says. His voice is rough, and he clears his throat and gives me a smile, but his stab at bravery only worsens the ache in my chest. My dad's attachment to Jonah is as deep as the ocean. What will happen to his heart today when he has to walk away, leaving his beloved boy behind? The thought is like an elephant stepping on my solar plexus; it takes my breath away.

I turn back to Jonah. "Give me a hug, sweetie."

He leans toward me and rests his helmet on my head. I put my arms around him. He smells like fabric softener and toast and jam. "I'm gonna see you real soon." But that's as far as I get before I break. I hold on to him, my eyes blurring. I rub his back, wanting him to make a noise, maybe to say *Bao Bao*, but he is eerily quiet.

"He's tired," my mom says gently, as if reading my mind.

I nod, but I suspect it's more than that. He knows something's up. He knows this isn't a normal day, and I am pretty sure his silent stillness is an indication of his confusion. He can't possibly imagine the change this day is going to bring to his life, and when I think of what it's going to feel like when he figures it out, it's more than I can bear.

I'm glad when I hear the tap of Cammie's horn outside; it's too hard to stand here watching the last moments. Wordlessly I hug my parents and, with a last regretful glance at Jonah, I head out.

The day passes with all the speed of a glacier in slow motion. In the late morning, my mother texts: On our way home. Nothing else.

It doesn't take a genius to imagine what her brevity signifies. What must it have been like for them, saying goodbye to Jonah, however he handled it (was he upset?). What must it have been like for them to get in the car and drive away. To put mile after mile after mile between them and the boy they love so tenderly and fiercely.

Unable to face lunch with my friends and Hunter, whom I haven't yet told about Jonah and don't particularly want to right now, and presumably unwelcome in the library, I spend my lunch period in the choir room, plucking out the tune on the piano for a solo piece I'm going to audition for in the new song we're working on. By the end of the period, I'm starving. An unlikely salvation comes in the form of a delicious slice of Black Forest cake, which Mrs. Padgett brings in from the teachers' lounge and offers me, saying she already had a piece but Mr. Cohen pushed another one at her as she was leaving.

Fortified by the cake, I push through the afternoon, including a spirit rally that gives me a headache. The marching band already stomped through the halls of the entire school, and now, watching the football players and cheerleaders and pom squad turning themselves inside out with enthusiasm for a *game,* for something that seems so small, so unimportant, I feel like an alien that dropped in. I have a sudden desire to bolt, to sprint to the studio theater and sit alone on the set of *The World Over.* I would rather be in a place that feels less tethered to my real world than at this pointless-seeming display of school spirit.

But I sit with Hunter and our friends, and in between whooping and hollering, they discuss plans for the weekend. I don't have anything to contribute to that conversation — it's mostly about the after-party, which I'm not going to, and about the girls' hair and manicure appointments, which I'm also not doing. I can do my own hair and nails, as my dad would surely (and rightly) point out. While a hundred-plus bucks for salon appointments is nothing to Cammie and probably to Syd and Erin, my family has a pretty strict budget.

My lack of enthusiasm for all of this makes me miss Sam even more. She'd understand what a waste of time it seems like, hanging with a bunch of drunk kids at a dance to celebrate a sports game, especially when my heart is somewhere else: with Jonah.

Still, that night I find myself at the football game, shivering despite the stadium blanket and Hunter's warm arm around me. He's waiting for the arrival of his brothers, both former West Hills football stars, both at University of Oregon, and he keeps checking his phone.

And all I can think about is my parents sitting alone at home. Guilt chews at me; I don't think they should have to have the first Jonah-less evening without me there to support them. But they urged me to go to the game, saying there was no point in sitting around feeling sad. And it's made Hunter happy, my being here. He seems to be trying to be a good sport about the overnighter, possibly so as not to let it ruin everything else. Still, things aren't quite right between us. I don't know if it's him or me or both. Stress twists through me. There is no way to be everything everyone needs, and I can't bear it that no matter how hard I try to make the right choices, I'm going to disappoint someone.

Rain needles off the overhang that roofs the bleachers. I have no idea what's happening on the field, although I can see the scoreboard. We're still in the first quarter, somehow, and the score is 0–0. It's going to be a long night.

I turn at the sound of my name. Erin is handing me a cup of hot chocolate, which is just what I need, but it's Erin, so I'm pretty sure it's spiked.

"Try it," she says, grinning mischievously.

The smell of peppermint hits me before I even have the cup halfway to my face.

"Schnapps," she says. "Taste it!"

"How strong is it?" I ask. I'm nervous about drinking it — both for fear of getting busted in public and for fear of my parents finding out — but I'm freezing and this smells really good.

She rolls her eyes at me. "Oh my god, it's not, don't worry."

So I take a sip. It burns a little more than I anticipated, but the warming aspects more than make up for it. "It's yummy," I tell her.

Hunter peers over to see what I've got. "Is that from Erin?" he says. "What is it, Everclear?"

I laugh. Erin's reputation as a partier is hard-earned.

He leans closer. "Okay, don't get mad, but I had an idea. What if you told your parents you were sleeping over at a friend's house?" He raises his eyebrows hopefully.

I bristle at the way his focus on this is so singular, at the way he just won't quit. "You want me to lie to my parents?" I snap. As if I haven't lied several times lately with incredible ease and grace. Somehow the truth of that just makes me angrier, even though it's not his fault. I think about how sad they must be right now, and I realize I probably should have told Hunter what's happened with Jonah. He might be more understanding. But I didn't want to talk to him about Jonah, and I still don't. And even though that's on me, I take it out on him. "Isn't it enough that I'm going to the dance?"

He looks like he's been slapped. "What," he says, "like it's some kind of *favor* that my own girlfriend goes to the Homecoming dance with me? Our senior year?"

"I have a lot going on, Hunter," I say, my heart starting to beat harder. Something wants out of me, but whether it's rage or tears, I can't tell.

"Like what?" His challenging tone puts me off from even considering sharing anything with him.

"Forget it." I look away and sip the cocoa.

"No, I won't forget it." I've pushed him over a line, and he's pissed. "You know, we're all stressed, Zoe. We're all worried about getting into college and trying to get through senior year."

I bite my tongue to keep from saying terrible things out loud. *Oh, poor baby. It must be hard to be the perfect athlete with the perfect family who gets to go to whatever college he wants.*

I'm not cold anymore. I'm starting to sweat inside my jacket, and my hands are shaking. I hold my cup in both hands, trying to steady it.

"Why are you being like this?" he says. When I look back at him, he's staring at me with complete incomprehension.

I don't really *know* why I'm being like this, but I just keep going. "I have things going on that you have no clue about," I say, vaguely aware of our friends tuning in to the argument and eyeing us nervously.

"How is that my fault?" He gestures and knocks the cocoa cup out of my hands. It splashes on my jeans.

"God—" I stop myself before I can unleash the string of curses I long to fire out. I pick up the cup. My right leg is soaked.

"Are you okay?" he asks, sounding stricken. "Was it hot?"

"No." I take a napkin that someone hands me, I don't even know who. And something about the concern being shown to me makes me crack, and I start to cry.

"Zoe?" Hunter says. He's clearly so confused by the way I'm acting.

I'm being awful. And it hurts. "My brother's gone," I finally mumble.

"What?" he says, leaning closer. "What did you say?"

"Jonah." My tears spill over. "We sent him away. To a home for disabled people."

He stares at me, his glasses covering over with tiny drops of rain as the wind picks up. The seconds feel like hours as he processes, and I hope his response is one of kindness and not anger, not that I don't deserve his anger. It wouldn't be the first time I struck out at him for something that wasn't his fault.

Finally, he shakes his head. "How did I not know any of this?"

I have no answer.

Suddenly everyone jumps up and screams. I clap my hands over my ears. I am barely functioning. I just want to leave. I wish Cammie had driven — she'd drive me home. But everyone seems to be drinking except Hunter.

When I look up, he's typing on his phone. He turns to me, but he doesn't quite meet my eyes. "My brothers are here. I'm gonna go sit with them." He stands up and with a short "see you," he's climbing over legs and feet and making his way out.

I feel a hand on my back. I turn to find Cammie, watching me with a very worried expression. She says, "Are you okay? Is Hunter being a dick? On the day Jonah left?"

My stomach sinks. I am such a terrible person. I wish I could say yes and watch her face take on that loyal, determined, *hold my purse* expression, but I have to tell her the truth. "He didn't know. I'm just being horrible."

She steps over the bleacher and plunks herself down, putting an arm around me. "Zoe, how did you not tell him? What's going on with you two?"

I shake my head. "We shouldn't be together. I'm no good for anyone."

"Stop that," she says, and her expression is stern. "You're the best person I know! I just think . . ." Her brow furrows. "Zo, do you even love Hunter anymore?"

I wish she hadn't asked. It's been a question encroaching perilously into my field of vision, but one I have mostly succeeded in ignoring. But I can't ignore it anymore. "He's not a bad guy," I say, searching for the rest of my response.

"No," she says. "He's not."

I use a napkin to wipe my nose.

"It's not a crime not to love him," Cammie says gently. "But if you don't . . ." She shrugs. "You don't want to string him along, right?"

"Right." It comes out a whisper.

"The timing isn't so great," she says. Her unhappiness is clear.

"I'm sorry if it messes up Homecoming."

She squeezes me. "Zoe! I didn't mean that. Don't worry about that! I meant because of Jonah and everything you have going on at home."

Her understanding is more than I deserve, and I lean in

for a proper hug. Another wave of cheers goes up in the stands, everyone springing to their feet, but neither of us moves.

When I pull back, I say, "I want to go home. I should be with my parents."

She nods. "Do you need help finding a ride?"

"It's okay." I pull out my phone and text my parents: I'm sorry—can you come get me? I've had enough, and I don't have a ride. If you're eating, I can wait.

My mom responds immediately that my dad is on his way. I get to my feet, glad for the rain, which disguises my tears and my spiked hot chocolate stain and blends it all into a single damp mess that represents me perfectly. I push through the noisy crowd, the air heavy with the smell of hot dogs and popcorn and rain, and then stand under the stadium lights in the parking lot, shivering. When my dad pulls up, I tumble into the warm car gratefully.

"There's my princess," he says, leaning over and giving me a hug.

Princess. I think of Sam with a pang.

My dad clucks because I'm shaking. "It's wretched out, isn't it?" he says, cranking the heat.

"Everything's wretched," I mutter, holding my hands over the heat vent.

He takes a breath to speak, and I cut in and say, "No pep talks. Please. I'm not in the mood for positivity."

My dad laughs softly. "I was going to agree with you."

I smile a little. Sometimes he surprises me.

"But we have to be strong for Mom." He glances at me. "Roger that?"

I nod. "I know. I'll try."

"That's my good girl."

But these words he's spoken so often suddenly chafe. *I'm not your good girl,* I think.

I'm not anybody's good girl.

My mom is already in bed with a book when we get home. It's barely eight thirty. Her eyes are puffy, and I know she's had a bath because I can smell her lime blossom bubble bath in the air, and because I know that she sometimes takes a bath when she needs to cry.

"Hi," I say from the doorway.

She glances up and smiles at me. "How was the game?"

I shake my head and climb onto the bed next to her, like I did when I was little. "I was having kind of a bad time."

She turns and pets my head. "What happened?"

I sigh. "I was cold and grumpy. And I had a fight with Hunter. I think I just missed you guys."

"Aww, come here." She closes her book and reaches to give me a hug, and I let myself melt into her.

"Mom? Was this morning awful?"

She shakes her head, letting me know she doesn't want to talk about it. "I finally stopped crying," she says.

"Okay, no worries," I say, an ache swelling in my throat.

"How's the set coming for STOTS?" she asks when she pulls away.

"Not actually terrible," I say. "A budget of zero dollars really inspires resourcefulness."

She laughs. "Truer words were never spoken. One of my

close friends in high school bought almost all her clothes at thrift shops, and our senior year she was voted Best Dressed."

"That's amazing."

She smiles and leans back, thinking. "She just put the effort in, you know? And she had style — there was no denying that Suzanne had style."

"What happened to her?" I ask. "Are you still in touch?"

"Actually, I had lost track of my high school friends, but this last year I reached out to some of them."

My stomach drops as I realize why she might have done that. Did she want a chance to talk to people who were once important to her, before it was too late? In case the cancer won?

"She's a partner at a top law firm in D.C. She has a five-bedroom house in Great Falls. And she still shops in thrift stores." My mom laughs.

"You didn't keep in touch with any of your high school friends?" I ask. Is it possible that I'd lose track of Cammie, Erin, and Syd someday? They've been my world for years; I can't imagine having no idea what became of them. But when I consider how much I've grown apart from them recently, it doesn't seem impossible that we could keep going in that direction, especially once we're not even in the same town or state anymore.

"Not really," she says, tilting her head. "A few college friends, but not high school." She must be able to tell I'm worrying, because she says, "It's probably different now. There's so much social media to keep people connected."

My mind goes to Sam, who isn't, as far as I know, on any social media. And maybe I've lost her already anyway.

But I miss her. I miss the way I can say anything to her. And I'm so sad about it that I find myself telling my mom what happened, tiptoeing around trying to explain what exactly my friends were making fun of, because it turns out it's hard to explain Sam, and even harder to explain how we are friends.

She lies on her side, listening, her face making all the right expressions. "Poor girl," she finally says. "And you apologized?"

"Over and over."

"In person?"

"No, in text. We mostly talk in text." I stop short of trying to explain Starworld, which, even if I didn't feel private and proprietary about it, might be kind of impossible.

"I don't really think texting is the best medium for an apology," my mom says. "That probably sounds old-fashioned, but . . ."

"Well, what can I do if she doesn't want to see me?" I say. "And don't say call her — that would freak her out completely."

My mom sits up. "What if you did something nice for her? Something to show you're thinking about her, and you're really sorry for what happened?"

I sit up, too. "Like what?"

"I don't know. I always baked something for your dad when I owed him an apology."

"Ha, bet that worked like a charm," I say, smiling. My dad loves sweets.

She grins. "You know it."

The idea interests me immediately, but then I think about Sam's wacky lunches and I wonder if I could make this work, if I could figure out a way to do this that won't challenge her mother's compulsions. I don't want to do anything that makes things worse at home for Sam, like sending over asymmetrical cookies in random stacks of unequal numbers or something.

"Maybe I could make Grandma Betty's shortbread," I say. We have a well-loved recipe in the weathered wooden recipe box that belonged to Grandma Betty before it was passed to Grandma Helen — my mom's mom — and then my mom. I just need to find the right shape, which shouldn't be hard. There's a giant bin of cookie cutters in the kitchen, many passed down on my mom's side like the recipes they go with.

"That's a great idea," she says. "I can help you in the morning." She lays a hand on my cheek. "You're such a good girl, Zoe."

I give her a weak smile, because while there is a part of me that chafes at this compliment, there is also a part of me that craves those words of praise.

She smiles. "Grandma Betty would be pleased we're still making her cookies." She goes off on a tangent about what a hoot Grandma Betty was, how she used to regale Mom with all her wonderful stories about her childhood, their farm, and Mom's bootlegging great-uncle. And of course all the much-loved recipes she passed down through the generations.

Also passed down among them all is the Wilson widow's

peak. Grandma Betty had it, my grandmother had it, my mother has it, and Jonah has it.

It's a terrible thing to admit, but I've always hated that widow's peak. It's just another reminder that they are all real family, and I'm a drop-in. I wonder if I have living grandparents and great-grandparents. And if I do, would they want to claim me? Do they even know about me? When I picture safe haven drop-off situations, I think of a girl (in my head she's young, maybe even my age) hiding her pregnancy, having the baby in secret, and dropping it off quickly at the safe haven spot, and maybe no one ever knows, or maybe just a friend or two. Did her parents know? My grandparents? Did my birth father know? Will I ever know any of them?

I feel the usual stab of guilt at the unabating feelings of loss and longing, and I push the thoughts aside.

I hug my mom good night, then retreat to my room, where I discover I have messages from Hunter.

I'm sorry for what you're going through, and even sorrier you never felt you could trust me with it. I wish I understood why. I've tried to be understanding, but I guess maybe I've fallen short at times. Anyway, I feel pretty shitty about everything. ☹

Do you still want to go to the dance? I don't want to pressure you to do something if you're not feeling it. Anyway, if you don't . . . Abernathy has mono, so Nicki's going without a date. If you don't want to go, I could offer to go as her "date." Just as friends, obviously.

Let me know. And let me know if there's anything I can do.

I don't know whether to be angry, hurt, or relieved.

Somehow I'm feeling all those things at once. But the over-riding feeling is one of not wanting to be an asshole. I owe him an apology. I think about what my mom said about apologies, and I know I should probably call him, but the idea of a real-time conversation about this stuff feels beyond me right now — especially because I feel like our relationship is probably coming to an end, and I *definitely* don't want to face that tonight.

So I take the easy way out and text: I'm sorry, Hunter. None of this was your fault. You're right — I haven't talked to you about things I probably should have.

And about the dance . . . Why don't you go ahead and take Nicki. That sounds like a better option for both of you. I wouldn't be much fun anyway. :-/

And now I need to tell Cammie and Syd and Erin. I can just imagine their reactions to my bagging on the dance, and I can't bear to face it. I wish they were more like Sam in some ways. . . . Sam wouldn't freak out or ask me ten thousand questions, and she certainly wouldn't gossip about it. She'd just listen.

I turn back to our texts, or mine, I should say. Since yesterday morning, it's all me. One apology after another.

I think about trying one more time, maybe letting her know that I need her. If she cares about me, she'll surely respond.

I turn off my phone and go to bed without texting. I'm too fragile to risk finding out I'm wrong.

Sam

It takes me about three nanoseconds into the Homecoming dance to realize I've made a huge mistake. Fear consumes me the moment we cross onto school property. What if I see Zoe? I'm hopelessly torn between wanting to and being disgusted with myself for that same desire. She betrayed me. I need to let go of any stupid notion that we understood each other, that we could be friends. Still, I disappeared on her during one of the hardest weeks of her life. I suck, too. I have no idea what to do.

Will has to forcibly drag me past the coat check and into the gym. The dimly lit Cavern of Athletic Suffering is loaded to the brim with silver and gold balloons tied to every stationary object, and tables along the side are draped with shimmery tablecloths. Fake candles glow inside vases dipped in gold glitter, and strings of tiny white lights are hung all around in a scalloped pattern. The atmosphere is magical — at least I assume it is for people who aren't bothered by the thumping bass of the DJ, the sound of three thousand half-shouted conversations at once, and pervasive clouds of the popular perfume du jour, which to me smells exactly like the nostril-violating flea powder we had to use on a litter of kittens Dad rescued when I was eight.

People stare as Will and I make our way through the crowd. He looks dashing in the three-piece suit he borrowed from his dad, who could probably dress the entire theater department with his vast costume collection. On the other hand, I look like a drunken furniture upholsterer swathed me in a bedazzled trash bag, because apparently that's what dresses looked like in the 1920s, and this unfortunate black-and-gold frock was the closest approximation I could find at the thrift store at the last minute.

But the biggest problem is that Will and I are apparently the only clueless idiots who took the *Gatsby* theme to heart enough to come in costume. Pointed fingers and snickers follow us everywhere we walk, and the burn of all those eyes is enough to fry my circuitry in less than ten seconds. I want to slam my hands over my ears and back up all the way to the coat check and disappear into the muffling layers of all that fabric and wait there until it's time to leave. But Will has me by the arm, and his height means that his earholes are up in a layer of the atmosphere that my voice is unlikely to reach without the help of a rocket launcher. So I stare at the far wall and try to pretend I'm a queen whose subjects are parting before her instead of a numbskull who can't even do something as simple as wear the right thing to a school dance.

James and Will greet each other with a hand gesture that falls somewhere between fist bump and Trekkie salutation. Caroline lurks behind James, looking only marginally more delighted than I am to be in attendance, and keeps nervously adjusting her glasses every five seconds. As for Kitty, I don't need telepathy to tell what she's thinking. She bites her lip hopefully and bounces on her toes as Will approaches. She's supposed to be there with Carlos, but the dude is so far lost in some puzzle game on his phone that he might as well be on a date with it.

"Unexpected commitment to the theme," James says to Will and me.

"Isn't Sam's dress awesome?" Will shouts back, gesturing to the beaded monstrosity engulfing me. I think he's trying to help me feel like less of a fuckwit, but unless he activates an obliteration ray that will reduce me to particulate matter, there's no hope.

I let go of Will and slip behind Caroline, whose full figure and explosion of purple taffeta provide the perfect blockade between me and the rest of the room. Syd, Erin, Cammie, and a couple of other equally pretty girls are already out on the dance floor having a fantastic time, but Zoe isn't among them. Ethan's talking so loudly, I can almost hear him even over the wretched echo of the music. He busts up laughing over some asswit thing he said to Connor and Hunter, and in the process nearly sweeps an entire tray of cookies off the snack table with a rogue gesture. He must be tanked. I hope Mr. Sherman or one of the other chaperones notices. I'll take my vengeance where I can get it. But it's Hunter I follow with my gaze as they move away from the table.

When he walks off with two drinks in hand, my heart lurches as he steps through the crowd. But it's not Zoe that Hunter hands the other cider to — it's Nicki Bowman. I blink in confusion as they disappear into the crowd. He can't possibly be here with her.

The DJ puts on a slow song and couples start to sway, prompting Kitty to eye-fuck Will into instant zombification. He leads her out onto the dance floor, and they mash their bodies together in an awkward entanglement of limbs. Kitty can barely reach his shoulders, even pressed right up against him, undoubtedly contaminating him with eau de haricot vert. She stares up into his eyes, smiling. Sometimes I swear there's little difference between lust and lobotomy. But Will looks a little blushy and very happy, so I don't want to quack it up for him.

I take the opportunity and slip away along the edge of the gym. I wasn't so sure about seeing Zoe, but now I'm not even sure she's here — and if she's not, I need to know. I weave my way through clusters of people until I catch another glimpse of Hunter. Sure enough, he's dancing with Nicki, and Zoe is nowhere to be seen. They sway together, chatting intermittently, until the song changes and then they finally break apart. She looks happy when she turns back to her friends, but something dark and troubled flickers over Hunter's expression until he catches up with his group, and then they're jostling each other and he's smiling and playing along like nothing's wrong.

I glance back to where Caroline was standing, but it seems James dragged her out on the dance floor. She doesn't even look too upset about it. Kitty and Will are flailing around to the beat, and Carlos is wandering toward the drink table with his face in his phone, bumping into people left and right. With the group dispersed, I'm on my own, so I find a chair in the darkest corner of the gym and plant myself to wait out the rest of this nightmare.

An hour later, I'm in an almost comatose state of space-out when my phone buzzes from where I stashed it in my bra.

It's Mom — she's sent a photo of what appears to be some cookies packaged in cellophane and tied with blue ribbon.

Someone left cookies on the front porch for you, the text reads. **The tag says they're from Zoe?**

I can't really process what I'm seeing. Zoe stopped by my house? To leave me cookies?

I slip out into the hallway, where it's approximately a thousand degrees cooler and several magnitudes quieter. The scent of linoleum floods my nose as I take a deep breath and turn my text notifications back on.

There are so many messages from Zoe, I can hardly take them all in. It's almost like she missed me, and, unexpectedly, my eyes sting. A lot of the time, I don't feel like anyone would notice if I suddenly disappeared.

She apologized — a lot. And explained that Connor grabbed her phone without asking. But the messages that make me feel guiltiest are the ones from Thursday night, her last night with Jonah, her last night with her family whole. I know that feeling — the moment when you know everything is about to change in a way you hate, but you can't do anything to stop it.

I lack the emotional capacity to respond to her messages with any level of articulation, so instead I write:

Um. My mom sent me a picture of these incredibly perfect cookies and said a girl named Zoe dropped them off?

Her response comes like lightning. I wanted you to know how sorry I am. I hope they work for your mom. The stars have six points, and I grouped them into fours . . .

My heart feels like it's pounding so loud, surely people can hear it over the pulsing bass reverberating from the gym. I write: *stares* Holy shitkettles. You really pay attention. *is at Homecoming in a very unfortunate costume, so things were already pretty surreal*

Zoe: Your mom said you were at the dance. That was surprising!

Me: *is desperately searching for the escape hatch* Anyway, thanks for the cookies.

I can't believe she took the time to make something just for me.

Zoe: I really am so sorry.

I exhale a long breath. Her friends were dickweeds, but I was, too.

Me: *is sorry, too* *shouldn't have gone MIA when you were going through such a hard time*

Zoe: *hugs* I'm just glad you're back. I missed you.

Me: *missed you too* I hesitate, then decide to be honest. *was afraid to check messages*

Zoe: Why? Why afraid? I thought you were ignoring my messages because you hated me. ☹

Me: *had turned off notifications* *thought you had showed my messages to your friends to mock*

Zoe: ??!?!?!? How could you think that??

Me: Because no one like you could ever want to be friends with someone like me.

It's the truth. The bitter, unadulterated truth. No one who could be the star of every show wants to befriend the nerd whose social circle has the depth and breadth of a mud puddle. I'm fucking weird, and I don't know how to be anything else.

Me: *doesn't know how to be human* *has a weird mom* *is dressed like a bedazzled potato sack in mourning*

I lean against the cold wall, letting the chill seep into my bones as I wait for her response.

Zoe: You're the most human person I know. Anyone would be lucky to be your friend.

Before I can respond, another message comes in.

Zoe: What is this dress you're wearing? Perhaps a photograph? *smiles fetchingly*

I don't have to think long about the response to that. I'd sooner ingest a box of staples than document it, thank you. ☺

Zoe: Ha-ha, then that's the only thing I'm sorry about missing at the dance. ☺ Any fun plans for after?

Me: I'm supposed to go to Carlos Mendoza's with the nerd-core gang. Will probably end up suffering through games on some ancient console while they play D&D.

Zoe: Sam? I never understand half of what you say. ☺

It's kind of cute that she doesn't have a clue. Or maybe there's just a thrill in the idea that I could be a mystery to someone. Or that Zoe could like me without having to *be* like me.

doesn't understand half of what I say either I write. *contemplates saddling up Humphrey instead*

Zoe: *hopes to hitch a ride to the stars*

I hesitate for a moment before responding. Somehow it doesn't seem like quite the right time to go off on a flight of fancy with Humphrey. I don't even know why she's not at the dance. Or why her boyfriend is dancing with another girl.

Me: I was kind of surprised you aren't here. Are you okay?

Zoe: Not really.

Me: *wonders where to send Humphrey to check on you*

Zoe: *is sitting on the porch swing at my house*

I remember our weird lunch in the library, and I get brave.

Me: Want company?

Zoe: Oh, you're so sweet! But you have your after-party. No worries, I'll be okay.

All I can think of is that she's sitting alone in the cold at a time she needs someone the most. Her friends are at the dance, her boyfriend seems to have ditched her for Nicki Bowman . . . Even I turned my back in her time of need. How can I let her be alone now?

Me: *hijacks Will from Kitty's succubus-like embrace to man my chariot* *bribes him with RPG DLC loot*

Zoe: *has no idea what that means* Do you even know where I live?

Me: *assumes Humphrey knows*

Zoe: 1516 Caraway Street. Near the middle school, close to the river.

She lives barely a mile from me. I never knew. I'll be able to get home easily even if Will can't drive me, and that plus her giving up her address so easily is all the encouragement I need.

I shove my way back into the gym, hoping I can talk Will into doing what I want. He and Kitty look like they just walked out of the photo booth, and she's giggling while he jumps to try to reach a heart-shaped foil balloon that's part of the arch decorating the entryway to the photo area. I roll my eyes. Knowing him, his best intentions of procuring a cute balloon for the girl he likes will result in the destruction of the entire arch.

I hurry over and poke him in the arm.

"I need to talk to you for a minute," I say, my heart already racing at what I'm about to do.

Kitty gives me a confused look as I drag Will off.

"I promise I'm not trying to cockblock you," I say, making him blush ten shades of crimson.

"I didn't assume you were," he mumbles.

"I think I'm going to skip the after-party," I say. "Can you drop me off on the way there?"

"At home?" he asks, confused. He knows I'll usually take any opportunity to be out of the house for a bit.

"Uh, no. Actually, at Zoe Miller's."

"What?" He looks at me like I've sprouted a second head out of my rib cage. "Are you serious?"

"Completely," I say.

"Zoe? The person whose friends were total jackasses to you at lunch the other day?" He gestures so broadly I'm half afraid he's going to accidentally knock me in the head.

"One and the same," I say, with more confidence than I feel. "But the lunch thing wasn't her fault. I guess Connor grabbed her phone. She feels really bad about it."

"Sometimes I can't even begin to understand you." He shakes his head.

"Well, I don't understand you either, since you seem blind to the fact that Kitty has been waiting all night for you to make a move." I chortle.

My comment makes him smile and blush again.

"If you want to hook up with Kitty, you should," I tell him. "As long as we still have Sunday afternoons, okay?" I want him to have something with Kitty if that's what he wants, but my afternoons gaming with him are one of the few escapes I have left — that and Starworld now that I'm back in touch with Zoe.

"Always," he says, the confidence in his voice unshakable.

Not much later we pile into the car. Kitty hitches a ride with us instead of the rest of the crew, but I make her sit in the back seat with the Dr Pepper cans. (Last-minute planning and limited funds meant no limo for us.) If Kitty is going to seduce her way into Will's pants, which she clearly intends to do, she might as well know what she's in for. She spends the whole ride leaning forward so she can talk into Will's ear, and I stare out the window and dream about worlds made of stardust — of Zoe with a crown of stars, queen of a much less complicated universe. One in which messes can be wished away and where the possibilities are as innumerable as the stars.

Will pulls into the driveway of one of the Craftsman-style homes prevalent in the older part of our neighborhood. The windshield wipers push off leaves dropped by the huge trees that arch over the road.

Zoe is sitting on a weathered swing on the covered front porch, bundled up in a puffy down coat that looks better suited to skiing.

I crack the door and peer out at her.

"Hey, Sam," Zoe says.

"Hey," I echo, my voice soft.

I climb out of the car, suddenly self-conscious about how like a sparkly hobo I must look in my ugly thrift store dress. Kitty jumps out of the back seat to take my place in the front.

"Hi, Zoe," Kitty says, her voice bright and cheerful.

"You look beautiful, Kitty!" Zoe says. "I love your dress."

"Thanks!" Kitty bounces on her toes, eyes glimmering with delight at the compliment. "Have a good night, Sam," she adds as she slips into the passenger seat.

Will's death trap on wheels backs out, hacking a cloud of exhaust into the rain. Through the blurred window I can see Kitty bid us farewell with a friendly wave. I really should try to be nicer to her.

"Look at you." Zoe tilts her head and grins at me. Her eyes are puffy. "I would never have the guts to dress that way for Homecoming. You're so . . . yourself."

"So, an idiot?" I ask.

She laughs and shakes her head. "No. Clear on who you are. Not a follower."

I never would have thought of it that way. I don't know how to be anything other than what I am.

She pats the cushion next to her on the swing. "Sit!"

I obediently take a seat.

"How was the dance?" Zoe asks.

"I don't know." I shrug, not really sure what to say that won't make me sound like a fuckwit or a sociopath.

"But what did you think of it?" She actually smiles a little, like she knows I probably hated it.

"It was on par with being slowly lowered into a sarlacc," I say.

"A what?"

"You know, the pit monster that digests its victims over thousands of years? In Carkoon? On Tatooine? In *Return of the Jedi*?" None of what I'm saying seems to be clarifying. "Thankfully you rescued me from the after-party," I add, hoping to divert the conversation from my own idiocy.

"I guess we have our own after-party. The Hermits' Club." A sad laugh escapes her. "I'm not great company — I'm sorry. Jonah's gone and we won't see him until Halloween. My parents are wrecked. Hunter probably hates me. It's been a banner freaking weekend."

"Try fucking," I say.

Her eyebrows shoot up. "Is that how you handle stress?"

I wheeze, clasping my hands to my head over the communication fail. Fucking as a coping mechanism!

She grins at me. "Because my chance for that is at the dance with someone else."

I can hardly stop laughing long enough to get the words

out. "No! God! I haven't even kissed anyone! I meant the swear word. Try saying that actual swear word. Instead of the mock one."

"Oh!" A laugh rolls out of her. "I can't."

"Sure you can. Fucking. It's easy." I may not speak that much, but I don't let that stop me from using a full range of vocabulary when I do.

"I—I don't . . ." She sounds stressed. "Okay, what the heck. I'll say it." But she hesitates.

"Fucking!" I prompt her.

"Um. Fucking!" Her hand claps over her mouth, which cracks me up. "Fucking!" she says again, louder. "Fuck! Fuck! Motherfucking fuckmonkey fuckers!" She starts laughing so hard, she can barely keep getting the f-bombs out.

I watch her, smiling, until she finally catches her breath. She might never have looked so beautiful or so free.

"That felt amazing," she says.

"*How* amazing?" I'm a terrible influence, but everything she does and says right now seems to turn up the electric intensity between us. I can't get enough.

"Fucking amazing!" She laughs.

"*You're* amazing," I say, and then I duck my head, feeling my cheeks flush. I hadn't meant for that to slip out.

A silence falls that we don't seem to know what to do with. Zoe glances toward her house, which is dark. "Hey. Do you want to come in?" she asks.

My heart grinds to a robotic halt, but I manage the slightest nod, wondering what it means that she's inviting me in. It doesn't seem to be an offer she makes often.

She stands up and I follow her into the dim house. She takes off her coat and hangs it in the hall closet, leaving her in a faded baseball shirt and yoga pants. I look away, uncomfortable about how much I want to stare at the way the fabric hugs her curves. Only the oven hood casts light into the kitchen and living room, both of which are decorated with incredible sparseness even by my mom's neat freak standards. I follow her inside and quietly close the door.

Zoe signals me to follow her, putting a finger over her lips so I know to be quiet. Somewhere in the house I hear a TV—a movie, maybe. Halfway down the upstairs hallway, she hesitates beside an open door as a flicker of intense sadness passes over her face. She keeps going, and I sneak a curious glance inside what must be her brother's room. The streetlamp outside the open blinds casts enough light that I can make out posters on the walls, mostly of birds, many of them torn and wrinkled. I remember Zoe's request for the Fairy Godbot—that it be able to send colorful birds to Jonah. He must love them. I'm already sketching one in my mind, more fantastical than anything he's ever seen. I wonder if he'd like that.

We go into her bedroom, which is the opposite of mine. Her bedspread is a pale pink, with an intricate floral design, whereas my bed coverings are just sheets and a haphazard pile of afghans knitted by Mom. Zoe doesn't have posters tacked up crookedly on the wall or random stacks of books all over the place. Everything is tidily put away, the books alphabetized on their shelves, the nail polishes lined up in color order along the back of her vanity. My mom would love this.

A shimmery aquamarine dress hangs from a hook on the outside of her closet door, the tags still attached. It's studded with tiny gems that grow more dense the farther up they go, and then the bodice gives way to sheer fabric at the top. If Zoe had worn it, she would have looked like a fairy or a mermaid, something too ethereal and beautiful to belong on this broken planet. The past few days must have been incredibly hard for her if she didn't feel up to going to the dance. I feel bad.

"Is that what you were going to wear to the dance?" I ask.

"Yeah. Stupid freaking dress," she mutters.

"Stupid *what* dress?" I ask.

She grins and opens her mouth to speak, then glances at her bedroom door nervously. *Fucking,* she mouths at me. She does it with such giddy exaggeration that I can't even come down on her for not saying it aloud. When I realize I'm beaming at her like a besotted wharf rat, I duck my head, my cheeks on fire.

"Do you want some sweats or something to change into?" she asks, nodding at my dress.

My heart leaps into my throat and tries to hammer its way out the side of my neck. "Uh, no thanks. I'm good." Undressing in front of her is absolutely out of the question.

"Are you hungry or anything?"

I shake my head.

She collapses on the bed. Her shirt rides up a little, showing the barest hint of creamy skin above the waistband of her yoga pants. I avert my eyes to the stuffed polar bear nestled among the throw pillows on her bay window bench.

"Sit," she says, gesturing at her desk chair, and again I obey.

On her desk is a lamp, her laptop, a bunch of framed snapshots of her with her friends, a set of photo booth pictures of her and Hunter, a notepad, and a white mesh container holding mechanical pencils and glittery gel pens.

I'm afraid to look at her, so I pick up one of the pencils and start doodling on the notepad. "Did you see Hunter at the dance?" she asks. "With Nicki?"

I nod, worried she's going to ask more.

"I hope he's having a good time," she says with a sigh.

I want to ask if they broke up, ask what happened, but I don't know how.

"What are you drawing?" she asks.

"Nothing," I say, which is mostly true.

"I wish I could paint like you," she says, her voice wistful. "You're so talented."

"You're the talented one," I say. "You could have a future on stage, if you wanted one."

"Ha, no. I'm not that good."

"But you are!" How can she be that beautiful and that talented and not know it?

"Agree to disagree," she says, smiling.

I smile, too, continuing my sketch. I steal a glance at her. She stares at the ceiling, lost in thought, her hair tumbling in waves over her pillow. For the first time I notice a small birthmark near her hairline, like someone pressed a kiss to her forehead and it left a mark.

"Can you turn on the lamp and turn off the overhead

light?" she finally asks, gesturing at the switch on the wall near me.

I'm happy to oblige; the ceiling light is bright enough to illuminate a small country. I've always felt more comfortable in the dark—perhaps because it makes it that much easier to be invisible. I turn on the lamp and get up to flip the switch off.

On the wall across from her bed, a whole galaxy of glow-in-the-dark stars comes to life, and my heart speeds up. It's the one and only thing our rooms have in common, except mine are on the ceiling. I think of all the times I wished I could step into those stars—fly through them into an alternate universe that's easier to live in. Maybe Zoe dreams of that, too.

"What do you want to do?" I ask, glancing up at her. "In life, I mean. Do you know?"

She shakes her head. "Not really. Do you?"

"Yeah. I want to be an aerospace engineer," I say, feeling stupid about how nerdy it sounds.

"Wow, like spaceships and stuff?" she asks.

"Maybe. But I'm also interested in rovers like the ones they've put on Mars—mostly how we get them there, how we make sure they can navigate and land safely, that kind of stuff," I mumble.

"Wow. I have no idea what's even involved in that."

I settle back into the chair. "Can I ask you something?" I say, before I can stop myself.

"Sure."

"Why can't you swear?"

She shakes her head and closes her eyes. "It's dumb."

"I doubt that." It's the mildest version of any of the things I'd like to say to her. She's so funny and huge-hearted and creative and clever. There's nothing dumb about her. She may have high walls around her, but the more I get to know who Zoe really is, the more I love the tender heart of her — the girl who is devastated by her brother leaving, the one who is willing to let me push her outside her comfort zone, the one who seems to like me in spite of my epic weirdness.

The person who sees me.

"Okay," she says. "So I have this theory about being adopted. I call it the Theory of Original Defectiveness. Because I was immediately deemed not worth keeping." She pauses. "I mean, nothing is more fierce than a mother's instinct to protect her young, right? Darwin and everything?"

"Right," I say. My mom's instincts are sometimes so fierce, they don't even make sense.

A pained look crosses her face. "So there was something about me that was not worthy of that. Of being kept. Hence, original defectiveness."

The thought of Zoe being defective or someone not wanting her doesn't compute. I'm probably the one who should worry about defectiveness — my dad knew me well and still chose to leave me behind.

"So I try to make up for it," she continues. "I try to be good. And good daughters don't swear. They don't cause trouble. They're not ungrateful; they don't get bad grades; they don't wish for things they can't have."

"Ah," I say. Now I get it. With the understanding comes a wave of sadness.

"Well, I guess the not-swearing part is out the fucking window." She grins at me.

A squeak of amusement escapes me. I can't meet her eyes, because everything she says only makes me want to be closer to her. "What do you know about her?" I ask. "Your birth mother? Have you ever thought about looking for her?"

She turns her eyes away. "I think about it all the time. But I wasn't just given up for adoption in the usual way. I was dropped off at a fire station the day I was born." She shrugs. "And that's all I know. I don't know her name or anything about her. And honestly, I'd be scared to find her, because she probably doesn't want to be found, after the way she gave me up. It's like she hated me. Like she just wanted to forget me, and as fast as possible." She pauses, pulling the covers up like maybe they can protect her. "And anyway, I don't want to hurt my parents. They're the best."

Her words gut me. I wish I knew what to say.

Her next words are spoken softly. "But I wonder what she's like. I wonder how old she is, and if she still lives in Texas."

"Texas?"

She nods. "That's where we lived when I was little. My dad used to teach at UT Austin. So I wonder if she's still there. And I wonder if I'm anything like her. If I look like her. If she's musical, or if she likes spicy food, or if she's afraid of bugs. But mostly, I wonder why she gave me up."

I hardly know what to say. "For what it's worth, you don't seem defective to me," I finally manage, only stumbling a little over the words.

"Oh — thank you, Sam." She looks like she might cry.

Desperate for a distraction from the awkwardness I created, I pick up the mechanical pencil again and turn to a blank sheet of paper. Zoe's face is so close it's an easy reference, and before I can think about it too hard, I let my hand fly. I draw until every curve and angle comes alive, until the stars I sketch into the night sky behind her hold as much light as the constellations on her bedroom wall.

In a way, I'm luckier than she'll ever be. I know where so many parts of me came from: the sci-fi-loving parts (Dad); the neurotic parts (Mom); the aptitude for mathematics and a tendency toward academic overachieving parts (both). I still haven't answered Dad's email, but I have an opportunity that Zoe might never get. I can still see him — if I want to. But I can't resolve the swirling tide of love and anger that surges every time I think of him, much less begin to explain it. Mom is the one I have to worry about anyway. So are the things I fear I've inherited from her.

She sighs. "The thing about not being a regular person — someone who was wanted — is that I'm taking up resources, and I'm not even supposed to be here. So I feel like I have to justify my existence."

The pain in her voice is hard to bear.

She glances at me. "But my brother — Jonah — he doesn't have to justify anything. He was wanted. He's their biological child. They're all real family. And I'm a drop-in."

Her life is no fairy tale, but I wish I could make it one for her. All the words of comfort that want to pour forth from me are too much. Zoe and I haven't known each other very long, and I have no idea why she's telling me all this, but I do know it would be way over the top for me to say even half of what I feel about how amazing she is. How worthy.

How wanted.

I sit there, stewing in the silence that comes from not being able to dial down my feelings to something reasonable, until finally she says, "Ugh, never mind. I'm just being stupid."

Cartoon balloons bloom all over my head, filled with words that I can't figure out if I should say. *You can always talk to me. Nothing you say is stupid. I love listening to you.* But as it turns out, cartoon balloons are silent. And maybe it's just as well, because a rogue interloper like *The smell of your hair makes me delirious* or *The way your collarbones look in the moonlight makes my heart race* could pop out.

"Anyway, thanks for listening. You know . . . it's strange having someone in my room. I've barely had people over in the past couple of years. It was too hard with Jonah here."

"I'd come over," I say.

She glances at me questioningly.

"If Jonah were home. I mean, maybe you wouldn't want me to, but I would if you did." I stare at the floor, afraid to look at her.

She hesitates. "He's not like disabled people you see on TV," she finally says. "He can't talk or do basic things for himself."

"It's okay," I say. He's a person who matters to her. When I glance at her, she's watching me, her brow furrowed.

"It's okay," I say again.

She turns away and wipes her eyes with both hands. "Sorry." She takes a quick breath.

I stand, trying to compute some kind of human reaction.

"Do you have to go?" she asks, misunderstanding my motion. She sits up and reaches for a tissue. "I'm probably freaking you out with all my drama."

"No, I . . . I was—I thought . . ." I take a sudden hard breath. "Do you need a hug?"

She glances up, surprised. Then she nods and says, "A hug would be good."

My heart pounds in my throat. I inch over to the bed, gingerly sitting beside her, then stop, not sure what to do with any of my limbs. "I'm not really very good at this." I stare at my shoes.

"At hugging?" Her voice is gentle.

I nod. I'm so awkward and shaky, she must think I'm completely weird. Mom hugs me. I used to hug Dad. But beyond that, I've always had a no-touching policy. I don't know where the proper boundaries lie for people who are outside of family.

"It's okay. You just . . ." She puts a hand on my shoulder.

Every nerve in my body is on fire. I keep staring at my shoes as if they contain the hidden secrets of the universe.

"You're supposed to put your arms around me, too," she says.

So I put my arms around her, letting them rest softly on her back, trying to ignore how good she feels against me. How much I love the way her curves press into me, how amazing she smells.

Finally, she pulls back and says, "Thank you."

"You're welcome," I mumble, grateful for my mother's conditioning regarding manners. "I have to go." I stand up, unable to think about what happens if I stay.

"Are you walking?" she asks, frowning. She's worried about me.

"Yeah. It's not far."

"Okay. Be careful. Hey." She smiles at me, and my insides go wonky. Being smiled at by Zoe is like stepping off a cliff. I have no idea how long the drop is, and no clue where I'll land. She says, "Thanks for tonight. I liked hanging with you."

"Sure," I say, because at this point it's going to be either monosyllabic words or desperate random noises. I give her a stupid wave.

And then I do what I do best: disappear.

When I wake up on Sunday, the house is too silent, and then I remember why.

I lie there, listening for signs of life. The coffeemaker beeps, signaling the pot is brewed, and down the hall the shower is running. My parents are trying to carry on, I guess. But I know that they, too, had this moment of waking up and remembering that Jonah isn't here. My heart hurts to think what that must have been like for them.

I'm so glad things are okay with Sam again, largely because I hope today holds lots of Starworld. Starworld will get me through.

I get up and find the sketch Sam left on my desk, and my breath catches. I know right away that it is meant to be a drawing of me — a very charitable version of me, with a perfect nose and delicate cheekbones and gorgeous hair, wearing a crown made out of stars. She's even included my birthmark, and somehow under her rendering it looks less like a flaw and more like an intentional particularity, a part of a thoughtful whole. I reach for my phone and write to tell her how incredible it is, and how much her company meant to me last night, but minutes tick past with no response. I hope she's okay. I hope she wasn't freaked out by everything I dumped on her.

I glance through my other texts. My friends sent messages of love and well-wishing last night, letting me know how much they missed me, which was nice. Still, it doesn't look like my absence killed anyone's fun, judging by the photos that whiz by my field of vision when I look at social media. I feel weirdly distanced from it all, like I never even belonged there anyway. But then I think of Hunter there without me and feel a small crush of regret. Does he feel abandoned, too? The idea of making someone else feel that way makes me want to die. Why does being human have to hurt so much?

I go downstairs, thinking I might have some oatmeal or some toast, but those things will just remind me of Jonah. My parents are too quiet, and the sounds of the house — the tick of the clock, the heat turning on and off — are too loud. I go back upstairs and hide out in my room with headphones on. I have plenty of homework to keep me busy.

Cammie messages me in the afternoon. I don't know how to respond without asking about Homecoming and the overnighter, which I don't particularly want to hear about just now, so I ignore the messages like the asshole I apparently am.

But after a while, she calls. "Hey, are you okay? Did you get my messages?"

"I'm sorry." I sink onto my bed. "I suck. I suck at everything."

"Oh, Zoe. I know how hard things must be. But I missed you so much this weekend. And I don't even know how you're doing."

"Are you home?" I ask.

"Yeah, I just got home. I got, like, two hours of sleep."

"Was it fun?" I'm not sure I want to know how fun it was, but I ask anyway.

"The dance was fine. It was fun; it was stupid; it was okay. Your friend Sam was there." She says it conversationally, not loaded in any way, and I feel a rush of gratitude at the way she is able to just accept things.

"She wore a flapper dress," Cammie says, "and her date was in period costume, too. It was great."

I hesitate to admit that I know what Sam wore. I realize that, in some ways, I feel like I'm cheating on Cammie. Like Sam is taking her place. I hope it doesn't seem that way to Cammie. Sam can't take Cammie's place, for a thousand reasons. But at the same time, I can't deny that there are things I love about Sam, things she gives me that no one else can.

"How was the after-party?" I ask, avoiding the subject of Sam entirely.

"Oh, you know. A little wild. Ethan was out of hand."

"I'll bet." I'm not sorry to have missed it. "How about Erin?"

"She's always out of hand."

I laugh. "Truth."

"I felt weird without you there. And with Hunter and everything."

I guess this part was inevitable. I lie back on my bed. "Did he have fun?"

"You'd have to ask him," she said. "I mean, there were times when he was laughing and screwing around with the guys, and other times he looked out of it. He thinks you guys are going to break up."

"He told you that?"

"No, Connor did. Zo . . ." She sighs. "I don't want to hurt your feelings, but . . ."

I sit up, girding myself.

"It's just that everyone feels bad for Hunter," she says. "And I don't really blame them? Because he did kind of get the screw here. But, like, I don't blame you, either. I think you're going through a hard time and you deserve some slack. That said . . ." She hesitates. "I mean, Zoe. You didn't even tell Hunter what was happening to you and your family. Or even Erin and Syd. It can make people feel like you don't trust them, or like they don't matter to you."

I start to object, but then I realize she's right.

I do put up walls so people can't see past them — that's true.

But it never really occurred to me that people could see the walls.

"So," she continues, "the weekend was hard because people were judging you and I kept defending you, but it wasn't easy to do. Because you don't want people to know why you do the things you do — why you bagged on Homecoming, why you keep to yourself a lot. And so what am I supposed to say? In defense of my best friend?"

My eyes sting with tears to realize not just the truth in what she's saying, but also that she's stood up for me in spite of it.

"If people knew what it's been like for you — with your mom's illness, and with Jonah . . . They'd understand, Zoe. I really think they would. Even boneheads like Ethan and Connor. I think you need to think about why you don't give anyone a chance."

That's not true, I want to say. Because I have trusted Sam with everything.

But nobody else.

She's right.

At school, I usually keep to myself, mostly, trying not to forge bonds that will interfere with the way I keep my family and home life in a silo, separate and away. I always hoped it came across like I was busy or preoccupied. Not like a slight.

My heart sinks to realize how futile my wishful thinking was.

"They don't know it's because you're so afraid of anything hurting your family," she continues gently. "But you don't trust anyone, you don't want anyone getting too close, and it shows."

I get up and close my bedroom door all the way before speaking again. "I just — you all seem so perfect to me and my own life feels so" — I pause, then finish — "fucked up." Because that's how it feels. Fucked up.

"Whoa," she says. "An f-bomb? From Zoe Miller?" She laughs, but she sounds kind of off. "What is happening here?"

"What's happening is I'm not perfect," I say, pacing around my room. "And I'm tired of trying to be."

"Who ever said you had to be perfect?"

I sit at my vanity, catching myself in the mirror. My hair is in a ponytail, and there's that birthmark.

I don't know how to make her understand. About the Theory of Original Defectiveness. About justifying my existence. About trying to be what my parents need, about being a good girl. About feeling like a drop-in. About everything feeling under threat. About the losses I've faced and am facing. About not knowing who I am or where I came from or who I'm meant to be.

How can she possibly understand that, when her life seems like the complete opposite?

"It's hard to explain," I finally say.

"Well," she says. "You don't have to be perfect for me. You're kind of a problem, to be honest, but I still love you."

I burst into laughter. A little levity was just what was needed. "Thanks," I say.

"You're welcome," she says, and I can hear the smile in her voice. "Zo? Are you doing okay? How is Jonah doing at the place? How are your parents?"

"I don't even know," I tell her. "Like, I literally don't know if we're okay. We're going to see Jonah on Halloween. Maybe after that I'll have a better answer."

"Yeah, maybe seeing that he's okay will help with, you know . . . accepting things, I guess?"

"Maybe," I say. I honestly can't imagine feeling okay about how things are.

"Listen, I had an idea I wanted to talk to you about. What if Sister Symphonies does an instrument drive for Little Lambs Village? Nothing delicate — not strings, maybe. But things like recorders and xylophones and maracas?"

My heart warms even as it twinges with sadness. She's doing what she does: finding a positive spin, finding a way to do something constructive and forward-moving. "That's really nice, Cam."

"And then I thought maybe you and I could do a road trip to deliver them all, and then we could also visit Jonah."

My chest hurts at how good she is, how hard she's trying to help.

She continues, "We could go, just the two of us, if you didn't want to involve Syd and Erin in that part. And then after seeing Jonah and letting everyone lavish us with praise over how awesome we are, we can come back, get some vodka with my new fake ID, and party! Because, you know, if we have to listen to everyone trying out the instruments, our nerves are going to be shredded."

I laugh. I almost feel bad, but it's true.

"We could start the instrument drive now and deliver things during the holidays."

"Maybe," I say. "It's a great idea."

"Okay, I'm taking that as agreement," Cammie says.

My phone vibrates with a message. "Fair enough," I say to Cammie, opening my messages. It's Sam. "Okay," I tell Cammie. "Well, hey, thanks for the talk."

"There's one other thing."

"Yes?" I say, trying not to sound impatient.

"Make it official with Hunter, if it's over. He doesn't want to break up with you — we all know he doesn't. But it's like he's just waiting for it, and it's an agony to watch."

A heaviness fills my chest as I take in what Cammie's saying. "No, you're right," I say. "I will. I'll talk to him tomorrow."

"Good girl," she says.

I ignore the echoes of that phrase I have such mixed feelings about.

When Cammie and I hang up, I push aside thoughts of Hunter for the time being and go straight to Sam's message.

Sam: *is glad you like the drawing* *is glad to be of help last night* *is basically a clusterfuck of gladness*

Me: THERE YOU ARE. *leans* Great timing! Ugh, I'm having a hard day. ☹

Sam: *apologizes for absence due to gaming appointment* *sends the Fairy Godbot to deliver a caramel latte* *demands coordinates for parties responsible for said hard day* *loads the Super Soakers with cat urine* *readies the army of dingo bats*

And just like that, she has me laughing.

Ha, I write. There's no one to avenge, really. It's me. I'm an asshole, basically.

Sam: *disagrees but admires language*

Me: RESCUE ME. *whistles for Humphrey* I need the way she lets me escape, the way she takes me to places that are amazing and magical and worry-free.

Sam: *pauses in castle workshop to fit Humphrey with a nitro engine, adjusts carburetor, launches us at the speed of a comet*

·179·

She keeps going, rapid-fire, filling my phone with unfathomable, fantastical beauty:

lands Humphrey on Planet XB-Z57 in a secret forest where the soft rush of an ocean is barely audible

leads you carefully through trees with frond-like leaves glistening with sentient drops of water that giggle and rush into crevices as we approach

points to the prismatic crystals hanging from branches as we emerge into soft sunlight that warms a beach of white sand laced with reflected rainbows

kicks up soft sand and scatters rainbows everywhere

dashes into the turquoise water and whispers to the waves until two water-horses rise from the sea

leaps aboard one and gestures for you to get on the other

races you under the three moons hanging on the horizon beyond the ocean

lands on an island in front of a worn wooden mailbox

pulls a letter from the box and points to script above the black wax seal that says "Her Royal Highness Queen Zoe of Starworld"

Sam finally pauses in her rapid-fire messaging, so I snap out of my dazed wonder and type: *regards curiously*

Sam: *reads from the missive*

If you seek the story of me, you must find objects three:

1. The key to a kingdom with rules beyond measure

2. The dungeon which housed the king's greatest pleasure

3. And last, but not least, Starworld's most perfect treasure.

My eyes widen. What's this? A riddle? What's she doing?

Me: *is intrigued* Who is "me"? Where are these treasures hidden? *peeks under tablecloths* MUST FIND OBJECTS.

Sam: *points to a sparkling trail across the island that leads back into the sky*

Me: *follows the glittery path* *whistles for Humphrey* *climbs on and pulls you onboard*

Sam: *steers him into the wilds of the universe*

She leads me on an adventure through multiple galaxies, in search of the key to a mystery only she knows, diverting me so completely that I barely look up until dinner.

Every sentence adds a new and unexpected dimension to the world. When it ends, I type OMG I LOVE YOU. I wish I could be more articulate, wish I could let her know how her words fill my heart and carry me away.

Despite everything that's going on in my real life and how painful it all is, with Sam there is always something extraordinary waiting for me, always a beautiful place where nothing hurts.

My mom calls in sick to work on Monday. When she sees the worry on my face, she is busted: she admits to me that she's not actually sick; she's calling in because she's too sad and upset to face the workday.

My dad's response is predictably the opposite: he buries himself in work, holing up in his office at home and leaving for campus early.

I want to call in sick or hide, too, but I can't do either. So we all do what we do: I try to be good and helpful, and my mother obsesses about Jonah's schedule and meds while waiting for a report on how his first night went, and my father loses himself in trade routes and trees and Jesuit missions.

The ride to school with Cammie is quiet, my stomach a tangle of nerves over not just my parents and Jonah, but over the terrible thing I need to do today, which is break up with Hunter. Midmorning, I text him, asking if he can meet me after school by the sculpture in the quad. He responds that he has a captains' practice until five thirty but could meet me after that.

I think about basketball season, and for a moment I almost second-guess what I'm about to do. Even before we started going out, I loved watching him play — he has such an ease on the court, such grace. I loved being the girlfriend of the star of the team — the player all the girls screamed over. It occurs to me that it gave me an identity, a place to belong. And it was fun for a while — the butterflies, all the firsts . . . But I think I was more in love with being Hunter's girlfriend than I was in love with Hunter.

He deserves someone who loves him in all the right ways, who wants the same things he wants. And yet, as sure as I feel about that, it takes all I have to press through the day, knowing what's coming at the end of it. The feeling of dread weighs heavy.

In choir, though, a distraction: I audition for — and get — the soprano descant solo in "Silent Night." But as pleased as I am to have gotten the part, there is as always that intertwined thread of wondering where this musical gift came from, if anywhere. Each good thing seems to be tangled up with a shadow side. Even with the things that make me special, it hurts to think I might always feel like I don't really belong anywhere.

After school, I sit with Elliot at rehearsal, watching the cast work through a couple of scenes from act 2 as I wait to meet Hunter. Elliot rubs his beard as he watches, an intense expression on his face. The set is starting to shape up nicely, and I have to admit that Serena is actually really good — better than I imagined. When he calls for a break, I tell him he did a great job with casting. He gives me sort of a sad smile. "It's working out pretty well," he says. "But I'll always wish you were in the show."

"Me too. But I doubt anyone else would have found you Sam Jones's painting," I say, trying to stay upbeat.

"Oh my god, that painting!" His eyes widen. "I couldn't have dreamed up anything more perfect."

"Right? And the crew is doing an amazing job with the walls. And that window!"

He nods. "I just hope the snow goes okay — remember in *Enemy?*"

I laugh. "How could I forget? I was picking it out of my hair that whole night." I glance at my watch and my stomach dives. It's almost five thirty. "Oh gosh. I have to go." I get up and gather my things, then give Elliot a hug goodbye.

It's time to meet Hunter.

It's a beautiful evening — clouds are scattered across a pink-tinged sky — which makes this all the harder.

Hunter is waiting at the sculpture for me, his hair wet from a shower. "Hey," he says. He smiles a little but makes no move to touch me.

A lump forms in my throat before I even speak, because it's clear he knows it's over, too, and somehow knowing that it's real brings a rush of hurt. "Hey," I say. I sit on the base of the sculpture, and he sits beside me.

"Beautiful sky," he says.

"Yeah." I glance at him. "Did you have an okay time? The dance, and the party?"

He looks away. "I tried," he finally says.

"Oh, Hunter," I say softly. "I'm so sorry. I never wanted to disappoint you. Or hurt you."

He nods. "I know."

A couple of his friends shout to him as they head toward the parking lot. He holds up a hand in a wave, but his expression remains stoic.

We sit in silence for a few minutes.

"This sucks," he finally says.

"Sucks donkey dicks," I agree.

I glance over to see his shocked expression. He shakes his head. "You're full of surprises, Zoe," he says. "I just never know with you."

"I know," I say. "I'm not easy."

He smiles at me, barely. "I always thought you were."

"Easy?" I joke.

"Ha, you know what I mean. You seemed so easy to be with. Maybe I didn't try hard enough. You know, to make sure you were happy, or . . ."

I shake my head. "No, you're fine, Hunter. I'm *not* easy. It wasn't you."

"It can't have been all you. I mean, I'm not perfect." He watches me, and I realize he has no clue what went wrong. And I'm not sure I have answers.

·184·

"It really was mostly me," I say. "I'm not perfect, either." It feels surprisingly good to say it out loud, although a part of me feels like I'm losing something—as if maybe I'd had Hunter fooled and now I was going to be lower in his estimation. "You were a good boyfriend," I say, and my use of the past tense catches in my chest, and I can see that it's hit him the same way.

He looks toward the deepening pink of the horizon, nodding slowly. "I did try," he says. I see him swallow hard, and I realize how much this is going to hurt, this whole ending.

"I know," I say, laying a hand on his shoulder.

He turns and tries to smile, but his eyes well with tears. "You were my first love."

I lean on his shoulder, letting my tears spill onto his coat. "You were mine, too," I say. "And I'm glad."

We sit like that for a few minutes, sniffling from our tears and the chill that grows as the sun begins to set. Finally he puts an arm around me. "Come on," he says. "I'll give you a ride home."

We stand, and I hold out my arms to him. We hug for a long moment, then walk arm in arm to the parking lot.

Sam

I can no longer deny that I'm utterly lost to Starworld and to Zoe. We exchange messages all night on Monday after she tells me she broke up with Hunter. I don't know how to take the news. While I feel bad that she's hurting, the truth is that part of me is glad. And then I feel like a shitcan for feeling glad, because being happy when your friend has gone through something awful is a jerk thing to do. But her breaking up with him did the worst possible thing: it gave me hope.

Every day at lunch I settle in at the library, planning as if I'll be alone like always, trying to tamp down the spark of excitement that Zoe might show up. And somehow, every day she does, and fans that spark into a flame. We mix our lunches up and make asymmetrical multicolored messes of questionable but entertaining flavor profiles. We dip randomly shaped chunks of granola bars into hummus and pour ranch dressing on peanut butter and jelly. It's disgusting. It's hilarious. And it makes my heart feel like a fucking supernova.

When we aren't together, the world between us continues to build, and the fairy tale I've written for her takes on a life of its own. We both have study hall last period on Thursday, and I use the time to tell the next part of her tale.

Me: *sneaks out of study hall, flees through the door in the sky, and beckons you to follow* *enters teleportation turret of castle to pick up where our quest for the key to the kingdom left off*

Zoe: *races after you*

My breath still catches every time she comes after me.

Me: *activates hyperdrive* *crash-lands in a dark and tangled forest, noticing that objects grow on the trees* *gets snagged on a weeping willow that grows fish hooks instead of leaves*

Zoe: *carefully extricates your ponytail*

I blush thinking about what it would be like if she touched my hair in real life. I'd probably implode. The first quest I set for her is to find the key to a kingdom, so we need a locked door . . .

Me: *finds a trail that leads toward a wall over which the turrets of a castle peek in the distance*

Zoe: Could this be the kingdom we've been searching for? *edges along the wall looking for an entrance*

Me: *tugs on ornate gate of metal and glass sealed with a rusting lock, but it doesn't budge* *presses ear to the keyhole but hears only the whistling of the wind*

Zoe: *notes that its tone is a G* We need to find the key!

Me: *hurries back into the forest* *passes trees growing

hacksaws, light bulbs, trowels, washcloths, and single-ply toilet paper* *scurries under the canopy of one blooming with glass chimes, another of bells, then stops under a third covered with keys tinkling against each other in the breeze*

Zoe: *notices that most of the tones are B-flats or E-flats*

Me: *tries to sing an E-flat but ends up sounding more like a Z-sharp* *gets clobbered on the head by a tiny silver key that also sounds like a Z-sharp but is clearly the wrong one for the gate we are trying to open* *hopes you can match the pitch of the wind on the other side of the gate*

Zoe: *sings a G*

Me: !!! *catches a gleaming glass key just the right size*

Zoe: *zooms back to gate* *jiggles the key in the lock until the gate swings open with a great creaking of hinges*

Me: *regards the sign inside the entrance with some alarm*

WELCOME TO THE DOMAIN OF KING LORDERUS DIPSHITTUS III

ALL RULES MUST BE FOLLOWED

ALL SIGNS MUST BE OBEYED

NO MUSIC

NO DANCING

NO ART

NO FUN

EXCEPT BY ORDER OF THE KING

Zoe: *isn't too sure about this place*

Me: *struggles to read the road sign at the first cobbled intersection with several hundred arrows pointing in different directions*

Zoe: *trots off in the direction of the sign with a painted crown* *prepares to inform the king that the rules of his kingdom suck*

With the first of our three quests completed, we explore

the strange kingdom we've entered, trading messages back and forth in the stars until the bell rings and the school day is over.

As I walk out into the crisp afternoon, I text Mom to remind her that I'm headed to Will's to game for a couple hours and that I'll be having dinner there. I leave out the subtext, which is *please fix something or at least order in so I don't feel guilty about one of my rare nights away from home.*

When Will drops me off later, I find Mom in her office with her work laptop open.

"Hi, honey. How was your day?" She jumps up from her chair and hugs me. I wish I could take comfort in it, but her arms feel like a straitjacket.

"Fine," I say, and wiggle out of her grip.

"Is your homework done?" she asks. "Did you eat dinner?" She searches my face, tucking back a piece of the dark-blond hair that came loose from her hair clip.

"Yeah," I say. "Will's dad made pizza. Did you have anything to eat?"

She shakes her head. "No, I had work to do. I'm finishing up our staffing projections for next year. Kerry needs to submit them tomorrow, and she wanted the numbers double-checked. I've got to stay on top of things. Prove that I'm VP material."

I peer over her shoulder at her laptop, where her browser displays a yarn website.

"Definitely looks like you've been working hard," I joke.

"Well, the white elephant gift exchange at work is coming

up soon," she says sheepishly. "I was thinking about crocheting a wine cozy."

"In puke orange and monkey-poo green?" I ask.

"Well, it is a white elephant . . ." The corners of her eyes crinkle when she smiles, and a pang of the deepest love runs through me, immediately followed by the usual accompaniment of darkest sorrow.

Her failure to eat dinner is a harsh reminder of why leaving for college is both the thing I want most and the thing I don't know if I can have — because if someone isn't here to make sure she takes care of herself, she won't. What then?

"Do you need help making something for dinner?" I ask.

"No, I'll get something myself in a little bit." She chews on her lip, then turns to her desk, to her work. It resurrects a dull echo of my earlier anger; I know she's not actually going to eat. Somehow she manages to hold things together when it has to do with her job, but never when it has to do with home, or with me. It's funny that she judges Dad so harshly for choosing his job over me when she does the exact same thing day after day.

In my room, I toss down my messenger bag and see a letter sitting on my pillow. I stare at the blue envelope, feeling the chasm inside me widen and stretch, a knife twisting in an old wound. Still, there's no way I can let it sit there unopened.

I slide my finger under the flap and pull out a card with a rocket ship on the front. My eyes sting. I hate that even after all this time he knows me — not because he stayed in close touch, but because so much of who I am was informed by the time I spent with him. Because he's half of me. Because even if I wanted to, I can't excise the memories or the strands of DNA that gave me my hopes and dreams. Inside he wrote:

Happy Halloween! Our favorite holiday has finally gained a lot of popularity across the pond, which means your grandfather is working on a prank for the unlucky trick-or-treaters who come to his house. Maisie, his night carer, had the scare of her life when she opened the broom closet and a straw-stuffed corpse fell out. Pretty sure Dad is still laughing, the sadistic arse. As for me, I'm going to resurrect my Doctor Who costume for the contest at work. Remember when I wore it to take you trick-or-treating? You were dressed as a TARDIS, and Mrs. Clemons from around the corner asked if you were supposed to be a Tampax box?

Anyway, I hope you and your mum are well and you have a happy holiday. I wish we could be together for it, but hope to see you in the summer.

Love, Dad

I drop the card on the bed and curl up beside it. Hearing from Dad is a punishment now. All it does is dredge up bittersweet memories I'd rather forget. Downstairs, Mom has moved on from her work to checking the windows, latching and unlatching, counting to herself in a murmur I can't make out but know by heart. Unfortunately, she is not an equation or a problem that I can reason out with logic. I mash my face into my pillow and think about what Will said a while ago about asking Dad what to do about her. I can't avoid my dad's email much longer, especially now that I owe him the obligatory thank-you for the card.

So I sit on my bed with my laptop and fill an hour with false starts:

How could you leave me with her?

Hope your life in London is super awesome without me.

Do you have a new family yet? Are they better than the one you left behind?

I finally settle on a few sentences along the lines of "thanks for the card and invitation," and "I doubt I can visit since Mom needs my help all the time. Was she always like this?"

I wish I could remember more about the time before my parents split up, but my memories of the divorce are fuzzy and dim. She counted sometimes, but that didn't seem strange; in kindergarten, we counted things all the time. But when you live with someone every day, it's hard to see the slow ways they change, the way the walls keep closing in until you realize you're trapped in the box of safety they've built around you. Did I just fail to notice how bad things were until Dad took off for England? Or did they get worse because he left?

I hit send on the email, then spend a while online searching for things like "help mom with OCD," but just like every other time I've searched, there's far more information about children with OCD than parents. I only find one article that has any advice, suggesting that family members should try to avoid accommodating OCD or participating in rituals. How the fuck am I supposed to do that when helping her complete them is sometimes the only way I can get her to calm down?

Refusing to participate would probably lead to accusations that I'm not doing what needs to be done to help the family.

But what if it would help her for me to stop?

I don't know.

Eventually I fall asleep in my clothes with my lamp on, curled up next to my backpack like it might offer the comfort of another person instead of just books stabbing into my spine.

I don't wake up until Mom creaks down the hallway a little before four a.m., which means it's almost noon in London. I can't help myself — I pick up my phone and open my email.

Hey kiddo,

What do you mean, "Was she always like this?" Like what? She and I don't speak that much anymore. I'm not high on her list, as you know, and I don't fault her for it — I know how hard it was for you when I moved back to England. That's why I'd love for you to visit. I miss you more than you can imagine. I know you'd rather saw off your own head than Skype, so I hope you'll consider visiting so we can talk face-to-face. I really think you'd love London if you gave it a chance.

As for your mum, she's always had some anxiety, if that's what you're asking about, but I thought she had it managed with medication and was doing fine. Can we please talk?

Love you.

No, he doesn't.

If he did, he would just fucking explain what led to this.

If he did, he would have stayed.

Sunday morning my phone rings on my nightstand, awakening me from a dream I didn't want to leave. Zoe and I were lying down in a meadow filled with fire-lit flowers — one of the imaginary places I conjured up for her this past week. We lay face-to-face, almost touching. The way she looked at me made me feel like I was drowning in those incredible eyes of hers, but in the dream I didn't need air. I didn't need anything except the way she said my name, the way she touched my cheek, the way she let me run a finger along the perfect arch of her eyebrow and down the soft curve of her cheek.

Phone calls can go to hell.

It's so unusual for anyone to call me that my first thought is that it must be a wrong number, but when I grab it, the display says "Dad." I drop it back on the floor without answering and press a pillow over my head. The only person I might have answered for is Zoe, even though the mere idea of that fills me with a warm feeling that can only be the symptom of impending nuclear-core meltdown.

A few minutes later I hear another vibration indicating that Dad left a message.

I press the phone to my ear and his voice floods in — the same warm, accented voice that read to me when I was small, everything from *Goodnight Moon* to *A Brief History of Time*. Losing that daily routine was one of the hardest parts of my parents' divorce.

Hey, love. You didn't answer my email yet, so I'd hoped to reach you by phone, though I know it's not your favorite. What kind of problem are you having with your mum? You should let me know if something's wrong. I know you haven't wanted me to come before, but I'll fly back in a heartbeat if you need me. But would you please ring me either way? Your message worried me and I'd like to hear your voice. I love you, Sammy.

My chest is so tight I can hardly breathe. I don't want him to come here, don't want him to see how pathetic my life is. I just want him to tell me what he knows about why Mom is the way she is. Even if I wanted to call him back, I doubt I'd be able to produce any words. I hate using phones for their original intended purpose. It's like Alexander Graham Bell wondered, *Hey, what could maximize the awkwardness of human-to-human communication?* And then answered himself by giving us the ability to speak to one another through stupid disembodied little boxes.

If only one of Zoe's summons to Starworld had been my wake-up call. I shove my phone into the pocket of my pajama pants and slink down to the kitchen.

Mom is sitting on one of the bar stools scrolling through something on her laptop, already close to the bottom of the pot of coffee she must have brewed at the asscrack of dawn or whenever she got up.

"Good morning, honey," she says.

I mutter something noncommittal and pour myself a bowl of Cap'n Crunch big enough to put a rhino into a sugar coma. I can't decide what — if anything — to tell her about the message Dad left. She'd probably be better off not knowing he reached out at all, but talking to her about visiting London might be a way to test the waters about leaving for good. Maybe I should try not accommodating her for once, like the article said.

"Dad invited me to visit London," I say.

Mom looks up, startled.

I grab the milk out of the fridge. "What do you think? Would you be okay here by yourself?"

"Of course," she says, like I'm bonkershit for asking. "But when did he ask you? I've told him to check with me first before doing things like that. All it ever does is upset you."

"What are you talking about?" I set the milk on the counter and turn to her. "It upsets me that he ditched me! It upsets me that I haven't seen him in years."

"See? You're upset right now. This is why I wish he'd talk to me before making plans. Traveling to London is a long trip. Does he want you to come over winter break? That's too soon, and the weather might be bad. You could end up delayed in Chicago or something awful. I can't have you stuck in an airport in some strange city alone. I'll have to discuss it with him." Her mind is already a thousand steps ahead of mine, seeking out any possible disaster scenario that might result from this suggestion. My heart sinks with every one.

"Forget it," I say. "It was a stupid idea." Mom just proved every theory I had about her reaction.

I splash just enough milk into my cereal to make Mom feel like I'm doing my part to stave off future osteoporosis, but my efforts are wasted because my sugar and calcium consumption seem to be the last thing on her mind. She's on her feet and headed to the stove before I even take a seat at the bar.

"One, two, three, four," she chants to herself, her hands fluttering over the knobs of the stove like lost birds. Maybe I don't have to worry about her when I leave — maybe she'll be so busy counting things that she won't even notice I'm gone.

I try to tune her out amidst all the other Sunday-morning white noise: the gutter dripping outside with the last of the night's rain, the kitchen radio softly playing the classical station, and the *whoosh* of the heater sending a blast of warm air over my socks under the bar. I shove a spoonful of future diabetes into my mouth as my phone buzzes with a message from Will. It's a photo he took at the pumpkin patch with his family and Kitty this morning before heading to Planet Quest Con. He's smiling right into the camera holding an enormous pumpkin, Kitty is looking at him adoringly with her arm looped through his, and Will's little brother, Dylan, is photobombing in the background with wide eyes and his tongue so far out of his head he looks like an anteater on crack.

The picture makes me wonder what it would be like to know that kind of happiness. I feel like I might have at one time, but perhaps it was just a dream.

Ha-ha. See you this afternoon, I write back to Will, not sure what else to say.

Hope you're ready to play meat shield, he responds.

I groan. That's what I get for bumming two rides home last week.

Me: **Prepare for friendly fire and revenge by chain saw.**

Will: **Whatever you want AFTER we beat the DLC.**

His messages are my only new ones for the morning, so I flip back to the older ones — the last I received from Zoe. Every time I read her words, no matter how innocuous or silly, gravity feels like less of a fact.

"I'm going to the grocery store," Mom says after finishing her burner routine. She slips on her shoes and picks up her purse. "I'll be back in an hour."

The clock reads exactly 10:40 a.m. Even numbers. Safe times.

After the garage door closes (twice) and she disappears, I rinse out my bowl and put it in the dishwasher, then go back to my room. I should call Dad back, while it's still a reasonable time in London, but I can't bring myself to do it. I don't know what to say.

The part of me that wants to see Dad has grown bigger than the part that's angry he left — especially now that I realize Mom had more to do with him not seeing or communicating with me than I thought. I don't even know who to be angry with anymore. Why did I ever trust Mom over him? She answers to a thousand inexplicable priorities before dealing with things that are real and important. Dad was never that way. Still, he can't come back now. I can't imagine how Mom would react if he showed up and how much worse it would make things.

Instead of calling him, I email a few quick lines:

Thanks for the message, but don't worry — you don't have

to come back. Mom and I are pretty good at managing
these days.

Then I try to talk myself out of caring whether or not he responds.

But when night comes, I fall asleep thinking of his voice, remembering the stories he read to me when I was small.

Zoe

Bao Bao!" Jonah stands in front of me, holding my always-cold hands in his always-warm ones, rocking back and forth. Afternoon light streams in from the bay window in the apartment unit at Little Lambs Village. It's a nice place—clean and comfortable—but I can't quite fathom that this is where he lives now. There is a new reality to adjust to, and at the moment, the truth is we might need to see him more desperately than he needs to see us.

"Yeah, I've missed you, too, sweetie," I say. And then I softly sing to him, although the worry that he misses me singing to him, misses me, misses home, puts a wobble in my voice. I sing him "Tonight You Belong to Me," wishing as always that either of my parents could carry a tune in a bucket, because it's really meant to be a duet. But Jonah doesn't mind. He doesn't know.

He looks good. He's clean, save a smear of ketchup on his cheek, but we did arrive just as they were finishing lunch. Someone tucked his T-shirt into his pants, which I think looks silly. It's just a small thing, and it's not nearly as important as his being safe and well cared for, but all the ways we'll be relinquishing control of his life . . . The realizations keep piling up, and no matter how small or inconsequential they are, they stab at me a little. It feels like more than the sum of the tiny parts. How can a tucked-in T-shirt feel tantamount to leaving Jonah alone in the wild?

But somehow it does.

As my parents discuss Jonah's adjustment, programs, seizure reports, and so forth with the residential supervisor over in the kitchen and work out plans to bring him home for my birthday, which is next weekend, one of Jonah's apartment mates paces around, twiddling his fingers in front of his face. He stops in front of me to lean close, coming almost nose-to-nose with me.

"Hi," I say, not sure what else to do. I notice he has something chocolate on his shirt, which comforts me a little. I hope Jonah is getting treats, too.

A staff person named Delores calls from the dining area, where she's cleaning up from lunch. "That's Jonah's sister, Austin. You leave them alone." She says it kindly, though. Austin makes a noise like a machine gun and spins away.

"Bao Bao!" Jonah says again. He's smiling and making happy noises. I imagine that if he could talk, he would want to know if we're all going home now. The thought snakes tight around my heart.

Jonah holds up his hands and touches one fist into his other hand. It looks kind of like the way he signs bathroom, except that's usually a one-handed sign. He turns to the dining area, where Delores is wiping the table. She is in regular clothes, but in the spirit of Halloween, she has cat ears on and whiskers drawn on her face. She glances up from her cleaning and says to Jonah, "What do you want, sweetie?"

Again, Jonah taps one of his hands into the other.

"Aw, you already had your cookie," she says. "You have to wait." She holds up her hands, palms facing in, and wiggles her fingers, signing *wait*. "But good signing, Jonah." She winks at me.

"That was 'cookie'?" I ask in surprise, warming rapidly to this woman, whose smile could light up a stadium.

She nods and demonstrates. Her version is a little different from Jonah's, but it brings a lump to my throat to know that she understands *his* sign, and that she responds to it and praises him for it.

"Is he using a lot of sign language?" I ask her. At home he only uses a dozen signs or so — mostly the basic ones we were taught years ago when he started school. It occurs to me that this is probably more our failing than Jonah's. We tried learning and using more signs for a while, but, maybe because we always understood him, we were never as ambitious or consistent as we probably should have been.

"Oh, yes! He does a great job with signing," Delores says. She turns to Jonah. "What other signs do you know, Jonah? Do you know *please*?"

Jonah bangs his hand on his chest.

"That's right, good job," she says.

Jonah shakes his fist — his sign for *bathroom*.

"Oh, you need the bathroom?" Delores asks him. She turns to me with a smile. "We'll be back." She lays a hand on Jonah's back, and as they disappear down the hall, Jonah makes a familiar *meee* sound. I hear Delores say, "Yeah, you're happy, aren't you? You get to see your family."

I stare after them, my eyes welling. She knows his happy sound. Her tenderness with Jonah . . . the way she talks to him . . . I don't know if everyone here is like that. It seems unlikely. But this already is much better than I had imagined.

It's a rare sunny day, so we make our way out of the apartment to take Jonah for a stroll on the grounds, which are beautiful — walking trails and benches and even a gazebo. After, we get him a sundae at the ice cream shop, which is an all-windows wing of the café where a number of LLV residents are employed. We're served by a young guy who I think has Down syndrome. He tells us that he lives in the Johnston apartments. I don't know what the Johnston apartments are, but he seems very proud of this, boasting that their media center is state of the art. He is cheerful and conscientious, and he asks Jonah if he'd like Halloween sprinkles on his ice cream. When Jonah doesn't answer, my mom tells the guy, "Thank you, that would be lovely. Just a little," she adds. I know she'd probably rather skip the extra sugar and mess, and Jonah probably doesn't care either way, but she wants to be nice.

It occurs to me that I would have done the same thing. In a lot of ways, my mom and I aren't so different. Is that just because she raised me to be like her? Has all my effort to please my parents molded me into someone different than I would have been with another family? I push the thought away, because like so many others, it nudges and haunts, whispering its inescapable question, *Who are you really?*

We settle at a table that overlooks the gardens, which are bright with orange and yellow mums. A girl in a wheelchair sits at a neighboring table, a cheerful middle-aged man feeding her chocolate ice cream. She smiles a lot and sometimes squeals. I think he's her father, based on his comfort with her and the way she gazes at him, and my throat tightens. There is something about this kind of love, this kind of situation, that is so particular, so piercing. Other families have survived this. Can we? Everything here seems so nice, so festive and warm and cheerful, and I feel a surge of something like hope.

Still, saying goodbye to Jonah back at the apartment is agonizing. More of Jonah's apartment mates are here now, and it's much louder and more frenetic. One of the residents is upset — he cries and slaps at the kitchen counter. Delores tries to calm him as a male staff member repeatedly tells him he needs to stop hitting, he needs to settle down.

My parents exchange glances. Delores leaves the boy to the other staff person and comes over to smooth our goodbye so we don't have to just leave Jonah standing alone in our wake. We hug Jonah and tell him we'll see him soon. We struggle to be positive, but my dad . . . If I could choose something to never have to see again in my life, the way my father's face looks when he's bravely trying not to cry would be high on the list. And it brings back a memory I'd give anything to erase, from when my mom was in the hospital. My dad and I were struggling, trying to manage Jonah and get through the daily routines without her, and it was impossible, literally impossible, and there was a moment when he just . . . lost it. I had seen my dad *moved* to tears before, but I'd never seen him all-out crying because he was upset. He stood in the kitchen, having burned dinner while tending to Jonah's bathroom needs. The smoke detector was going off, but he just stood there, crying like a little boy, his sobs full and loud, arms hanging at his sides.

I had never felt so helpless, so scared. At that moment, the reality of life if my mom died fell on me like a great cosmic anvil. I actually prayed for a remission, and I'm not really the praying sort. Maybe there is a god and he was like, *Well, fair-weather friend, you can have a partial remission, but that's the best I can do for you.* And I'm so grateful that she's doing okay, but what I wouldn't give for the relief of a full remission. I worry every day that the cancer has decided to start growing again, and we're all just going about our business, oblivious to the sickness growing inside her. What then?

It occurs to me that, with Jonah being cared for, it might be possible for my father and me to survive the loss of my mother. Unbearable and untenable, but possible. And for the first time, I understand how my mother could make the most agonizing choice of her life — moving Jonah into a facility. This was the only way to assure that he would be okay. The weight of it bears down on me as we stand there, trying to say goodbye to Jonah, trying somehow to leave him behind.

Jonah doesn't throw a fit when we go, which I worried

he might. But in a way, it's worse. He stands still and silent, like a tree, and I imagine he doesn't understand what's happening. How could he? When I hug him, I wish I could make him understand how sorry I am that we're doing this, that we have to leave him here, that any of this has happened to him. Instead, I just squeeze him extra hard and try not to cry.

As we leave, Delores herds Jonah off to put on one of his nature videos.

My parents walk ahead of me to the car. My mom is crying, and my dad puts an arm around her. When we reach the car, he pulls a handkerchief out of his pocket and blows his nose with that terrible loud honk of his. My heart feels like a giant fist is crushing it to mulch. The amount of collective devastation in the three of us, despite how positive everything seems, overwhelms me.

It's going to be a long ride home.

I pull out my phone. There's only one person in all the world who could make me feel better right now, who could get me through this misery. And I need her more than ever.

I type: *gazes out car window on way back from Little Lambs Village* *heart breaks*

Her reply comes instantly: *stokes Humphrey's flames with shredded homework and flies over to get you* *sets coordinates to our castle in the sky*

The kind of startalk I love most of all. My heart lifts. Starworld is always a place I can find refuge. There she gives me a fairy tale to get lost in and quests we can undertake together. She gives me a reprieve from the silence left in

Jonah's wake . . . the ache of worrying about him . . . the agony of watching my parents' hearts break . . .

I can even temporarily forget the pain of breaking up with Hunter, which is even worse than I thought it could be. There are reminders of him everywhere. The photo on my mirror. Two shirts of his that I have, neither of which I really want to give back. The star necklace he gave me for our one-year anniversary. The stuffed polar bear he won for me at a carnival game over the summer. So many things.

Me: *buckles up* *clings to you as we careen gloriously through countless light-years of space*

Sam: *swoops into the kingdom of King Lorderus Dipshittus in a rush of stardust* *hops down Humphrey's spikes and jumps off*

Me: *bounces along after you*

Sam: *creeps through the palace* *follows a dust mote from sunbeam to sunbeam streaming through the high windows of the hall*

Me: *opens random doors in search of the king* *the FUCKING king*

Sam: *ducks through one into a secret passageway that leads through three interconnected rooms:

One with empty manacles chained to the floor, the walls stacked with canvases painted with unimaginable glory

One with stages at different elevations throughout and mirrors on every wall

One filled with enormous hanging cages where the sounds of the most perfect songs still echo*

Me: *listens for familiar melodies*

Sam: *stops in front of the largest and most gilded cage* *runs song through an intergalactic translation algorithm*

A long time ago I sang like a bird
Only for the king at his royal word
The rules of this kingdom mean a gift is a curse
Those left uncaged facing death or far worse
But when you were born, I knew you would sing
And I couldn't let you be enslaved by the king
With a last tearful hug and kiss I set you free
In hopes that you would fare better than me.
With a heart crushed to pieces, I let you go
Though I loved you far more than you'd ever know
I gave you away first thing at dawn
And every song's been for you from that sad day on.

The verse sparks a pain in my chest that sears like fire. I reread the poem, and then reread it again, my eyes welling with tears. It clutches hard at something in me, something raw and crucial.

It's the story of a relinquishment, and it echoes deeply in me, all the way to the marrow.

And then I realize what this is.

It's a counter theory to my Theory of Original Defectiveness.

Sam is telling me I am not defective, that I was never defective. She wants me to trust that I was let go so that I could have a better life. She wants me to believe that my birth mother loved me.

I'm unraveling in ways I don't know how to handle.

I type to her: *weeps*

Sam: *sends the Fairy Godbot to dispense tissues*

Me: Sam. I don't know what to say. How are you so good to me? Thank you. *hugs*

Sam: *grabs Humphrey and flies you back to home planet for comfort food*

She sends a snapshot of a trio of tacos from Taco Bell with an enormous pile of sauce packets alongside them. I laugh a little even as I swipe tears out of my eyes.

Me: *hopes there's enough to get back to outer space*

Sam: *saves some for the FTL fuel cells in our interdimensional rocket* *gets food to go, loads you into the rocket's sidecar, and careens out of orbit toward a far galaxy*

How I long for it to be real, to be somewhere far away — not here in this life where everything is too much.

I write: I don't think there's enough Taco Bell hot sauce in all the world to take me as far as I'd like to go.

Halloween night, it's just Mom and me — my dad has a dinner with his department. My friends are out doing all the Halloween things, and Sam went quiet a few hours ago. I hope things are okay for her at home. I hope, to be honest, she's quiet because she's working on Starworld. That she puts so much thought into it makes me feel like it means as much to her as it does to me. I can't wait to see where the quest takes us next.

For dinner, Mom and I decide on enchiladas, which we both love. In between trick-or-treaters (or "the crumb-snatchers," as my dad calls them), we snack on guacamole, which is meant to be for the enchiladas but will be history before dinner, because we never can stop eating guacamole until it's gone.

"How spicy do you want the filling?" my mom asks as she starts to chop jalapeños.

"As spicy as you can stand it," I say. I'm well aware that I'm the only one in the family who can handle the heat. I hold out a chip with guacamole. "Hit me."

She laughs and puts a fat slice of chile on my chip.

The doorbell rings and I go to answer it. When I open the door, a tiny princess smiles shyly at me, and her dad nudges her. "What do you say?" he says to her, his tone warm and encouraging.

"Trick or treat," she says in almost a whisper.

I give her a whole handful of candy because I love her. "Happy Halloween!" I tell her as she bounces off. Her dad gives me a wave.

Back in the kitchen, my mom is chopping cilantro. She says, "What should we make for your birthday dinner? Something Jonah likes."

"Nothing too complicated," I say. "You don't want to wear yourself out when he's here." She looks tired to me, which always sets me to worrying. "The play's next weekend, too," I remind her.

"Oh, shoot." She turns to me. "Will you go both nights?" I nod.

"Hmm. Maybe we can do a birthday lunch on Saturday?"

"Sure, that sounds good." I think about Jonah being back

at home and am overcome with mixed feelings. "Do you think it will be confusing for him?" I ask her. "What if he doesn't want to go back?"

Her brow furrows as she opens a package of tortillas. "I know. I'm worried about it, too. When we were there, the staff told me that he's getting much better about variations in his routine — you know, different days, different activities, stuff like that. They suggested we try new things here, too — keep exposing him to changes. It's harder for him to adapt when he gets set in a routine."

"That makes sense," I say. "Although it's sort of the opposite of everything we've done his entire life."

She nods sadly. "I was just always trying to make things easy, trying to keep things manageable. You know how he is when he expects a certain thing and doesn't get it. I should have worked harder at a lot of things — using sign more consistently, exposing him to more people and places . . ." She looks guilty and my heart goes out to her. And I feel guilty, too; I worked harder than either of my parents to keep Jonah isolated from the rest of my world.

"You've always been amazing with Jonah," I say. "But we're learning new things now. It's okay."

The doorbell rings, and my mom glances up toward the door. "I've got it," I say. But instead of trick-or-treaters, three familiar grinning faces are stacked in the side windows. Cammie crosses her eyes, sticks out her tongue, and waves.

"Aren't they a bit old for trick-or-treating?" my mom calls. She gives me a wry grin.

When I open the front door, the three of them yell "Surprise!" Cammie is holding a cake box from Papa Haydn's, Syd a pizza box, and Erin grocery bags with unknown contents.

"I thought you guys were going to Fearlandia and then that party at Kucharski's," I say.

Cammie pushes in. "We decided you need a night of fun. Your life has been a veritable suckfest!" With her hands full, she gives me a kiss and leans in for an armless hug, then parades into the kitchen.

I pause in the open doorway, staring out at the Halloween lights and jack-o'-lanterns glimmering across the street and breathing in the smell of wood smoke and wet leaves. The girls' high-pitched voices emanate from the kitchen as they greet my mom, who is, of course, gracious like she always is. I fill with guilty resentment at my friends' gesture. I know they're here because they care, because they love me. But Mom and I were having some rare "just us" time — we had an evening planned. It felt good, felt important. I don't want to desert her in the middle. And what if she wasn't feeling well today? They didn't even consider that.

"Come on, Zo, what are you doing?" Cammie calls. I take one last deep breath and close the door. When I return to the kitchen, Cammie has opened the cake box and everyone is *ooh*ing and *ahh*ing over what's inside: a raspberry chocolate gâteau, the entire top covered in glazed fresh berries that gleam like rubies. "We had it at my aunt's baby shower," Cammie says, closing the box. "It's amazing." She glances toward the stove. "God, that smells good, Mrs. Miller."

"But," Syd says, holding up the pizza box, "we have pizza. Zoe, we got pineapple and jalapeño — your favorite!"

"Great," I say weakly. I don't know what to do about my mom and the dinner we planned. I feel guilty bagging on her, but she's the one who taught me to put guests first.

True to form, Mom helps them put the Cheetos and M&M's they brought into bowls that my friends ferry off to my room. I hold back for a moment. "I'm sorry," I tell her. "I had no idea."

"I know," she says softly. She steps over and gives me a hug. "It's fine. Go have fun."

She returns to the stove, and my heart hurts. I wish she had friends to hang out with, too. Her closest friend is my aunt Eileen, who has lived in Barcelona for the last six years. I know how much she misses her, how hard it is not seeing her, not being able to talk to her easily, outside of their Skype talks when time zones and schedules permit. Especially during my mom's cancer treatment — that was the worst. But now, thinking of her at the table, alone with her dinner and her worries about Jonah, I think it's stupid that Aunt Eileen lives so far away, stupid that their mother died when they were young, stupid that their dad is too busy with his child bride to be a proper dad and grandfather. Thinking about how hard my mom tries, how hard life has been on her . . . Why does everything always have to be too much?

I rush over and hug her from behind, hard, before heading up to my room.

The girls have put music on and laid towels on my bed, picnic-style, the snacks arranged in the center.

"Zoe, your mom looks so great!" Syd exclaims.

"She really does," Erin adds, her blue eyes wide. "I didn't know what to expect, but she seems good!"

I nod. "Yeah, she is," I say. But it's a relief to hear them confirm it.

My phone buzzes from the dresser, and I lunge for it, hoping it's Sam with some undoubtedly hilarious Halloween update. But it's just my dad sending my mom and me a photo of a nineteenth-century pie safe at a colleague's house. Thought my girls would like to see this, he writes.

"Oh, no — no way. Not tonight." Cammie shoves a bite of pizza into her mouth. "Set it aside for a while?"

Syd nods and reaches out a hand. "Come on, Zo. Tonight is just for us. Okay?"

"It's my dad," I protest, but I let her take the phone from me, even as mild panic and irritation prickle in me. If Sam messages me, I don't want to miss it. What if tonight is the night we find the dungeon in Starworld? And if it comes when my friends are here, I at least want to be able to tell her I'm waylaid and will be back ASAP, so it doesn't look like I'm just ignoring her. But Syd slides my phone into my desk drawer. I don't want to make a scene, so I do nothing.

Erin opens up her paper bag. "Guys," she says softly, with a nervous glance at my door, "you are not going to believe how delicious tonight's drinks are going to be."

I hadn't anticipated booze, but then it's Erin, so I should have known. I wonder how my mother would advise my handling guests' contraband in my bedroom. How am I meant to be both the perfect hostess and the perfect daughter?

Syd bounces on the bed. "What is it? What is it?"

Erin pulls out a bottle of caramel-flavored vodka, followed by little bottles of Starbucks Frappuccino.

"Oh. My. God." Syd turns to me, flapping her hands with excitement. "Get ice!"

"Just three glasses," Cammie says. She makes the sign for the letter D against her forehead. "I'm driving."

I get up and do as I'm told, increasingly unhappy with the invasion. I love my friends, and I'm grateful for them, but I'd rather be having a quiet night with my mom, or questing with Sam in Starworld. And I'd rather *not* be sneaking around so my friends can drink in my room.

In the kitchen, my mom is filling and rolling the enchiladas, craning her head to see the TV in the living room. She suspects nothing when I get glasses with ice, which makes me feel even worse. She trusts that I'm a good girl.

Back in my room, Erin has turned my dresser into a make-shift bar, and I decide to have one of her drinks partly to be nice, partly because the idea of a caramelly alcoholic beverage is hard to resist, and partly because a buzz maybe wouldn't be the worst thing in the world. Cammie is right: my life has been a suckfest lately.

The quantity of vodka Erin adds is just this side of ruining a good thing, but I top it off with more Starbucks and it's actually kind of yummy. We gather around the snacks on the bed and shove our faces full while we chat.

"Zoe, how would you feel about us skipping the cast party

after STOTS?" Syd asks. "So we can celebrate your birthday?"

"Yeah," says Erin, pausing to cough and make a face at how strong her drink is. "We want to do a sleepover at my house. Can you?"

I quickly run through it in my mind. Jonah will be home, but I'd mostly be gone while he's sleeping. "That sounds great!" I say. I've been on the fence about the cast party anyway, feeling not really a part of the cast but also not really a part of the crew. "Thanks, Erin." I reach over and give her arm a quick rub. "That's really sweet of you."

"We are making *amazing* plans," Syd says, exchanging a conspiratorial look with Erin. "Can we tell her?"

Erin leans over to me, her long blond hair nearly falling into my drink. "Jell-O shots," she whispers.

Yikes, I think, but I try to respond with enthusiasm. I catch Cammie's eye, and she's smiling at me, but there's something in her expression that makes me realize she might know I'm ambivalent about it.

I do my best to get with the spirit of things, and to my surprise, the evening *is* fun. No one brings up Hunter, which I'm grateful for — especially because I know that's probably largely what motivated this intervention. And no one mentions my absence from the cafeteria these past couple of weeks. I'm sure they assume I'm just avoiding Hunter.

But my thoughts keep returning to Sam, despite the distractions. It tugs at me kind of uncomfortably, imagining what she'd think of this superficial, boozy gossipfest. At one point I get up to check my phone, which no one even notices. But there is nothing new from Sam, and I can't help fretting a little. Did I do something? She's been quiet so much longer than usual.

But what if it's not me? What if something happened? What if her mom is stuck in a circuit of counting to four into infinity? What if Sam needs something? Or someone?

I chew on my lower lip, unsure what to do. But then Syd notices what I'm doing and I'm busted. I rejoin them on the bed and nibble at the bits of pineapple and jalapeño that one of them — Syd, probably — pulled off and left in the box. After a while, I'm actually kind of forgetting myself and starting to laugh at Syd's impressions of the teachers at school when my mom knocks on my door. Erin quickly shoves the vodka bottle under the towel.

"Zoe?" my mom says, poking her head in. She opens the door wider and holds out a paper bag. "I found this at the front door."

"Maybe it's from Hunter," Syd says as I get up to take the bag.

It's not from Hunter. I can tell right away because my name is written on the bag in a beautiful, sparkly purple script. I'd know it anywhere.

There is a large laminated poster poking out of the top, plus a huge Ziploc of something. I'm afraid to take it out in front of everyone. I don't know what it is, or how my friends might react. The idea that it might be something that embarrasses or humiliates Sam sends a wave of panic through me, but before I can figure out how to avert disaster, Erin is peering into the bag. "What's this?" She pulls out the poster and my heart stops.

"Jesus," Syd mutters, staring at it with an expression that brings to mind her awful remark in the car — *that girl's weird as shit.*

"Zoe?" Mom says, stepping closer.

I stare at the work of art in Erin's hands, the world going gray and hazy around its splendor. I have never seen anything so beautiful. So bright. So fantastical. So astonishing.

"Oh my god. Is it Sam Jones?" Erin asks. "It is, isn't it? She does paintings like that — I had her in an art class a couple years ago."

My mom steps over to look at it, shooting me a questioning glance. I can feel everyone's gaze on me.

"Did she, like . . . draw that for you?" Syd asks. Her tone does nothing to conceal how weird she thinks that idea is.

"It's for Jonah," I say softly.

I know, because it's birds. There are three of them, each one glittering with so much detail I can barely take it all in. The orange one in the center rises with wings of flame outstretched as though to cradle the others — one blue, like it's made of water, and the other one green as a spring garden, gilded with blossoms in every color.

My mother's eyes find mine. I see wonder and confusion in her expression, and I feel the squeeze in her heart about Jonah.

I am paralyzed, even as Cammie reaches into the bag and pulls out the Ziploc.

"What the heck?" she says, squinting at it. It's enormous — it must weigh five pounds.

When I see what's inside, heat rushes to my face and my heart speeds up. *Oh, Sam.*

The bag is filled with what has to be a lifetime supply of Taco Bell hot sauce. On the outside, a label in her unmistakable pen reads, *FUEL TO ANYWHERE.*

Sam

The message from Zoe after my delivery might be my favorite of all time. Late Saturday night, long after the trick-or-treaters stopped coming, she thanked me for the artwork I made for Jonah and then sent a picture of herself sitting on her bed holding the giant bag of hot sauce. The smile on her face makes my stomach flip because I know I put it there. The caption reads: **Ready when you are.**

I have never been more ready for anything in my life.

I revisit the photo often in the following days, trying without much success to toe the line between fondness and obsession. But who am I kidding? That single delivery required me to take TriMet buses to three different Taco Bells, sacrifice my paladin armor to Will in exchange for free lamination at Copy Stop, where he works, and lie to my mom about my whereabouts for the better part of four hours.

The days pass in the usual flurry of classes and homework and Mom and Will and Starworld. I continue to dance around the second quest, because though I've worked out some of the details in my mind, I don't want the magic of the story we've created to slip away. So as we message this week, I build distracting galaxies and planets and places where waterfalls of stardust run in sparkling reverse, where saber-toothed rats are the best possible pets, and where we can have cloudball fights far more fun than ones with snow.

My head is so far in the stars that on Wednesday, after I'm settled in art class, it's not until I've mixed several new colors on my palette that I notice the folded piece of paper clipped to my easel.

Who would leave me a note?

I look around, but everyone else is minding their own business, or at least one another's and not mine.

The paper is crisp and neatly folded, and when I open it, I barely stop a snort of laughter. I get a couple of disturbed glances from other students nearby who are confused by the strangled squirrel sounds coming from my normally silent corner.

Zoe has done the most spectacularly terrible drawing I've ever seen. She used a green sparkly gel pen, and it looks like something a five-year-old did with her nondominant hand and her eyes closed. I think it's supposed to be a dragon, maybe even Humphrey, but to the untrained observer, it more closely resembles the love child of a wiener dog and a cactus.

A thought bubble above the dragon's head reads *Must not scorch ticket!* And a Friday ticket to *The World Over* is stuck through a slit in the paper between the dragon's teeth. Below that Zoe wrote, "Please come? Love, Zoe."

Love.

My stomach turns inside out and upside down.

My mind chases itself in circles, comparing facts that don't add up to anything I understand:

She's statistically straight.

But she broke up with Hunter.

She's out of my league.

But she said she *loved* me.

This invitation means something, doesn't it? The effort she went through to draw something for me, the single ticket, like maybe she'll sit with me if she's not backstage. . . . The possibilities make me hope for so many things I never thought I could.

I pull out my phone and send her a message: *has Humphrey burn a hole through Friday's previously scheduled events* There weren't any, but she probably already knew that.

Zoe: *hopes this means you're coming*

Me: *wouldn't miss it for Starworld*

Zoe: *would miss almost ANYTHING for Starworld* See you at lunch in the usual spot?

My stomach flutters. That's how much Starworld means to her. How much *I* mean to her.

She's even still coming to eat with me most of the time, which I barely believe until I round the corner of the sci-fi section and she's there already laying out the day's lunch fuck-ups: Cheetos, peanut butter, a chunk of blue cheese, and a few packets of Diablo Taco Bell hot sauce she must have grabbed from her now-infinite stash. Plus a container of curried chicken salad with grapes — enough to share.

"Hey!" She brightens when she sees me.

I flop down next to her and pull out my brown paper bag. "Let's see what color we have today," I say. I groan when I peer inside. "Green."

"Oh my god. What *is* that?" she asks when she sees my sandwich.

"Looks like green hummus, sprouts, cucumber, and avocado," I say. "At least the bread isn't green . . ."

Zoe laughs. "Things could always be worse."

I pull out green tortilla chips (which I actually don't mind), celery, and some maybe-lime butter cookies sprinkled with green sugar.

"Who even eats celery?" I ask. "It's the most pointless vegetable of all time."

"But it can be a vessel for better things," Zoe says, already reaching for it. "Crispy buffalo-wing celery? Coming right up."

We go about making everything more edible and less monochromatic, and I am stunned by her creativity when she mixes Diablo sauce into the blue cheese along with crumbled Cheetos and piles it onto the celery, creating an incredibly buffalo wing–like snack. We talk about plans for Friday while we munch away. I'll meet her at the theater, and she'll be right next to me through the whole play. I try not to be weird about it, but it's hard when I've never looked forward to anything more in my entire life.

"How are things at home?" Zoe asks gently.

"The same, I guess," I say. "You? Are your parents doing okay?"

"I don't know," she says, fiddling with a zipper on her backpack. "It's pretty terrible."

I nod, not knowing what else to say. "I wish I could help," I finally manage. "It must be so hard to be separated from someone you love so much."

She nods, and we're quiet for a moment. Then she says, "That thing you wrote. I don't know how to tell you . . ."

She must be talking about the poem in Starworld. I was so nervous about sending it, so worried it might miss the mark, that she might think it was silly, or maybe even that it might hurt her somehow. But I can't bear her thinking there's something wrong with her.

"She had to have loved you," I say, feeling flustered. "I know she did." I chance a peek at her, and I can see she's on the verge of tears.

"Thank you, Sam." She clasps her hands together. "That was . . . just . . . a really beautiful thing to do."

I manage to croak out a *you're welcome* through all the drunken frogs in my throat.

"I've been thinking about something," she says, shifting to face me. "I turn eighteen on Saturday. And there is so much ahead of me that's already plotted out. I know I'm going to Reed. My friends will go away to school. I'll come home a lot on weekends. I'll keep singing in college, and maybe I'll even get to do theater."

"But?"

She gives me a mischievous smile, but I can see she has

serious things on her mind. "It's kind of your fault," she says. "Because of the poem you wrote. Because of Starworld."

I think I know where this is going.

"I keep thinking about maybe trying to find out where I came from." She glances down and picks at a thread on the hem of her shirt. "I know there's no information from the adoption, but . . . What if I found something through a DNA test? There are so many places that do that now, and you can find matches online. I sometimes lurk at a couple of forums for safe haven babies, and some of them have found relatives that way. Through a simple saliva test!"

"Science is amazing," I say, because it's the only thing I can say with confidence. I don't want to spook her when she's trying to process something that could change her life forever.

"But the thought of telling my parents I want to find my biological family . . ." She trails off.

Silence hangs between us for a moment, and there is loneliness in it that I feel almost as acutely as if it's my own. Because even though she has friends and family who love her, there is a part of her left unexplained and unaccounted for that keeps her feeling untethered, like she doesn't quite belong. And if there is anything I understand, it's what it feels like to be on the outside looking in.

"Yeah," I say. "How do you even start that conversation?"

"I don't know. I'm just so worried that they'll take it wrong."

"I guess there's always that risk." I think about what I know about myself and wonder if it would be different if I didn't know anything about my parents. What would it be like to live without fear of inheriting my mom's anxiety or to not know that we both hate cantaloupe and are good at math? Would I be a different person if I hadn't known my dad was an engineer, or would I have turned out just the same if I'd still had a parent who encouraged me to build things? Would I be a different person who actually had social skills if I'd been raised in another family, or would I just feel lost and out of place — a drop-in like Zoe sometimes describes herself?

The questions are pointless, since I won't ever know the answers. But I guess they make me grateful for what I have, and I wish Zoe could have that same knowledge of who she is and why.

We finish off our food in silence, lost in our own thoughts, but the quiet isn't uncomfortable. It's just us, and all the things we know about each other, and Starworld somewhere out on the horizon giving us a safe place to hide when we need it.

To cut down on time spent fielding Mom's doom spirals, I don't tell her about the play until dinner on Friday when very little time remains until I need to get myself to the school. Mom made curried tofu and vegetables over rice, and we each start with eight perfect squares on our plates.

"How was school, honey?" she asks.

"Fine." I shove a chunk of tofu in my mouth. It's kind of bland. "Can you put hot sauce on the shopping list?" I ask. Zoe's been a bad influence.

She looks at me quizzically. "Since when do you like spicy food?"

I shrug. There is no short answer to that question.

"Your dad used to love my spicy venison chili," she says, her voice distant.

I feel a little pang of sorrow. Sometimes I want to rewind time back to when Dad was here, I had fewer responsibilities, and life was less complicated. I miss the days when I could lean on my mom without worrying that it would make her spiral. I miss the way I used to feel like her arms around me could protect me from the world, the way she whispered silly things in my ear to make me laugh when I was afraid.

"What do you think about doing something together this weekend?" she asks. "You could invite one of your friends over and we could watch a movie. Or maybe play board games. Do you still like that — whatsit — Carcass Home?"

My heart drops. "Carcassonne," I correct her softly.

"Yeah, we could play that," she says, like it's not the worst idea on earth.

"No, that's okay, I don't want to invite anyone over." More like I can't. Even Will isn't equipped to deal with two hours of my mom fretting about the uneven patterns created by placing tiles in a way that would actually allow someone to win the game.

She takes a deep breath, and my guard is up before she even speaks.

"Or . . . we haven't been to OMSI in a long time, and I know you want to see the exhibit on satellites," she says.

I look up, startled at the suggestion. Going out places with her is always so stressful — trying to figure out how to avoid things that might set her off on a routine, trying to be vigilant enough to prepare for it all.

"Maybe," I say. Can she really handle an excursion to a place full of kamikaze children? Can I?

She must sense my hesitation, because she tries again.

"What if we go to the game shop after dinner tonight? Wasn't Friday usually when they had those tournaments for that card game you used to play?" She's trying so hard, it breaks my heart a little bit.

"I have a ticket to the school play tonight," I say.

"Oh!" Mom says, blinking, clearly not sure how to respond.

"I need to take the car," I continue, shoveling another forkful of curry down my hole.

She frowns.

I clamp down on the frustration lurking nanometers under the surface.

"I can drive you," she says.

"I don't need you to," I say. "It's not a big deal. It's not very far. And I might want to go somewhere with my friend Zoe afterward."

I see the calculations running in the back of her brain, the cogs and wheels turning ever more rapidly as they determine every possible catastrophe that could result from letting me out of the house behind the controls of a 2,500-pound piece of machinery she's barely let me touch.

"But what if—"

"What could possibly happen between here and school?" I cut her off in exasperation. "It's like two miles."

"A lot of things could happen!" Her voice rises. "Most accidents occur within one mile of home! Did you know that?"

I recognize the look in her eyes. It's the one she gets before going into full rampage mode—the kind where the entire china cabinet gets cleaned out and rearranged, or the living-room carpet vacuumed until the lines are just so, or something else equally pointless and loud.

"No, a lot of things can't happen. I will drive safely to the high school, I will see the play, and I will spend time with my friend. I want to be normal. Why can't you let me have that?" I ask, proud of how steady my voice stays.

"You're not an experienced enough driver to go off alone in the car at night," she says. She taps the butt end of her fork on the table. One, two, three, four. Each tap crashes through my eardrums with the force of a battering ram.

"Whose fault is that?" I throw up my hands. "I've had my license for over a year. I got a perfect score on my driving test, no thanks to you." I ought to stop there, but I don't. "Thank goodness for Will's parents, who took me out to practice driving, and Will's mom, who drove us to the DMV on *his* birthday—almost six months after mine!" Any semblance of control I had over my feelings is gone.

"Will's parents let you drive?" Her face is ashen.

"Didn't you stop to wonder when you signed my driver's

license application how I got fifty hours of practice behind the wheel after driver's ed?" I explode. "Did you even know I needed to log fifty more hours to apply for the license?"

"I knew they were taking you to the DMV, but you didn't tell me they let you drive," she says, her voice sharper. "I would have taken you myself."

"No, you wouldn't! Because every time I asked, something else was more important. Work. Reorganizing the craft room. Burners. Window latches. You barely pay attention to me unless I'm breaking the nonsensical rules we live our lives around! Do you realize how lucky you are that I'm not a drug addict or a dropout? How would you even cope with that?"

"You would never do those things," my mother says, her tone clipped. "And just because things could be worse doesn't mean you suddenly get a free pass to do things with Will's parents that I wouldn't let you do."

"Too late!" I yell. My heart is pounding like it's going to punch a hole through my ribs. "If you won't help me, I have to take care of myself!"

"Taking care of you means keeping you safe." Her voice shakes.

"Safe from what? From ever becoming independent? From knowing my father actually loves me? Safe from seeing him? Safe from imaginary germs? The things you insist on don't even make sense. You know that fruit doesn't have to be washed with soap before being put in the refrigerator, right? I don't wash the things I bring home from the store. I don't even always disinfect the cutting board twice after I cut meat. And we aren't dead yet!"

She reacts like I slapped her, then scurries to the sink and starts scrubbing at the cutting board as though bleaching it now will somehow make up for all the times I didn't.

"This is why you and Dad divorced, right? And apparently you spent years discouraging him from emailing me because it upsets me? *You're* the one upsetting me!"

"He chose to leave," she snaps, dropping the cutting board into the sink. "We don't need him. You have me. I have you. That's all that matters."

"He's staying away because you told him to! And I've never had you. Your job is more important than I am. So is shutting the garage door properly. The time. Even alphabetizing my books! Everything else!"

"That's not true. Nothing is more important than you! I love you." She leans on the counter, swiping at her eyes, her hands trembling.

"If you loved me, you would have told me that Dad wanted to visit. You would have gotten help. Therapy. Something!"

I've rendered her speechless. She gulps at the air like a dying fish.

"We can't go on like this." I push back my chair and stand up. My chest feels so tight, I can hardly breathe. "I'm going to the play now," I say, swatting at my stinging eyes with the sleeves of my shirt. Mom makes no move to stop me.

So I leave.

Guilt follows me, deepening the farther I get from home.

Darkness seems to have come early, even though the skies are mostly clear. Only a few leaden clouds drift like ghost ships overhead. I drive to school five miles per hour under the speed limit with a white-knuckled grip on the steering wheel and an enormous burden of paranoia. I'm at least an hour early, which is good since I need to calm down. I find a spot in the nearly empty parking lot and sit there in the car until I feel like I have my emotions under control again.

When the time comes, I trudge through the parking lot, impervious to the cold front that came in last night. The evening smells faintly of smoke winding its way from chimneys. I'm the only person walking in alone — the only one untouched by the familiar jostle and laughing words of family or friends. But I have Zoe, and her words, and her invitation. Maybe even her love, the thing I've begun to hope for more than ever.

Those things are a promise, and tonight they're all that keep me warm.

My breath catches when I slip into my seat in the black box theater beside Zoe. The small space and dark walls make her feel that much closer to me. Her cheeks are rosy, and that beautiful dark hair of hers cascades over a lavender sweater made of something that looks so soft, I can barely stop myself from running my hand down her arm.

"I'm so glad you came," she says, her eyes sparkling with excitement. "You really need to see your painting on the set. We had the crew paint the wall a buttery cream color, and they built a heavy frame for the painting with a dark mahogany stain. Wait till you see how it makes your painting pop!"

"Thanks for inviting me," I mumble, barely able to form words with the warmth of her smile frying my capacitors.

Zoe opens a program and points to the scenes that take place on the set that has my painting, walking me through the basics of the plot. The story captivates me immediately, and I have trouble containing the magnitude of my feelings over how much thought she put into incorporating my artwork. When the lights go down, I'm immediately mesmerized by the way the story comes to life, the way that people I see every day are inhabiting other bodies, other lives and times. And part of that is what Zoe did — the ways she helped create a place for them to exist, the illusions that make the story feel real.

We're sitting close enough to the stage that I can just make out the crew, all dressed in black, smoothly and silently changing out the set in the dark between scenes. I'm amazed to consider all that goes into making a play the seamless experience it is from the perspective of the audience. When the third scene begins, the stage lights go up to reveal my artwork. My pulse races. The small studio stage makes my painting look larger and more vivid than it ever did lost in the canvases of the art classroom, and Zoe's right about the frame: it has an assertive presence that both contrasts and highlights the art within.

When I glance at Zoe, she's watching me, a small, knowing smile on her face. When I smile back at her, she leans toward me and nudges me with her shoulder, her eyes returning to the stage. Heat suffuses my body, radiating out from where she touched me.

The scene is a dramatic one, the actors' energies rising to meet the escalating tension, but I am helpless to take my eyes off my contribution, which serves as a symbol for the main character's forgotten past, the sense of "home" he longs for but forever eludes him. In this context, my painting is evocative and moving in ways I never could have imagined or envisioned. I marvel at the way Zoe understood that the moment she saw my painting, the way she knew how right it would be. Seeing that juxtaposition between appearances and truth so brilliantly illustrated makes something shift deep inside me. It's something both Zoe and I understand and live with every day—the ways our outward lives don't reflect who we truly are.

When I chance a peek at Zoe, she's riveted by what's happening onstage, eyes wide, knuckles resting on her lips. I remember that she used to be in plays, and I wonder if she's sad not to be up there. And even though I love that she's right next to me, I kind of wish she were acting tonight, because then I could watch her the whole time, and it wouldn't seem weird if I was captivated by her every word, her every move.

During the short intermission between acts, I try to articulate to Zoe all the ways I'm feeling, but there are too many thoughts tangling in confusion, and I stumble over my words. Zoe is as understanding as ever, but I'm not satisfied. I want to dig deeper into all the ways we seem to understand each other without trying, but I need more time and space—somewhere we can be by ourselves. Gathering all my courage, I ask her, "Do you maybe want to go to Taco Bell after the show?"

The upward movement of her perfect eyebrows suggests that I've surprised her, and I gird myself for her rejection. I rush to continue, "I guess you might have a party to go to tonight." There's probably some correlation between performances and parties. I don't know how these things work.

"I'm not going to the cast party tomorrow," she says. "My friends are doing a thing for my birthday. There's a party tonight, too, but . . ." She hesitates, frowning a little. "Honestly, I wasn't really looking forward to it. It still feels kind of weird, not being in the show." She tilts her head at me and then smiles. "Let's do it."

Before I can say anything, the lights go down again. I'm relieved, even though it seems unlikely that the cover of darkness can obscure the warm glow in my heart.

When the play is over and Zoe has to run backstage to make sure things get safely put away, I go outside and wait by the exit doors. I shiver, but it's more from anticipation than from the cold. I take out my phone to compose a message to her about the possibility of Humphrey losing his genitals to frostbite, but there's a notification from Mom.

My heart drops into my shoes when I see what she wrote. **We should talk. I'm sorry we fought. Please come home?**

Guilt weighs on me like ten tons of rock. I pushed her too hard. I was too mean. But the hurt is still there, too — the hurt I never gave voice to until tonight. I can't deal with this yet.

I write back: **Going to Taco Bell with Zoe. Will be home by 11. I'm sorry, too.**

Zoe finally emerges from the building, just in time to save me from writing more.

"Thanks for waiting — sorry it took a while," she says. Her breath mists in the air.

"It's okay," I say. The cold means nothing with her so near

me. All I see is a milky moonlit cheek, the flutter of night-dark eyelashes — pieces of her that I want to snatch out of the dark and capture and commit to a blank page with colors too vivid to be real.

"The show was incredible," I say as we walk to the car.

She smiles. "I'm glad you liked it."

We get in and buckle up, and as I pull out, I proceed to embarrass myself by blathering at warp speed about everything I loved and how much her work helped the play come to life, about the intersection of setting and story. It's so much easier now that we're alone.

"It blew me away, too, and I've seen it before!" Zoe says. "I identify so much with those characters. Fiona, who tries so hard to smooth things, to make everyone happy, and Chris, who feels like a drop-in and aches to reconnect with a past that will always be hidden from him." She turns to me and says, "Is it just me and my particular issues, or were a lot of the themes kind of universal? I mean, wasn't it kind of amazing?"

"It was everything," I say. But I hope she knows what I really mean when I say that.

You're everything.

Zoe

Sam's enthusiasm about the play fills me up — and helps distract me from the ache of not being in the show. The way she appreciates even the small details of the set makes me feel like my contribution was more valuable than I realized — although honestly the best thing I brought to the set was her painting. And I couldn't bear the idea of her never seeing her artwork in the show, never witnessing the way it sang on that set and imbued the scene with meaning and richness. I hope this helps her confidence, hope it helps show her how good she really is. She's so brilliant, and she's the last to know.

I want her to know.

She is unusually animated in the car, despite her death grip on the wheel and granny-like adherence to the speed limit.

"Do you like driving?" I ask her.

She sighs. "That is not a simple question."

"It seems simple," I tease.

"You're right," she says with a laugh. "It's a simple question, but the answer is complicated. I *should* love driving. It's me and a piece of machinery, and I control it and I decide where I go. It's almost perfect."

"So what's the flaw?"

"One guess."

The dark expression that clouds her face is clue enough.

"Your mom," I say.

"Bingo. Oh, shitballs," she mutters as we approach a merge sign. She signals and glances over her shoulder to move into the other lane. "See, this. *This.* My mom won't let me drive, so I have barely any experience at something I should be really good at. The only reason I was able to get my license at all is that Will's parents took me out to practice with him."

"Wow." Her words make me realize how sheltered and limited she's been. "When my mom got her cancer diagnosis, she made me drive everywhere, even when she felt fine. I think she needed to know I'd be okay if, you know . . ." The reality of it hits me fresh, choking me up a little. It occurs to me that my mom's first thoughts upon learning she had cancer were for her two children, for making sure Jonah and I would be okay if she was gone. I'm overwhelmed at how unselfish and brave and good she is — and I realize, for the thousandth time, how incredibly lucky I am. I try to pull myself together and focus on what's right in front of me. "Anyway, I'm glad you have Will. He seems really sweet, and I guess his parents must be, too."

"They are. Good thing, too," she says wryly. "I might need a place to live after taking the car tonight."

"You didn't have permission?" I ask, suddenly worried that I'm an accomplice in whatever rules Sam broke. The last thing I want is to make anything harder for her at home.

"Nope. But how am I supposed to function in the future if she won't let me drive while I'm still close to home? I see how some of her rules are reasonable, like never eating salad at McDonald's or closing the toilet lid before you flush so germ spray doesn't contaminate your toothbrush. Those things make sense. But I don't want to be an incompetent loser who can't handle real life once I'm away from her, you know?"

My heart hurts for her. "I think you're really brave," I tell her. "I couldn't defy my parents if my life depended on it." No detours for me. "But then again, they're mostly pretty reasonable."

"Yeah, well . . . Who needs permission when you have keys?" She grins, but I know she must not be having the easiest time. She's trying so hard to both take care of her mom and take care of herself, and clearly sometimes those two goals are in complete conflict.

"I'm really proud of you for taking the car tonight," I tell her. "Really *fucking* proud," I add.

She smiles at my choice of words. "Thanks. I am, too."

As if on cue, her phone vibrates, and the brightness in her eyes dims.

"Is she going to survive this?" I ask, my worry increasing. The truth is, I feel bad for both of them.

"She has to," Sam says. "I'm determined to try to act like a healthy person. Whatever that is. I might need some help figuring it out."

I reach over and give her arm a squeeze. "You're doing fine." As she pulls into the Taco Bell parking lot, I add, "When you see how much hot sauce I use, you might reconsider how healthy you think I am."

She laughs as she carefully pulls into a space. "Let's do Humphrey proud."

Inside, we order various burritos and tacos and have them put jalapeños on everything. Sam insists on treating because it's my birthday tomorrow. She messages her mother while she waits for the food, and I claim a table and gather a heaping assortment of sauces, recalling with guilty humor that ten billion packets were recently appropriated on my behalf.

When Sam sits down with the food, she asks, "Does your family have plans for your birthday?"

"Jonah's coming home tomorrow, so we're going to have a birthday lunch. My mom's making lasagna, which is one of Jonah's favorites." I smile just thinking about it. He's going to be so happy about lasagna.

"Are you excited about Jonah coming home?" she asks, unwrapping a burrito.

I nod. "I'm excited and nervous. I'm really happy he'll be here for my birthday, but I have no idea what this change in his routine will do. Sometimes when he doesn't want to leave, he'll plop down on the floor or the ground, and there is no getting him up until he decides to get back up."

"I admire that," Sam says.

I almost spew Dr Pepper all over the table.

She smiles. "I'm serious. It shows character to stand up for what you want. Or sit down."

I wipe my mouth as I try to stop laughing. "You're my favorite," I tell her.

As we eat, we pile all the empties into a small mountain on the tray. "Humphrey would be impressed," I say, adding a Diablo sauce packet to the pile.

"It is rather extreme," Sam says, squeezing more hot sauce into her burrito. "This is not how Taco Belling with my mother goes at all. She wipes off and stacks her empties. This random pile of drippy packets would make her brain explode." Her brow furrows as she looks at the packets, then she glances up at me and asks in a small voice, "What if that happens to me?"

My heart goes out to her. That kind of ever-present threat must be a heavy burden to carry. And I don't know what to say—I can't assure her that it *won't* happen to her.

"You'd watch for it," I say tentatively. "And if something like that started manifesting, you'd get whatever treatment and help you needed to be as healthy as you can be. You'd be okay."

She looks dubious. "You think so?"

I nod. "I really do, Sam. You're incredibly strong and brave."

I can tell by her expression that my words mean a lot to her. "Thank you," she says softly.

"Of course." After a moment, I add, "I wonder what kind of mental health things there might be in my history. I spent my whole life thinking about things like eye color and hair and height and stuff . . . even my voice and quirks and things. But I never really thought about mental illness."

It's silent for a moment. She folds and unfolds a packet of sauce. "You could try to find out. I think some of the DNA test kits offer health screening, but they're more expensive."

"I might, someday." If I can ever figure out how to navigate the issue with my parents.

She looks at her phone. "Legally, 'someday' is in about two hours."

"Two hours?" I ask, wiping my fingers on a napkin.

"To take a DNA test on your own, you just have to be eighteen." She glances up at me, and that old expression is back—the one that's pure self-doubt. "I checked online. It only took a few minutes. I just . . . I know you have a lot of questions about where you came from, and I wanted you to know that"—she glances down at her lap—"if you wanted to do it . . . I'd be there for you."

My heart fills with warmth. "Sam. Thank you." She has been unfathomably supportive and thoughtful—of course she'd help me.

She takes a deep breath, and her eyes flit around a little bit before landing back on the table. "There was this sale," she says, "and free two-day shipping. So I just got one in case you wanted to have it, in case you wanted to think about it." The rest comes out in a rush. "And if you don't, that's totally okay — I'll use it myself and maybe it'll finally confirm whether or not I'm a cyborg."

She pulls a small box out of her coat pocket and hands it to me, and a rush of adrenaline courses through my entire body. I struggle to form words, and Sam's brow furrows.

"I'm sorry," she says. "It was presumptuous. Just pretend I never —"

"No! Sam. It's not that." I squeeze the box tighter as I realize my hands are shaking. "This is an amazing gift. But it's just . . . It's also terrifying."

"What are you afraid of? Apart from hurting your parents, I mean," she adds.

"Well, that." I take a slow breath, hoping to calm my skyrocketing heart rate. "But also, everything — all the endless what-ifs that run through your head, you know? What if I'm the product of a rape? What if my parents were drug addicts? What if they're dead? What if I find out something terrible?"

"You'd be okay," she says quietly.

"How do you know?" I ask.

"Because you already are." Her hazel eyes glow with warmth and certainty.

I mull over her words and wonder if she's right. Could I handle whatever truths might emerge? Maybe I could — and I have supportive, caring parents who will love me no matter what. And what if I learn good things, meaningful things? Things that inform my sense of self — or even things that connect me to relatives who want to know me? I think about the story Sam created in Starworld and wonder for the ump-teenth time if I come from a musical family . . . If I share traits with them. . . . If they want to know me. . . . Any or all of those things would be incredible.

"I don't know how to thank you. You're . . ." I shake my head. "I've never known anyone like you."

She ducks her head; I've either pleased her or embar-rassed her — or both. "It's not one of the health screening ones. It's about ethnic background, mostly, but you can enter the database to find DNA matches, if you want to."

I reach across the table and squeeze her hand. "This is perfect. This is just what I needed, and I don't know if I ever would have had the guts to do it alone."

Her cheeks flush as she smiles at me. "I hope it brings you good things."

"Me too."

Sam gathers up her trash and finishes her water. "I'm sorry — I told my mom I'd be home by eleven. I have to get going."

"Oh, of course," I say, tossing napkins onto the tray and standing up. We throw out our garbage and head back into the night. "Can I reimburse you for the test?"

She shakes her head as we approach the car. "Consider it a birthday gift."

"Thank you." I pull her into a hug and laugh as she stag-gers a little, obviously surprised.

"You're welcome," she says breathlessly.

The ride home is quiet, although I know there's nothing quiet about what's going on in our heads. When Sam pulls into my driveway, I turn to her. "Thank you," I tell her again. "Thank you for being . . . well, you."

She stutters on a reply; I've probably tripped her robot circuits or something. But it's just minutes before eleven and I don't want to make her late, so I climb out of the car. "Good luck with your mom," I say, leaning in for a moment. "Let me know how it goes, okay?"

"I will," she says. "Thanks again for everything."

It seems crazy that she's thanking me, when she's the one who has done so much for me. I watch her drive off, hoping nothing terrible is in store for her at home.

Inside, my dad is in the living room watching something on the History Channel. "Hey, sweetie," he says when I come in. "How was the show?"

"It was good," I say, plopping down next to him and leaning on him.

"I miss seeing you in shows," he says, putting his arm around me.

"You'll get to hear me sing a solo in the holiday concert," I tell him, settling into his warmth. "A descant in 'Silent Night.'"

"A descant." He tilts his head. "Is that from the Latin *discantus*, I wonder?"

I gaze at him fondly. "No clue."

He doesn't give up. "Is it a song apart from? Apart from the melody?"

"Yes! Exactly. Good work."

He beams. "And it's a solo? Just you?"

"Yes, Dad. Just me. Solo, from the Latin *solo*."

"That's awesome sauce," he says, nudging me a little.

"Dad, no." I laugh, shaking my head. He uses what he thinks is hip lingo strictly as a means to torture me.

"Well, speaking of Jesus . . ." he says.

I scoff. "When were we speaking of Jesus?"

"'Silent Night'!" He gestures, like *duh*. "'Round yon virgin? Mother and child'?"

Ugh, he's got me.

"Why don't you watch the end of this show with me? It might change everything you ever thought about Pontius Pilate."

I roll my eyes. "I barely know who Pontius Pilate was," I tell him, which is a rookie mistake. He is only too delighted to pause the show to give me some not-abridged-enough version of Bible history.

"Thanks, Dad," I say, getting up. "You can tell me how it ends over breakfast."

"But I can't!" he says. "We have to head out early in the morning."

"Oh, darn."

He mock-glares at me as he realizes I set it up. He makes a fist and says, "Why I oughta . . ."

I lean over and hug him. "Good night, Dad."

He holds on to me a beat longer than usual. "Good night, seventeen."

I smile at the acknowledgment of my birthday tomorrow, but when I pull away, my heart tugs at the emotion on his face.

"I love you, Zo," he says, trying to smile.

"I love you, too, Dad."

Up in my room, I change into pajamas and think about the things Sam and I talked about. There are so many aspects to consider. There is the whole unknown, which is most of it: the infinite field of things I could find out, the question of who they are and what they're like . . .

But there is a smaller field of what is more knowable (or guessable, anyway), which is how my parents will feel if I search for my biological family. I can't bear the possibility of their being hurt, of their thinking this reflects in any way on them — that they aren't enough, that I don't think they've been good enough to me.

I am so lucky. So fucking lucky. They love me so much. They have taken such good care of me. If I do this thing, I have to make sure they know that they're the best parents any kid could ever wish for.

And that isn't what this is about, after all. It's not about my wanting something else, or even wanting something more. Wanting to know about my history doesn't mean wishing for a different one. And who appreciates history more than my parents? They both majored in history!

If I do this right, they will understand. I have to believe that.

I open my computer and find several websites where I can upload my DNA to be connected with anyone who shares my genes. My heart pounds at the idea of being able to send off a sample as soon as tomorrow.

It occurs to me that my parents will be gone at least four hours in the morning — more than enough time to mark my birthday in the most important way possible. But as the possibility threatens to become a reality, the grip of anxiety tightens, and I find myself leaning toward the source of comfort and support I've come to depend on so much these last weeks.

I write: Sam? Are you free in the morning? I know it's dumb, because it's just putting my saliva sample into a mailbox, but I'm a nervous wreck. Could use the moral support.

Her reply comes quickly: *will be there with the swiftness of a hot-sauce-fueled dragon bearing a hot-sauce-fueled robot*

I smile. She's nothing if not reliable. 10:00?

She says: Perfect. Hey, Zoe?

Yes? I write.

She responds: Am I the first to say happy birthday? *points at clock*

It's exactly midnight. I write: You are indeed.

She says: Happy birthday, Zoe. I'm awfully glad you were born. *robot heart sings in the key of Z-sharp, causing cacophony of atonal rings and beeps*

I laugh at her goofy startalk, and of course I want more. If she's up for it, there's nothing I could use more than some startalk or maybe even a foray into Starworld.

I write: *tightens wires in an attempt to tune* *clutches ears as you start trilling Happy Birthday in a minor key*

She responds: *shoves burrito into facehole to reduce noise pollution emissions* *ducks as Humphrey swoops in, having smelled hot sauce*

My heart soars. We're off! I climb under my covers with my phone.

With the first quest complete, we're on to the second — to find the dungeon where the king kept his greatest pleasure. I have a lot of questions for the king, like why he has so many stupid rules. And more importantly, why the cage where he kept my mother is empty. Where did she go? What happened to her? I know it's not real, but I still want to know, more than I've ever wanted to know anything.

When Humphrey has zoomed us off to Starworld, I pick up where we left off.

Me: *looks in the throne room but finds only dust* *sends Humphrey on a scouting mission to chase the king out of any hidden rooms*

Sam: *follows a spark of light back into the kitchen and down the cellar stairs*

Me: *lights a torch to guide us through the darkness*

Sam: *crawls through a low space and bursts through a grate into the dungeon*

Me: *hopes there aren't any spiders* *coughs on dust*

Sam: *holds torch up* *points to a sign on the wall*

ANY WHO DARE TO DISOBEY

WILL BE CAGED HERE TO ROT AWAY

Me: *shudders*

Sam: *notices a piece of paper poking out from behind the sign* *breaks the king's seal, then unfolds paper and reads*

To: My Favorite Songbird,

Your imprisonment here was not my desire
Your songs and your love are all I require.
But foolishly you loved my knight and not me

Now no one is happy, and none can be free.

Only your daughter has escaped by your grace

With your kiss goodbye forever marked on her face.

I touch my hairline with trembling fingers. My birth-mark. Rather than a flaw, Sam is depicting it as the mark of a mother's love.

My eyes well with tears. How does she do this? She not only gives me hope that the things that hurt me most may not even be true, but she dismantles my fears and insecurities and reassembles them into beliefs that make me special, worthy, even beloved.

Me: *hugs* *is fucking leaking again*

Sam: *applauds language* *hugs you back*

Me: That fucking king. What a fucking asshole.

We found the dungeon and now only one object remains: Starworld's most perfect treasure. I'm excited, but also hoping it doesn't come too soon, because I am not ready for the story to end, and because I don't know how many more of these tales I can handle. How is she so good to me when she can so clearly see these broken pieces inside of me?

The next morning, I'm up before eight, but my parents are already gone. One of them must have tiptoed in, because there's a card propped against the lamp on my bedside table. I pick it up, wondering which of them chose the card. It will be clear immediately: if it was Mom, it will be flowers or butterflies or birds, with sweet words. If it was Dad, it will be a *Far Side* card or something gross or based on a bad pun.

I sit up and slide the card from the envelope. Mom. It's dragonflies and flowers, and it says, *Wishing you a birthday as bright as your smile.* My dad has added his personal touch, though. He has drawn an arrow to "smile" and made an orthodontia joke: *$7,200 worth of bright, not that anyone's counting.*

On the inside, my mother has written, *I can't believe it's been eighteen years. What a joy you have been. I love you with my whole heart. Mom.*

And my dad added, *Slow it down, sunshine — the years have gone too fast. Love you lots, Dad.*

A lump forms in my throat, especially as I consider my morning plans. I remind myself that this isn't betrayal or ingratitude. It's just information. Well, potential information — there's no guarantee it will even lead anywhere.

I'm just packing up the completed test kit when the doorbell rings at the stroke of ten. When I open the door, Sam holds out a large cup from Coffeehole. "Caramel latte, m'lady," she says. "Happy birthday."

"Oh my god. You didn't!" I pull back the door to let her in. "What a perfect start to my birthday."

"Well, the BOY-FRND01 was on the fritz, so I had to get it myself."

I take the cup and give her a quick hug. "You're way better than any boybot. Come on in. Let me just grab my stuff." I head up the stairs and she follows me. "How are things with your mom?" I ask.

She comes into my room, sets down her messenger bag, and sits on my bed. "Not terrible," she says. "She didn't object to me taking the car this morning."

"That's great! Sounds promising." I sit at my desk and sip the latte. "Mmmm, so good! Want a sip?"

She shakes her head. "That's okay."

A message dings on my phone. I turn around, looking for it. Sam finds it on my bed and hands it to me. It's from my mom.

Are you up? All is well! Arriving back earlier than expected. Dad and I couldn't sleep, so we got up and headed out early. We should be home in less than an hour.

The sudden time pressure exacerbates my nerves over doing the test in the first place. I write back: **That's great! But fyi, Sam is here. We were doing something together this morning. But it won't take long.**

She writes: **Sam is over? Don't kick her out on our account—we'd like to meet her. Would she maybe want to stay for lunch?**

I glance at Sam, who is busying herself looking at the books on my shelf. I write to my mom, **Do you think it's okay if she's here right when Jonah gets home? It won't be confusing?** As soon as I send it, I remember what Mom said about changing things up, not letting Jonah get too attached to routines.

She writes: **He'll be fine. You know him—he'll mostly care about seeing you and about eating. What do you think? You said Sam is good about Jonah.**

"Hey, Sam," I say. "Do you maybe want to stay for lunch?"

She stares at me like I have just spoken an ancient language, or perhaps asked her if she would like a herd of wildebeests for Christmas. "I don't want to impose on your family time," she finally says.

"You wouldn't be. My parents would like to meet you," I say. "And then you could meet Jonah."

She hesitates only a moment before she gives me a small smile. "I'd like that."

I type to my mom: She can stay! See you soon.

"Okay, let's get our errand done!" I say, jumping up and grabbing my things. I spot Sam's bird poster on my bookshelf. "Hey, would you like to give Jonah your poster?" I step over and pick it up. "It would be nice if he understood it was from you." I hold it out to her. "You don't have to, if you'd feel uncomfortable. I just thought maybe—"

"I'd love to," she says. She takes it from me and gazes at it. "I hope he likes it." She sets it on top of her messenger bag.

"Ha," I say. "You'll see how much he likes it."

We head downstairs, but as we're leaving, her brow furrows, as if she's thought of something.

"What is it?" I ask.

She chews her lip for a moment. "It's just that your hair is still wet. Won't you be cold?"

I smile and touch her arm. "I'll be *fine*. Don't be such a worrywart." And then I want to kick myself, because what if my calling her a worrywart reminds her of her mom and sparks her concerns about having OCD?

But she nods with a smile as we climb into her mom's car.

The day is unusually bright and sunny, which I hope bodes well. I sip my latte and clutch the box. Sam must sense my nervousness, because she talks more than usual, yammering about a video game she must know I am clueless about. Still, I know why she's doing it, and my heart warms at her thoughtfulness and understanding, at how hard she tries to comfort and help.

By the time we reach the post office, I feel like I almost understand why blowing up robosquirrels is such a good method of stress relief.

"Do you want to go inside? Or just drop it in one of the boxes?" She gestures to the mailboxes out front as she parks the car.

My stomach seizes up when I realize the moment to turn in my DNA test is suddenly upon me. "I think I'd feel better handing it to an actual person," I say. "If you don't mind waiting in line?"

"Of course not."

Inside, we stand in line, and I try to follow as Sam explains the difference between casual, core, and hardcore gamers. She is aghast when she discovers I've never been clear on the difference between *World of Warcraft* and *Dungeons & Dragons*. When I'm called up to the counter, my heart gives a great lurch and I reach for Sam's hand. Her warm squeeze gives me the courage to hand the box over, thereby taking a giant step into my post-DNA-test life.

Whatever that might be.

Sam

Even once we're in the car headed back to Zoe's house, my hand still tingles with the memory of hers in mine. It felt so special to be there with her for a moment that might change her life forever, and if I could be with her for a hundred more, I'd do it gladly. My body sings with nerves over how close I feel to her, and with anxiety about meeting the rest of her family. I hope they like me.

Just as we arrive at her house, Zoe gets a message from her mom asking her to do some things to get lunch started. I wash my hands so I can help, but when she asks me to put the baby spinach in a bowl and slice some strawberries, I freeze.

At home, my mom insists on soaking greens in cold water with vinegar added before rinsing four times. That's probably not normal. The problem is, I don't know what *is*. So when

Zoe hands me a large bowl and a plastic container of baby spinach, I ask, "Should I clean the spinach?"

She glances over from rinsing the strawberries and says, "Um, we don't. It's organic and triple washed."

"So I just put it in the bowl?" I ask, still hesitating for some reason, like if I don't follow my mother's steps, the food might be ruined.

She laughs. "Yes, that's all you have to do. Can you pat these berries dry and slice them?" She hands me a colander full of rinsed strawberries.

I do as she asks, wondering if they have separate cutting boards for meat and produce like we do at home. Zoe mixes dressing in a jar — balsamic, salt, honey, a small spoonful of Dijon, and olive oil. She opens the jar and pokes a finger in to taste it. "Nailed it," she says, holding out the jar to me.

I don't know what to do.

"Taste it," she says.

"With my finger?" The thought would appall my mother.

"Oh, do you want a spoon?" She starts to reach for the silverware drawer, but I interrupt her. I don't want to accommodate the ways my mom has trained me. I don't want to stay in my comfort zone.

"No, it's okay." I reach into the dressing with my forefinger and taste it, feeling like I'm breaking the law. "It's perfect," I say. "You didn't even measure."

She tosses her hair, unleashing a dizzying, invisible field of flowers. "Not my first rodeo."

It's all I can do not to gaze at her like a love-struck space clown.

When the salad is ready to toss and her mom's lasagna is in the oven, we go upstairs to Zoe's room. She sits in her window seat, pulling a large stuffed rabbit into her lap to make room for me. She pats a spot next to her on the inviting cushion. The green of the pine trees outside her window does her hair and complexion every favor somehow, but I don't think there's a color on earth that could mute her beauty.

My messenger bag sits on her floor, and a nervous thrill runs through me at the thought of what's inside. I keep thinking about the gift and wondering when to give it to her. I hope she loves it.

She pulls her legs up and sits cross-legged, facing me, and I pull up my legs and mirror her.

"I wonder how long it will take before my data comes in," she says, clutching the rabbit to herself. "Every time I think of it, my stomach does cartwheels. Just the idea of knowing my ethnic background is so exciting — and that's only the beginning, right? I could sign up to find DNA matches. I might find actual relatives!"

"Anything's possible!" I say, wanting to seem enthusiastic and confident. This morning we did something that could alter the entire course of her life. I don't know what to say to reassure her. Her knees are so close to mine, it would be easy to reach out and lay a comforting hand on one, but I don't have the ease of touching that she does. Just thinking about doing it makes me break into a sweat. Instead, I pick up a stuffed chipmunk and run a finger over its soft head.

My greatest hope is that whatever comes of this will disprove Zoe's Theory of Original Defectiveness. If she finds out why she was given up—if it was because the situation was impossible and not because they didn't want her, just like the story I told her in Starworld—then maybe that hole in her heart can begin to mend.

We talk quietly as the sunlight climbs over the house and the smell of cheese and meat wafts from the kitchen. Finally, I hear the sound of a car pulling into the driveway, and Zoe jumps up. "They're here! Grab the birds!"

I pick up the drawing I did for Jonah and follow her as she runs down the stairs. My heart pounds as my nerves engage in some kind of biological warfare. Will he like the art? Will he like me? Can I fake being a normal person long enough to impress Zoe's parents? Through the living room window, Zoe and I watch as her mom helps Jonah out of the back seat and her dad pulls a duffel bag from the other side. When Jonah emerges, he's wearing a helmet, and he's bigger than I expected—much bigger. He dwarfs Zoe's mother, who is awfully slight, and he's even larger than her dad, who is not a small person. Jonah stands for a moment in the driveway, rocking back and forth on his feet, and his mom gives him a gentle tug toward the house.

I glance at Zoe, who has a hand laid on her chest, her fingers at her collarbone. Her expression is one of happy anticipation, and it makes my heart squeeze. When her family reaches the door, she opens it and says, "Jonah!" She pulls him inside and hugs him tight, then steps back and looks up at him.

"Bao Bao," he says, and I'm surprised by his voice, which

is strong but also somehow pained. Maybe that's just how he sounds. He leans his head down and presses the front of his helmet to Zoe's head.

I am so mesmerized that I scarcely notice Zoe's parents slipping in the door around us.

"Happy birthday, Zoe," her mother says. "This must be Sam!"

"Yes," I say, holding out my hand awkwardly. "Nice to meet you."

Zoe steps back, holding on to Jonah's hand, and says, "Sam, these are my parents."

Her dad reaches over to shake my hand. "Sam, great to meet you."

"And this is Jonah!" Zoe says, beaming at him.

Jonah is facing away from me and he doesn't turn, so I step over to see him better. "Hi, Jonah," I say. I don't know whether to shake hands or not, but I don't want to seem rude, so I hold out my hand. "It's nice to meet you."

Zoe helps him shake hands with me. "This is Sam, Jonah. Can you say hi?"

He doesn't do anything, but I'm not finished. I pull the poster out from behind me and say, "This is for you, Jonah."

I hold the drawing up to show him. "The orange bird in the middle is a phoenix — a magical immortal firebird that is reborn in flames every time it dies. But I thought if there could be a bird of fire, then there needed to be ones made of other things, too." I trace my finger over the birds made of water and leaves.

Jonah holds very still, his eyes on the picture.

"Jonah, what do you say?" Zoe's mom prompts him. "Can you say thank you?"

He sort of smacks himself in the chin.

"Yes, good boy." She turns to me. "That means thank you."

"You're very welcome," I tell him.

He makes a sound and raises his hand, opening and closing his fingers.

"Yes, Jonah!" Zoe exclaims. "Birds!"

"Good signing, Jonah," Zoe's dad says, patting Jonah on the back.

Zoe smiles at me. "That's the sign for *bird*." She demonstrates making what looks like a little opening and closing beak with her thumb and forefinger.

Zoe's dad steps in and admires my drawing. Jonah takes it in both hands and makes a sort of keening noise I don't know how to interpret.

"He's happy," Zoe whispers, smiling at me. She tugs me by the sleeve to follow her into the kitchen. Her mom propels Jonah in and says, "Jonah, do you smell something good? I made lasagna."

Zoe's eyes widen and she exclaims, "Mom! He just made the sign for eating." She demonstrates moving her closed fingers to her lips. "Jonah! Good job."

"They say he's become quite consistent with signing," her dad says. "Maybe we just weren't persistent enough with it at home. He's doing great."

Zoe's dad takes Jonah to the bathroom, and her mom

washes up and puts in breadsticks to warm. "Thanks for putting this in and making the salad, Zo," she says, pulling the foil off the lasagna.

A waft of garlicky steam makes my stomach growl.

"Sam helped," Zoe says, pulling what must be Jonah's dishes out of the cabinet. They're plastic and sort of strangely shaped. "He has adaptive equipment," Zoe explains when she sees my puzzled look. "It makes it easier for him, but it's still going to be messy, so gird yourself."

"I could use a little more mess in my life, as you know," I joke, immediately regretting it when I see the quizzical expression on Zoe's mom's face.

"Her mom is kind of a neat freak," Zoe says.

Understatement of the century.

"Ah," her mom says, pulling out a spatula. "Well, this will be different." She gives me a wry smile.

And it is. Mealtime with Jonah is . . . not tidy. But he loves his food and he loves his family and his family loves him and I love Zoe. There's so much love at the table that it almost hurts. I want to live somewhere like this. Somewhere I can just be and exist without following rules, where the only guidelines are to enjoy the food and the people around me.

It doesn't take long to get used to Jonah's messiness and the way everyone pitches in between conversation and bites of food with wiping Jonah's chin or helping him get a forkful of salad. It's loud and there's a lot of laughter, and the food is delicious and asymmetrical, and everyone has seconds of everything. At one point I ask Zoe's dad about his field of study, and when he catches Zoe giving me an alarmed shake of her head, drawing her finger across her throat, he almost falls out of his chair laughing.

"The *short* version, Dad," she says, brandishing a threatening breadstick at him.

I try to follow along when he talks about Jesuits and trees and agriculture and gold, but it's like he studies all the parts of history I have the least interest in. It's all I can do to keep my eyes from crossing. Thankfully, he soon asks me what I'm interested in studying in college.

"Art, I assume?" he says. "By the way, I had to practically wrestle that drawing away from Jonah to get him to wash his hands, didn't I, Jonah?" He grins at his son, then turns his attention back to me. "You're really talented."

"Thank you," I manage to say. "Actually . . . I want to design rockets."

He's surprised and impressed as I tell him all about the aerospace engineering programs I'm applying to, and soon we're discussing the differences in launch protocols for probes and satellites. Zoe's dad listens to me like my dad used to, asks good questions, gives thoughtful responses. I almost fall down a rabbit hole of wondering if my family might have been like this if my parents hadn't divorced, but I know this is not the time for that. This is the time to enjoy one of the best, happiest days I've had in years.

When we finish eating, Zoe's mom gets up and takes off Jonah's bib. "Sam, can you stay for cake? It won't take us too long to clean up."

"I can help," I say, standing and picking up my plate. I'm accustomed to it. This is part of the routine. Then a little bit of panic rises as I second-guess my ability to help. What if the way my mom has taught me isn't right? Do other people wipe their counters down twice? Are they as particular about how their dishwashers are loaded?

"I wouldn't hear of it," she says. "You've both done plenty. You and Zoe go on upstairs, and we'll call you for cake."

Zoe nods at me, so I say, "Thank you so much for lunch. It was delicious, and I . . ." I hesitate, choking up like the worst excuse for a robot in the history of technology. "I'm having a wonderful time."

I glance at Zoe for reassurance because I'm pretty sure I'm coming off like a weirdo, but the smile she gives me is as gentle and warm as ever. Seeing it floods me with relief. She's so patient with me. So understanding. She seems to like me in spite of all the ways I routinely fail to function. Every moment I'm with her, she helps me figure out who I want to be.

When we get to the top of the stairs, Zoe steps into the bathroom, saying, "You can go ahead — I'll be there in a minute."

Her door hangs open like an invitation, so I walk right in. The afternoon light filters through the windows, not bright enough to illuminate the room. I can't help closing my eyes and taking a deep breath, filling my lungs with the now-familiar smell of Zoe. It's sunshine and spring and hope and a longing so deep, I can't find the bottom.

I wish there was a way to tell her how she's changed my life.

I wish there was a way to tell her how I feel.

When I open my eyes, the answer is right in front of me.

The glow-in-the-dark stars on her wall are just barely visible against the ivory paint. They come off easily, and my hands work fast as I take apart constellations she's probably had since childhood and build something new.

I rearrange the stars for her the way I do every day in Starworld.

I tell her what I could never speak aloud.

I tell her something that will only be visible in the dark and on her way to dreaming.

I tell her the truth.

By the time she returns from the bathroom, I'm perched at the edge of her bed with the box I wrapped for her in my lap. My heart pounds like a mace being slammed into an anvil.

"What's that?" she asks, her eyes wide with curiosity.

"Your birthday present," I mumble. "Nothing big." But it kind of is.

"Sam!" She looks moved. "You already gave me the DNA kit! You didn't have to do anything else."

"No, I really had to," I say. She'll understand when she opens it. She sits down right beside me on the bed, so close that her weight makes me tip closer to her as the mattress sags. I hand her the box.

I can hardly hear anything but the sound of my pulse drowning out my thoughts. I wish that somehow I could give her the most precious treasure in Starworld this very moment, too, but it's not yet time for the third quest to be over. And I want that third treasure to matter most. I don't just want to show her something incredible. I want her to feel it and know it with every fiber of her being, just like she did with the other stories.

She gasps when she opens the package and unwraps an antique silver powder box, the first piece of the vanity set I got her. The design is ornate and feminine, but with a twist: a dragon winds through the pattern of leaves and flowers. She looks at me. "Where did you find this?"

"You can find anything on the internet if you look long enough," I mumble. My cheeks are burning like they're on fire. Maybe this gift was too much, but I knew from the moment I saw it, she needed to have it.

She digs in to see the rest. There's a boar-bristle brush with an ornate silver back, a jewelry box, and a silver tray. They gleam even in the weak light from outside.

"They were a little tarnished, but I found a trick online to get them clean. I know you haven't been able to have a lot of fancy things here, but soon you'll be in a dorm, and I thought . . ."

"They're beautiful," she says. "I love them." She sets the package aside, and before I know what's happening, her arms are around me.

Cautiously, I return her embrace, sure she can feel the way I'm trembling with adrenaline. When she doesn't let go right away, I let myself feel the draw of her breath as I hold her, in and out. I have never loved anything as much as the way she feels under my hands. I breathe her in, feeling the warmth of her neck beneath her hair.

I want to be against that skin.

My breath hitches and rattles around in my lungs like a dying thing as I run my hand through her exquisitely soft hair and down the gentle curve of her back. I am so dizzy with the smell and the feel of her that I can barely think. But I don't want to. I'm done with that.

She pulls back just a little to look at me, a question in her eyes.

"Zoe," I whisper in response, and close the distance between us until my lips meet hers.

Her mouth is warm and soft, the smell of her even more intoxicating right up close.

But instead of kissing me back, she pulls away.

The expression on her face is one I would give anything never to have seen. Is it disgust? Horror?

"Sam. No. I — I like you, but I don't . . ." She shakes her head. "I'm not . . ."

Numbness courses through me from head to toe, and there aren't enough multiplication tables in the world to save me. My heart is in my throat and my spleen is halfway out my ass, and all I know is I need to get away.

I leap up from her bed.

"I'm sorry," I choke out. "I need to go."

I grab my bag and race out of her bedroom and down the stairs, slowing only briefly as I pass the kitchen where Zoe's parents are sticking candles into a bakery cake festooned with flowers and confetti.

"NicetomeetyoubutIhavetogo," I say in a mumbled rush. I glance over to the living room where Jonah is watching something about penguins. He still has my drawing clutched to his chest. My heart pounds the breath out of my lungs.

I burst out of the front door, holding myself together until my ass hits the leather driver's seat of my mom's car. My vision blurs and my face explodes with a number of bodily fluids that robots most certainly should not have.

I was wrong about everything. Wrong about Zoe, wrong about her seeing me and understanding. Wrong to think that she might like me as anything more than a friend, or that the magical world we created might be able to overcome my weirdness or my gender or any of the other mile-high obstacles between us that now are clear as day. But most of all, I was wrong to kiss her. My stomach churns with shame. How could I have been so stupid? Everything could have stayed perfect if I just hadn't done that.

I pull out of the driveway, racking my brain for some way to fix this. Maybe if I apologize enough, try to explain that I was confused by what was happening, that it was an accident, that none of it meant anything, she'll understand. Maybe she can forgive me for being stupid and pathetic, and I can disappear quietly, forgetting all of this.

But then I remember.

The glow stars.

The message she won't yet have seen, the one I wish I could tear from the wall. If it weren't for the stars, I might be able to preserve at least the tiniest modicum of dignity. I should have remained invisible, kept my distance, stayed somewhere safe. But as soon as she sees that message, it's over. The final blow is yet to come, and there is nothing I can do to stop it.

By the time I stumble through my front door, sobs are choking me. I go into the first-floor bathroom and rip into the box of Kleenex like a raccoon.

"Samantha?" Mom calls from her office.

I look up in panic. I can't let her see me like this.

I flee to my room, only to feel like a trapped animal when I get there. The walls can't contain my feelings, and my floor looks like the recently vacated nest of a pack of sock-shitting lemurs with a frightening appetite for high fantasy books. Even the mess seems to be mocking me, telling me, *You did this. You fucked up. The disaster that is your life is your fault, just like the chaos in this room.*

But the loss of Zoe is so much bigger than this mess, and it's not just her — it's my entire life.

A knock sounds at my door. "Are you all right?" Mom asks.

"No," I whisper too softly for her to hear.

"What are you doing in there, Samantha?"

"Cleaning," I say, my voice high and tight.

"Really?" She sounds dubious. "Do you need help?"

"No!" I barely stop the sob that rises to choke me. "I need to turn on some music and focus."

"Okay. Let me know if you change your mind." She clomps down the stairs, satisfied by my explanation — at least for now — leaving me in the midst of the disaster that is my life. And even though it was a lie when I said it, I start to think maybe I *should* clean.

So I start tidying, and once I start, I can't stop. For the first time I have an inkling of what it's like to be my mom. I feel that if only I can get everything put back in its place, maybe my life will rearrange itself into something bearable. Maybe my mom is on to something—maybe that kiss would never have happened in a world that had some order in it. Maybe if I get rid of all the reminders of what a freak I am, I won't feel like such a freak.

Maybe I'm already just like her.

I clean with shaky hands and let the task take away all my thoughts except decisions about where to put stuff. This book on that shelf, these pencils in the holder I've never used, and that last uneaten bag of shortbread from Zoe into the trash to be buried under subsequent detritus. Fantasy novels piled in my closet, video game posters pulled from the walls and shoved behind bookshelves where they can't be seen. When I'm done, the place doesn't even feel like it's mine anymore. I'm living in someone else's room, someone else's life.

I fall face-first down on my bed, consumed with fear that I'm doomed to turn out just like my mother—perpetually organizing my life to stave off disaster while only deepening the pit of my own dysfunctional reality, the black hole of my existence. The pointlessness of it all is so vast. I am a fucked-up robot incapable of human interaction. I am a girl with a mentally ill mother and a father who didn't love me enough to stay. I just destroyed the only relationship I had that gave me any hope someone could love me. None of that is ever going to change.

There is no cure for the cruelty of the universe, and no way to rearrange these broken stars.

Zoe

I sit frozen on my bed, staring after Sam.

My mind is full of so many ricocheting thoughts that I can't follow a single one to completion — unformed questions that start with *how*, or *why*, or *when*. I am almost numb with shock. I am vaguely aware of the sound of her car starting outside, the grinding of the transmission as she steps on the gas before the gear has even engaged, the squeal of tires. And even though I'm stuck on what just happened, a part of me wants to run after her and comfort her and make sure she's okay, make sure *we're* okay. She raced out so fast — but not so fast that I didn't see her expression, the impact of my response.

She's not okay. Obviously.

I have no idea what I'm supposed to do.

Suddenly my mother is in front of me.

"What happened to Sam?" she asks, her face creased with concern.

I realize how tense I am, my arms pressed tight to my body. I try to relax.

"Zoe?" She sits down next to me. "Is everything okay?"

I nod.

"She looked upset. Did something happen between you?"

I can't find words. I don't even quite understand what just happened. Except I do. It's starting to seem obvious.

I don't know what to say to my mom. I know I need time to think, but I don't have it. So I go with the only way out I can find: I lie. "She got a message from her mom. Her . . . her aunt was in an accident." I regret the lie already, but I see no way around it.

Her brows draw together. "Oh, no!"

My mom's concern makes me wish I'd gone with something less extreme, but the thing is, I don't know what happened downstairs. Was Sam crying when she ran out? Did she say anything to them?

"Was it bad?" she asks.

"I'm not sure."

"Well, tell Sam we're here if she needs anything." She moves my hair over my shoulder and I stiffen a little, recalling Sam's hands in my hair.

Did I do something to give Sam the impression I liked her *that* way? My mind reels, untethered, looking for something solid and unmoving to hold on to.

"We really like Sam," my mom says. "I'm glad you became friends."

I nod mutely.

"What's this?" she says, noticing the vanity set. "Oh, it's beautiful."

"Gift from Sam," I mumble.

"Wow." She picks up the pieces to examine them. "This set is really old — I'd say turn of the century, if not older." She glances at me. "This is really special, Zoe." She stands up. "You ready for more gifts? Jonah's not going to wait long for cake."

"I think I should hold off a bit and make sure Sam's okay," I say. I am not ready to go down and be with my family. I can't even think clearly. "You can give Jonah a piece if he can't wait. I don't mind."

"What? Not before we sing to you! I can give him a granola bar or something if push comes to shove." She kisses my head. "Take your time. When are you leaving for Erin's?"

My stomach drops. I had almost forgotten: tonight's the Jell-O shot sleepover. "I'm going with Cammie from the show, and then we're going to Erin's after," I say.

"Okay." She lays a hand on my cheek, just briefly, then stands up. "Come down when you're ready."

She closes the door behind her, and I curl up into a ball on the bed. I don't want to think about what happened with Sam, but until I do, until I process it, I am sort of immobilized.

I hadn't thought about the possibility of Sam being attracted to me. Most of the time it seemed like touching me at *all* was a struggle for her. And now suddenly she kisses me? How did I ever signal to her that I wanted her to do that?

Did I do something that gave her the wrong idea?

My phone vibrates on my nightstand, making me jump about a mile. I grab it, hoping it's Sam, but it's just Syd. She's sent a photo of red-pink Jell-O shots and a message that says: HAPPY BIRTHDAY, ZO. WATERMELON JOLLY RANCHER JELL-O SHOT OMG YUMMMMMM. I CAN'T WAIT TILL TONIGHT.

I can. Enjoying myself at a party? It's the last thing I can conceive of right now.

I wonder if I should reach out to Sam. When someone kisses someone who didn't want to be kissed, what's the protocol? Will she reach out and apologize? Should I reach out and say no hard feelings? Should *I* apologize?

I have no idea how to handle this.

If she had *talked* to me, or if she had somehow given me any clue of what she was feeling or thinking, then I could have stopped this before it was too late. But I never saw it coming.

I can hear my dad struggling downstairs with Jonah, who wants cake, and I know I should get down there. But my mind quickly goes to that drawing Sam made for Jonah. It's so thoughtful, so detailed — it must have taken her such a long time to do. She didn't even know Jonah; did she do it because of me? Because her feelings for me were not just those of a friend?

With a jolt, I recall her sketch of me. I pull open my bedside drawer and take it out. It's so beautiful — I have half acknowledged to myself that part of the reason I love it so much is because it's so flattering, that she overlooked my imperfections and made me more beautiful than I actually am. But I have always felt Sam sees me the way I am, accepts me the way I am. Which of us sees me more clearly?

I have no idea.

I am lost.

I glance at the top of my bookcase, where I set the giant bag of Taco Bell hot sauces. "FUEL TO ANYWHERE." Is that what Starworld has been all this time? Some sort of, like, romantic fantasy? I never dreamed it didn't mean the same thing to both of us. An escape. A place where we could forget our troubles. A safe —

I stop, stumbling over the term I'm realizing defines Starworld perfectly.

A safe haven.

That's what it was to me. And it's what I wanted to make for her, too.

I think with horror about some of the things I wrote to her in Starworld, the way I clung to her on Humphrey's back and expressed so much love for the places she dreamed up. My god — I even told her *I love you*. Did she think I meant as more than friends? A lot of things I've said could in fact sound sort of romantic, if one wanted to see it that way. But I didn't mean them that way! If I had known that's how she was feeling, I would have been more careful.

I can't bear the thought of losing her friendship. When I consider the many ways I care about her, depend on her . . . She is in everything now — not just my habits and my heart, but my home. My family.

I pick up my phone to check it, even though there have been no alerts since Syd. Nothing. I keep seeing Sam's face, the way that expression of love and hope so quickly morphed into hurt and mortification, and my chest aches for her. To feel that way for someone and be rejected . . . And she was so fragile already, socially. How will she recover from this? How can I make things okay again?

What I need is to talk to someone. But I know there's no one I can talk to, not without giving Sam away. If she's not straight and not out, then that's by choice. My mind goes to Jared Abrams, a theater kid who came out last year just before he graduated. Before that, though, I remember the jokes and teasing, and how he seemed to flinch at the way people pushed and prodded at something he wasn't ready to share. I didn't understand how normally nice-seeming people could be so thoughtless. It still hurts to think of some of those moments, and what that must have been like for Jared.

I would never want Sam to experience something like that. I will just have to figure this out for myself.

I go downstairs and manage to autopilot my way through cake and gifts. My dad chose the cake — from St. Honore, the French bakery we both love — and it has all my favorite things: chocolate, caramel, and almond. It might as well be cardboard, for all I enjoy it. Mom, who avoids sugar since her diagnosis, has an obligatory sliver. Thankfully Dad and Jonah enjoy it enough for all of us.

My main present is the promise of a new laptop for college next fall. Fall seems so far away as to be unreal, but I manage to express my gratitude. There are other gifts, too: earrings, chocolates, books . . . My mom gives me a hand-drawn certificate for a "girls' day" together: lunch and pedis. And my dad, not to be outdone, gives me a certificate for a FREE LUNCH WITH DAD, ANY DAY. He sketched the Reed griffin in the upper-left corner. He's looked forward to our lunches at Reed since he got tenure there when I was in seventh grade.

"What if I don't get in?" I joke. I know my scores and grades are well within range.

"No chance," he says. "Who wouldn't want my brilliant daughter?"

I don't give the answer that always comes to my mind — *my birth mother* — although it amazes me that he doesn't understand what he's saying. The important part is that he honestly can't imagine anyone not wanting me, and so, in a way, that kind of thoughtless remark is the greatest gift of them all.

With a stab of guilt, I think about the DNA test. I need to tell my parents. The discomfort I feel over having done it without telling them first makes me know I need to make it right. But I can't face it yet. The idea of another emotional upheaval on top of what's happened with Sam is too much.

"Zoe?" My mom pauses from cleaning up the cake plates and tilts her head at me, her expression concerned. "Are you okay? You're really out of it. Have you heard from Sam about her aunt?"

I avert my eyes. "Not yet."

My dad comes back in, stirring Jonah's crushed medications into a little container of applesauce. "I like Sam a lot.

She seems mature and thoughtful. And that drawing she did for Jonah . . . She's a keeper."

I flinch a little, as I always do at that word. A *keeper*. Another thing my dad doesn't understand. To an adoptee, the word *keeper* is loaded. Relinquished children were not "keepers." I was not a "keeper." It goes to the Theory of Original Defectiveness.

But now there's Sam's counter theory — the belief that I was not defective at all, that in fact someone loved me enough to do the impossible. If she's right, maybe somewhere out there my birth mother has the same agonized feelings about the phrase *keeper* as I do. The thought fills my heart with pain and hope in equal measure.

Jonah has made his way back to the living room, and he's clutching the bird poster again. I swallow a lump in my throat. "You'll bring that back to Little Lambs Village, right?"

My dad glances over at Jonah and says in a low voice, "It might come in handy for coaxing him into the car. I'm a little worried about that."

I fill with dread at the idea of Jonah not wanting to go back. If he flops down and refuses to go — or, worse, cries — it will be unbearable for all of us. And it seems perfectly reasonable that after a relaxing weekend of good food and cake and lots of love, he might not want to leave.

This is all so brutal. So fucking brutal.

All afternoon, thoughts and worries about Sam fill my head. I wish she'd reach out. I don't know if hearing from me would just make her feel worse. But I also don't want her to think I'm upset with her.

I lie on my bed, chewing on it for a while, before I finally fire off a message: Sam, everything is okay, okay? Can we talk?

Nothing.

The whole day passes without a word from her. I'm still watching and hoping for a response when Cammie pulls into the driveway early that evening to go to the play and then Erin's.

Happy fucking birthday to me.

I flip off my light and start down the hall, but no sooner do I reach the stairs when I realize I forgot my overnight bag.

I go back to my room, and something pops out at me before my hand even reaches the light switch.

Something is different.

My glow stars. They aren't the way they were, the way they've been for years. I blink, taking in the new pattern on the wall across from me.

The message glows bright in the dark room: I ♥ YOU.

My breath catches and the ache in my chest sharpens.

Oh, Sam.

The thing is, I love her, too. But I love her as a friend.

It seems impossible that love cost me what I had come to treasure most.

"You're quiet," Cammie says in the car on the way to Erin's. She has been yammering on about the play, and I have had little to contribute, which must seem strange. "Are the realities of adulthood weighing you down?" she jokes.

I come far enough out of my stupor to laugh. "Yes," I say. "Eighteen is so much harder than seventeen was."

Little does she know it's the truth.

In my mind's eye, Sam's message glows still. Can we get past what happened? Is it naive and foolish to hope that someday we might laugh at this? Even if we never laugh about it, I need to believe we will find our way to the other side. There are too many things ahead that I don't want to face without her.

When Cammie and I arrive at Erin's, I'm surprised to find her parents and her twin brothers home, watching a movie in the living room. There is enough popcorn on the floor to fill a silo, although Jackson, their aging Lab, is surreptitiously lapping it up at a fair rate of speed.

"Happy birthday, Zoe!" Erin's mom calls from the sofa. Her leg is propped up and bandaged from recent ACL surgery. With her fair skin and blue eyes, her resemblance to Erin is unmistakable.

"Thank you," I say, but already the dog is jumping on me. "Hey, boy," I say softly, squatting down and letting him lick my face. He probably only likes me because I unfailingly sneak him scraps of food every time I'm over, but I'll take it. He rolls over for me, and I stroke his belly until Erin tugs me by the coat collar.

I needn't have wondered how Erin planned to get all the Jell-O shots past her parents: when we're settled in the finished attic, she rolls a giant cooler out of a low closet in the slanted wall and lifts the lid.

"You sure your parents won't come up?" I say, worried as always about getting in trouble.

Erin counts off on her fingers: "My mom won't because

she's still recovering from the knee surgery. My dad won't because he literally never does. He says setting foot in this room will instantly suck the testosterone out of his body."

I can see why. The renovated attic, or the "lady cave" as her dad grossly calls it, is done up in an exaggerated French country style with floral wallpaper and plush furniture and pink throw pillows and little antique finishes. It's . . . girly.

"My brothers won't," Erin continues, counting off on a third finger, "because I told them the attic is full of spiders." She does her cheesy grin where every tooth shows.

"Well played," Cammie says, pulling a lidded plastic cup out of the cooler and shaking ice water off it. She peels the lid off and tips the cup back. When the shot doesn't shake loose, she plunges her tongue in dramatically and runs it around to free the Jell-O.

"Gross," Erin says to Cammie, laughing.

"Dibs on the first massage," Cammie says, plopping on the floor in front of Syd, who is still messing with her phone.

"Just a sec," Syd says, petting Cammie's hair absently. Cammie leans her head back into Syd's lap, smiling with her eyes closed. Erin settles in on Syd's other side, cross-legged, and feeds Syd a Jell-O shot. Syd is trying to work her phone at the same time, and she's laughing, her mouth open, her head tipped back. Finally Erin sticks her finger into the Jell-O to loosen it and slides it into Syd's mouth, then licks her finger. They're all laughing.

And I'm just watching. Thinking.

We are all so affectionate, so tactile. So comfortable. We have a whole history of hair play and massages and cuddle puddles. Touching, so much touching. And then there's Sam, who could barely handle a hug. Is it because of her home life, her history? Or because she likes girls? I never considered that things like hugs and touching might be confusing to her for that kind of reason.

I glance up as a flash of glinting red appears in front of my face.

"Zo?" Erin holds out a Jell-O shot.

Alcohol. I hesitate only briefly. "Sure," I say. I tip the Jell-O shot back, and the flavors explode. "Wow, those are good," I say after I swallow. "I can barely taste the alcohol."

I slurp down another. Erin goes downstairs and comes back with soda and buttered popcorn, which we devour. As we talk and laugh and rub shoulders and braid hair, I work my way through all the flavors of the Jell-O shots, and then I repeat the ones I like best. The more of them I have, the less I care about how many I'm having. It feels like a small consolation on a truly crappy day. No, a shit day. A fucking shit day.

When the conversation turns to who's hooking up with whom, I step away to go to the tiny powder room. I don't want to think about human sexuality, let alone talk about it. I flip on the light, which is an ornate little antique chandelier. The room is done in pink subway tiles, a pink pedestal sink, and a pink tile floor. It's a lot of pink and it's kind of swimmy. I lean toward the mirror and stick my tongue out. It's an alarming dark shade of red and green, mixed. I catch sight of my star necklace, which I still wear because I like it. *For my superstar*, Hunter had said when he gave it to me on opening night of *Enemy*. I finger the pendant, remembering how my heart soared with the knowledge of his belief in me, and with the romance of the gift. I loved the romantic part of our relationship so much that it clouded my view of what was real. What else am I failing to see?

I stare at my face, trying to imagine myself twenty years older, searching for my birth mother in my reflection. I can't find her. I look at myself until my face goes strange and foreign and I don't even know who I am. But then, I've never known who I am. Not really.

I get out my phone, and in the process lose my balance and stumble into the door. So I sit down on the toilet and scroll through my messages until I get back into the ones Sam and I were exchanging when she was talking to me, making me laugh, making things beautiful for me.

I don't want to lose that.

I type: **Sam? Are you okay?**

I wait a minute before adding, **I'm sorry.** I'm not sure I've done something I should apologize for, but does it matter? I *am* sorry. Sorry if Sam had the wrong impression, sorry if I hurt her, sorry if I did anything that led to this.

The sounds from outside the bathroom are so happy — music and laughter and screwing around. Random words make it through the closed door. *Everclear. Hunter. Asshole. Watermelon. Necklace. Sorority. Blow job. Nachos.* And hysterical laughter.

But my heart is heavy with worry for Sam.

I write: **I don't want to lose your friendship. You're so important to me.**

She's the first person I've truly been myself with, even when I don't know who "myself" really is. She listened. She understood. She accepted me as I was, as I am. She made me feel like anything is possible. Will I ever have a friend like that again?

I ache to connect with her, to know she's okay. And then it occurs to me that there has always been one thing that Sam responds to, one place I can always, always find her.

I write: Besides, we haven't fulfilled the third quest and we can't leave that unfinished, right? *raids bag of hot sauces and prepares to fuel Humphrey for quest*

I wait a few minutes.

Crickets.

I'm thirsty. I turn on the cold water and drink right out of the faucet. I wipe my mouth on my sleeve and lean back on the door.

"Zo? Are you okay?" It's Cammie. She taps on the door. "Sweetie? Are you sick?"

"No, I'm fine. I'll be out in a minute."

"Okay."

I hear her footsteps retreating, hear her telling the others what I said.

I bend over my phone and type again: Sam, come on. SAY SOMETHING. Please.

I wait, staring at the screen, then add: If you had just TOLD me . . . Why didn't you tell me? I told you everything.

I amend that: Fucking everything. <3

Apparently I'm crying. A tear falls on my phone. I told you

stuff I never told anyone. I introduced you to Jonah. I trusted you with everything! You can't just go away.

She's not going to answer, and I can't bear it.

Please don't be gone.

But she is.

Sam

Starworld has collapsed in on itself.

So has my heart.

I manage to hold myself together enough to survive dinner with Mom — some sort of Crock-Pot chicken gruel full of frozen vegetables that has the appearance and appeal of cat vomit. I tell her my puffy eyes are due to allergies, so she stuffs me full of antihistamines and doesn't question me when I retreat to my room to "study." When I get there, I bypass my books, put on my pajamas, and climb into bed.

The messages don't come until later. Each time my phone buzzes and I read what Zoe says, my heart breaks into smaller pieces. She's trying so hard to be kind; she's opening the door to Starworld and hoping I'll follow her. But I can't banish the memory of the horrified look on her face after I kissed her. The look of incomprehension, maybe even disgust. Woven in with my shame are fragments of memory I can't seem to push aside: the way she smelled, how soft her hair was, how warm her lips were during the nanosecond they were pressed against mine.

I thought there was so much more between us, that she surely felt what I did — that tug that kept me always gravitating to where she was. The pull of Starworld, more deep and insistent than anything I'd ever known.

I am such a fool.

Part of me wants to answer her messages, pretend it was all just a dumb mistake, like that kiss never even happened. The problem is that I can't be near her perfect curves without every part of me feeling like it's burning up. I can't look into her kaleidoscope eyes without getting lost. And if I make her smile, it will completely undo me. What kind of friendship can we have if I'm consumed with desire for her and she never feels the same?

Even after Mom goes to bed and the house goes silent, I lie awake with my stomach churning like a pit full of venomous snakes. All I want is sleep. Oblivion. I don't want to wake up until I know there is something to get up for, but every time I close my eyes, they pop open again. Sleep is impossible, but there's no one I can talk to at this time of night, not even Will. If I texted him, he wouldn't respond; he sleeps like a sack full of corpses.

Feelings climb and writhe over one another until I can't figure out where one ends and another begins. I want to fast-forward my life to college, when I'll be far from here, where I can start over and try to be a different person. I wish I could leave—just walk out the front door and not come back. But like always, there is nowhere I can go.

Then my mind leaps ahead eight hours—to London. Dad invited me, but did he mean that? I glance at my clock. It's midnight here, which means he might be just starting his day in London.

The bright light of the phone screen makes me squint when I pick it up from my nightstand. I select my dad's name from my list of contacts, and tap the call button with shaky fingers. It rings four long times, and I'm about to hang up when finally a voice comes through.

"Sammy?" he says. The familiarity of his voice stirs up forgotten memories. Tears sting my eyes even though I thought I'd surely run dry.

"Hi," I say.

"It's so good to hear your voice, love. Wait . . . isn't it the middle of the night there?" He sounds confused, and I know he probably hasn't had his first cuppa—Earl Grey with a splash of milk, like always.

"It's a little after midnight," I say.

"Is something wrong?" His voice is worried.

Everything is wrong.

"No," I lie. "I just—I think I'd like to come visit sometime." It takes everything I have to keep my voice steady and calm.

"Oh, splendid! That would be lovely. When can you come? For Christmas, perhaps?" He sounds excited now, and for some reason all it does is make a bottomless sorrow well up in me.

I think about visiting him for Christmas and picture Mom wrestling the tree onto the roof of the car by herself, then heaving it into the driveway, where she'll have to wash it at least four times to remove imaginary contaminants before bringing it into the house.

"I'm not sure Mom can manage Christmas by herself," I say.

"I'm sure she wouldn't mind letting me have you for the holidays just this once," he says, completely missing the point. "We used to trade off when I still lived in the States."

As if I could forget. Christmas at his place was always the opposite of Mom's. Mom can barely stand the disorder that comes with opening gifts, but Dad and I used to leave shredded wrapping paper on the floor all day until we used it to get a fire going in the evening. Then we'd make s'mores and end up sticky with marshmallow and chocolate. He always caught his on fire and then pretended he liked them all charcoally like that.

"Things are different now," I say. "Holidays are nothing like when you were here." I feel a little guilty, like I'm betraying Mom's confidence by telling him.

"What do you mean?" he asks, sounding genuinely baffled.

"Her OCD," I say. "It'll disrupt everything if I leave. She'll fall apart." I explain how Mom is now. I tell him about her routines and about how I don't know how I'm going to be able to leave for a visit, much less college. I tell him how isolated I am, that I don't feel like I can make new friends, because what if they find out about Mom and don't understand? I tell him I don't know how much longer I can live my life this way, but that I also feel like I can't escape.

"Oh, Sammy—why didn't you say something?" he asks, his voice full of concern. "I'm so sorry. Do you want me to speak to your mum? If there's anything I can do to help, I will."

"No, not right now. I think I have to talk to her about it myself first." Even if he could effectively intervene, which I know he can't, I don't think I want him to. I need to talk to Mom on my own, because I need to figure out how to deal with humans, even her.

"All right, but if you need me, I'm here," he says. "It sounds like you've been dealing with too much on your own for a very long time."

"Okay," I say, my voice small. He's right.

"You always were so independent and brave." There's a smile in his voice, and I can perfectly picture the glimmer in his hazel eyes.

Ha. "I'm not brave at all." And the only time I was—with Zoe—it was a complete disaster.

"Nonsense. Remember how fearless you were when we went camping? You and Will always led the way and explored for hours. I'm fairly sure you gave your mum a few gray hairs every time you came home with new tales of misadventure." He chuckles. "That's what life is for—to explore. To make your own stories."

His words are a shock to my system. Somewhere in the last five years, I lost track of the Sam who could do things like that. I barely remember her.

"I'm so glad to hear your voice," he says again. "I've missed you terribly."

A lump forms in my throat. "I've missed you, too, Dad." Memories flood back of everything we used to have — favorites, jokes, adventures. I'm not the same girl he left behind, but now that I'm listening to him again, and feeling heard, I want his memories of me. I want exploring and adventure. I want to regain what we've lost.

I just hope it isn't too late.

"Call or email me and let me know how the talk with your mum goes, all right? I'll be here if you need me. In the meantime, I need to go rescue Maisie so she can have her day off. Your grandfather has tried to steal the car keys three times this week, so I'd best take him to the pub later to meet his mates for a pint."

I smile a little. Dad's stories about Grandpa were always wild, and it seems like the man hasn't changed much in old age. "Okay," I say. "Tell Grandpa I said hello."

"I will," he says. "I love you, Sammy."

My battered heart swells a little. Hearing those words in his voice, knowing he wants me to visit, and all the memories of me he carries — for the first time in a long time, I believe those words when he says them.

"Love you, too," I answer.

After we say goodbye, I'm finally able to fall asleep.

I wake up to Mom knocking on my door late the next morning. The sun slants through the window, making one of its rare breaks through the clouds for the winter. I jerk the covers over my head to block it out.

"Samantha, are you awake?" Mom calls.

I groan into my pillow.

"Samantha?" Mom knocks again, more frantic this time. "Are you all right? I'm coming into this room if you don't open the door."

A surge of worry tangles my stomach up. Last night, talking to Mom seemed possible when Dad was listening to me all calmly and rationally. But now? She's already upset, and my feelings are rising to meet hers. I pull the covers more tightly over my head and pretend to be asleep, even though I can hardly breathe.

"I'm coming in," she says, and then the door swings open. She steps inside, but her footsteps stop right after she crosses the threshold.

"What happened in here?" she asks, taken aback.

"I cleaned," I mumble from under the covers.

But instead of praising me for finally doing what she's constantly asking me to, she says, "I'm worried about you." She crosses the room and peels the blankets off me. Her hand on my forehead is cool and dry. "You've hardly left your room since yesterday afternoon," she says. "Have you been drinking water? Does your head hurt? Are you dizzy? Dehydration can be very dangerous." She pinches gently at the skin of my arm.

I shrug away. Her worry feels abrasive. Misguided. She's so clueless about what's wrong with me. She won't even talk to me about what's wrong with her. Perhaps I should reach for her to try to extract the sort of comfort that mothers are supposed to provide, but I'm as rooted to the bed as a tree to the earth. My branches don't stretch far enough to touch her. And even if I could, I am no shelter to her, and she is none to me. How can I break through this to have an honest conversation with her?

"Do I need to take you to the doctor?" She wrings her hands. "You don't look well."

"I'm fine." I want her to go away. I can't deal with her right now.

"Don't you have plans with one of your friends today? Games with Will?" she asks.

"Will's at the Blazers game today," I remind her. "I'm meeting him tomorrow after school instead."

"What about that girl Zoe? She seems nice."

I roll back toward Mom and jerk the blankets up tight against my chin. "In case you haven't noticed, I don't have friends. I can't have friends because I'm a freak and a robot!" Even though I try not to, I choke on the words.

"What do you mean?" she asks with a shocked expression. But I can't tell her what happened with Zoe. I can't explain that if I were normal none of this would have happened. I can't explain that an entire world, a universe, has been destroyed because of what a stupid robot I am.

She pats me a few times, but before I can take much solace from it, she starts moving the stuff on my nightstand around with her other hand. "Maybe I could help you finish up your room," she says.

"My room is done." I didn't know my heart could drop

even further, but it does. I try to tell her how fucked up I am, and all she sees or acknowledges are objects out of place.

"We have to put the books in proper order. And surely there are some you're ready to sell at Powell's or give to Goodwill?" She frowns at the rainbow of books on my shelf, which I organized by color in defiance of the alphabet.

"I like the books how they are," I say.

"But how will you find anything?" she asks. "You need them organized alphabetically. It won't take long." She stands up and starts thumbing over them.

"Stop it!" I throw myself out of bed and edge in beside her, enraged that she can't comfort me without needing to put things in order. Why can't she accept me as I am, even if that means messy or book-hoarding?

"I want them like this," I say, and start yanking books off the shelves and putting them back all cockeyed and crazy. I stack some of them on their sides in groups of five and seven. "What if this is how things feel right to me?"

"Why are you being this way? I was only trying to help," Mom says. There's hurt in her eyes, and no sign she understands that helpful is the opposite of what she is. Because of her, home has never been somewhere I can relax. Something is always out of place, in need of cleaning, in need of checking.

Starworld was a much safer place to live than this. Zoe gave me the gift of somewhere to hide, somewhere to be myself without judgment, where mess and magic could go comfortably hand in hand. But now I'm back in the real world. No Zoe, no Starworld. Just my mom with her twitchy hands itching to reach for my shelf and fix things that don't need fixing.

"I can't do this anymore," I say. My chest feels so tight, I can hardly breathe.

"What do you mean?" She blinks at me in confusion.

"I can't go on being the weirdo with no friends who can't invite anyone to her house. I need to be able to go out without you texting me three thousand times. How am I supposed to go away to college with you like this? What is going to happen to you?"

"You know your friends are welcome here," she says. "And college is next year. We don't have to worry about that right now."

"Who is going to make dinner when you get distracted making sure the garage is closed right? Who is going to help you check the windows? Who is going to find the twelfth fork when it's fallen under the china cabinet to keep you from counting into infinity? Do you have any idea how much work it is living with you? And maybe somehow this all ties back to the divorce, but you won't talk to me about it. If I don't know what's wrong, how am I supposed to do anything to fix it? I want to spend my time learning how to design rockets instead of spending entire evenings trying to rescue you from your routines. Counting to four a thousand times doesn't make the stove burners more sufficiently turned off!" I'm starting to sound a little unhinged. I definitely feel it.

"I . . ." She struggles to find words. She sits down on my bed and stares at the floor. A thick silence hangs between us.

Finally, she looks up at me, her expression confused and

wounded. "You never invite anyone over because of me?" She taps her thumb across her other fingers. One-two-three-four. One-two-three-four.

My heart pounds deafeningly in my ears as a feeling almost like panic rises at the sight of her counting. "Just tell me how to fix this," I beg her.

Tears well in her eyes. "It's not your job to fix anything, honey."

"Then at least tell me how this happened! What happened with you and Dad? What piece of the puzzle am I not seeing?" I just want to know why she's like this.

"I don't know if I can talk about it." She looks scared and small in a way I've never seen her. Could whatever happened between my parents really have been so big she can't think about it, even now?

"I need you to try." I need this more than I've ever needed anything from her.

She's shaking now. She stands up and paces the room, and I can see an internal battle waging.

"Please," I say more softly.

"Okay," she finally says, not sounding at all certain. "Okay," she says again, seemingly more for herself than for me. "Maybe it's time we talked about some hard things you don't remember. Maybe it'll be easier if I show you."

My heart pounds with fear, because suddenly we are in completely uncharted waters and I have no idea what she's going to say next.

"Come to my office," she says.

I obediently follow her down the stairs. She flicks on the

light in her office, and we enter the small room. Her desk is so organized that it looks like the distances and angles between objects were measured. Everything is neatly filed, and anything too big to fit in the filing cabinet rests on a big bookshelf beside it. School papers and stupid drawings I did as a kid are all lined up in chronological order on the middle shelves. Photo albums are on the bottom, also in chronological order — starting with her childhood and ending with mine. She quit bothering to print photos years ago, and any she's taken since then are probably filed away on her computer in equally meticulous order.

She sits down on the floor in front of the shelf of photo albums. "Do you remember these pictures?" she asks, pulling out a blue one.

"Yeah," I say. We've looked at these together a thousand times before, and I've looked at them on my own a time or two as well. She hands the book to me and I flip through the familiar photos of me doing stupid little-kid stuff: Wearing my mom's giant sunglasses. Sitting in my dad's lap trying to grab his baseball cap. Petting a cat at someone else's house. Standing outside on a summer morning with my arms outstretched like I believe the world has promise, not knowing just how wrong I was. I wish I could go back in time and warn my younger self that her world is going to unravel and she'd better prepare to try to hold it together.

But the thing that strikes me most are the pictures of Mom: her and Dad at their college reunion, smiling with glasses of champagne in their hands; Mom laughing, on the floor in one of Dad's old shirts, splattered with paint, her roller poised to cover another wall in robin's egg blue (a color I don't even remember seeing in our house); Mom eating corn on the cob at somebody's barbecue, her fingers covered in butter.

This is not the mother I know now. The mother I know now is counting under her breath beside me: one-two-three-four, the rhythm of a song I would like to never hear again.

"What do these photos have to do with anything?" I ask, confused.

"Sometimes I just need to remember what it was like before," she says.

"Before what? Before me?" If she tells me I'm the reason she is how she is, I have no idea what I'm going to do. I can't help existing.

"No. Before him," she says. I think she's talking about Dad until she pulls out several other photo albums and sets them aside on the floor. There's a spiral-bound book hidden behind them, leaning against the back of the shelf. She picks it up with shaking hands, then gives it to me.

The cover stops me cold.

On the front is a picture of a baby on a cloud, and the script reads *In the Company of Angels*. A constricted feeling in my throat spreads until my arms don't feel attached to my body anymore. I try to breathe, but the tightness won't ease.

"What is this?" I whisper, and open the book to a random page.

It falls open to a blobby-looking black-and-white picture. The sonogram has my mom's name at the top: Jones, Lillian.

And a date — from three summers after I was born. I flip a few more pages and find one entitled "Thoughts on Your Name." And right there at the top in Mom's frighteningly neat penmanship it says, "Sebastian Richard Jones."

"We were so excited at first," Mom says, her voice trembling. "We'd always wanted two children, planned for two. We painted the room as soon as we found out we were having a boy."

As she says it, I realize the photo of Mom covered in paint must have been taken in the guest room, which we've never used as anything but storage for her yarn and craft supplies.

It was supposed to be a nursery.

"I was far enough along then that we thought we were safe to tell people, safe to celebrate and plan. To come up with a name. But then I started bleeding." Her voice shakes harder. "I went to the doctor right away, hoping it wasn't anything serious . . ." She can hardly keep speaking. My mother seems so frail all of a sudden, like so much as a word from me might break her.

"But it was?" I ask gently.

She nods. "When the doctor told me there was no heartbeat, I thought my heart was going to stop, too. If I hadn't had you to come home to, needing me . . ."

I cycle through feelings too fast to process them: denial, that this could even be true; anger, that no one ever told me; grief for the loss of a family member I never had the chance to know. Our lives might have been so different. Things add up that never made sense before, like my mom leaving the car seat in the car long after I got too big and moved to a different one. Was it some kind of placeholder for Sebastian? And Dad moving out — I never knew why they first separated, but Dad had made it clear on the phone he had no idea about the severity of Mom's OCD. Mom's miscarriage had to be part of why they split up — the timing was right. Was losing Sebastian what pushed Mom over the edge?

"The doctors couldn't tell me why we lost him. I did everything right. We wanted him so much." She sobs, snapping me out of my head and back into the moment.

"I'm sorry, Mom," I whisper, and I am. For her, for Dad, and for me. I awkwardly hold out my arms and she embraces me, no longer trying to hold back her tears.

My throat tightens.

I had a baby brother who died. Part of my mother's heart went with him.

"There should have been four in our family," she says, weeping into my shoulder.

Four in the family. It snaps into place.

Her obsession with fours isn't random at all.

It's the perfect number because in her head, that was how it was supposed to be.

After Mom and I make a slow recovery and put away the photo albums, I go back to my bizarrely clean room. I try to do some homework, then to read a little bit, but nothing can hold my attention with so many thoughts and feelings crashing through me.

Dad'll be at Grandpa's now, so there's no point in calling him again, but I decide I have to email him while everything is still fresh, before I can change my mind. In the end, it's only a few simple lines:

Dad,

I talked to Mom and she told me about Sebastian.
Why didn't you ever tell me?

After I hit send, I have to lie back on my bed for a minute. As it turns out, I'm not done crying yet. Maybe I'm making up for all the years of being a robot.

I fall asleep for a while and wake up to a photo message from Will that is captioned *YOU'RE MISSING OUT*. He's at the Blazers game with his family and some of his little brother's friends, and the awkwardly angled selfie shows the whole lot of them screaming something or other sportsball-related as a shower of French fries erupts from some indeterminate location off-screen.

And even though I don't like basketball and the scene in the photo looks like the opposite of what I consider fun, I can't help but think that this time, he's right.

I am missing out.

That should have been mine. Mother. Father. Little brother. My eyes are open for the first time, and now I see that the quiet in my house is not just because there are only two of us here. It holds the silence of a tomb and the emptiness of a life that never came to be and the broken promise of a family that should have been.

This is the world my mother has been living in all along.

My phone pings with an email notification, snapping me out of my reverie. I open the message. Dad. He must be up late.

His email reads:

I always felt it was your mother's choice to decide when she was ready to talk about it, and honestly I didn't know how or what to tell you. That time is hard to look back on, even now.

Remember that episode "Vincent and the Doctor"? Sometimes when things are hard to bear I think of this quote: "The way I see it, every life is a pile of good things and bad things. The good things don't always soften the bad things, but vice versa, the bad things don't necessarily spoil the good things and make them unimportant."

I wish things had gone differently, and I'm sorry for how hard it's been for you since I left. I wish I'd known, and I should've come back to visit more often even though you didn't want me to. I haven't been the father you deserve. I know I can't make it up to you, but if you give me the chance, I'll be there for you any way I can from here on out.

I'm so sorry, love.
Dad

I can feel the pain and regret in his words, and where once there might have been anger, now I only feel grief. I want to escape to Starworld, where nothing is real and everything can be shaped by whims and magic, where wounds can be mended and nothing has to hurt.

But the door in the sky is closed. Starworld is gone, and Zoe can't help me now. What we had is just another broken thing I don't know how to fix.

I wish my dad had stayed in Portland and that we had remained as close as we once were. I can't help feeling that if he had, he might have told me about Sebastian years ago. He would have been there for me to confide in about Mom as her rituals worsened. He would have helped me figure out how to help her. At least I might have had one parent who let me have friends over and make messes and be normal.

Maybe I wouldn't have screwed up with Zoe if my life had been like that.

But it's too late now. There is no TARDIS, and I can't go to the past and fix all the broken things that led me here. Only the future is ahead, unknowable and impossible to predict. I'm going to have to scrape up the mechanical detritus on the floor and put myself back together and figure out who I want to be.

In a show of unusual generosity, Mom lets me skip school on Monday and takes a sick day so we can go to OMSI. I'm too tired to argue against it. I barely manage to shower and drag myself out of the house, but once we're there, I admit I'm glad for the distraction from the shitspiral that is my life. There's still a fair amount of unease between me and Mom, but also a sense of relief. The truth about our family's history is all on the table, even if we don't know what to do with the mess yet.

We navigate the crowds of field-tripping elementary school kids, stopping once or twice to check out some of the interactive exhibits. Mom can't resist wiping the touch screens with bleach wipes, but I only notice her counting under her breath once, when she catches sight of a child of maybe six or seven who seems to be confused and alone. Fortunately, his mom appears from behind another part of the exhibit and takes his hand before Mom can go into freak-out mode, but I still watch her like a hawk, waiting for the other shoe to drop.

She finally mellows out a little when we get to the more sophisticated exhibits where it's quieter. The satellite one is indeed awesome, but I surprise Mom and myself by having something to add to the information on almost every display. Talking keeps her focused on me instead of our surroundings, and I find that it's actually kind of a relief to narrate the exhibit. My knowledge is something I have control over and can articulate, unlike the fallout dominating every other area of my life. Lost in explanations of orbital mechanics and propulsion systems, I don't notice the three little girls and their chaperone eavesdropping on us until we exit and head for the café and I catch the edge of their conversation.

"Does that girl work for NASA?" a kid asks the chaperone with awe. "She knows everything!"

I blush, embarrassed, when I realize the little girl is talking about me.

My mom squeezes my shoulder. "Maybe someday, eh?" she says, and I can see in her eyes how proud she is of me.

"Maybe," I reply, ducking my head. There's nothing I've looked forward to as much as leaving, but now that I know everything about what happened with my parents, it's bittersweet. She's trying so hard today—taking me somewhere I like, listening to the things I care about, and putting a lot of effort into not letting her OCD derail our day. Knowing the truth finally gives me space to see her more clearly — how much she loves me, and how much she's lost.

That evening, Mom lets me take the car to Will's. I'm surprised, but not about to look a gift car in the tailpipe. Being able to drive myself should be a tiny thing, but it feels huge. Getting to use the car three times in one week is unprecedented. I could tell it still made her nervous, but between her behavior at the museum and her permissiveness about the car, she seems to be trying. Maybe it's a sign of better things to come, but I don't want to get my hopes up. I can't. Too much of me is still weighed down by the epic fuckery of what happened with Zoe. How am I ever going to rise above that?

When I leave, Mom is settled on the couch winding hanks of yarn into balls in preparation for a new project. It gives me some comfort to see her like that. It's ordinary, it indulges her need to count, but it's safe and organized and harmless. Still, I hesitate in the doorway.

"Are you sure it's okay if I go to Will's?" I ask. Honestly, I considered canceling on Will after the emosplosion of my Sunday with Mom on top of Saturday's disaster. Plus, I feel guilty about skipping school even though it was sanctioned.

She waves me off. "Get out of here for a while," she says. "I guess I'm going to need the practice."

"Practice?"

"At letting you go." Her hands pause on the yarn, and when she looks at me and smiles, I know she's trying to be brave.

I also know she's scared to death.

All in a moment, I understand what our lives have been about. The routines, the anxiety, the suffocating grip. No wonder she couldn't leave anything to chance. No wonder she can't bear to let me go.

"I'm not gone yet," I say, and smoosh in next to her on the couch for a quick hug before I head for the door, taking the deep ache in my chest with me. I still don't know what I'm going to do with all the broken pieces of my life. I don't know how I will ever be okay.

At Will's, I park on the street and trudge up the steep path to the front door, evading the creepy half-eroded garden gnome on the steps. I ring the bell, and a series of terrifying sounds echoes from the other side of the door until Dylan finally answers it with one of his friends alongside him, both of them on inline skates and padded up like a couple of miniature Jaegers, carrying foam hockey sticks that look capable of vast amounts of damage.

"Hey, Sam!" Dylan says. "Will's in the dungeon." Behind him, his friend swings around his hockey stick, punctuating each motion with sound effects that indicate some sort of nebulous violence about to be visited upon the hapless flower arrangement nearby. They zoom off down the hall, skates clattering over the hardwood floors, leaving me to close the door behind myself.

"No skating in the kitchen!" I hear Will's mom call from the living room.

And even though the house is one hockey puck short of total chaos, a sonic boom of loss pounds in my chest. Maybe my home was supposed to be like this, too. Instead, it's always felt too quiet, too regimented — empty somehow, like there was something missing. For a long time I thought it was because Dad left, but now I know it's so much more.

I scurry to the left and take the familiar stairs down to the basement, skipping over the creaky one.

Will's already on the couch playing a platformer puzzle game that I in no way have enough patience for, and his hair looks like Kitty has been making bird nests in it with her tongue. The familiarity of his face pulls me back from the edge a little.

"Hey, Sam!" He hits pause on the game and turns to look at me as I plop down on the couch beside him. "Whoa. Are you okay?" His expression morphs from its usual easygoing smile into a frown of deep concern. I must look like shit.

No doubt my eyes still have dark circles under them from the rough weekend. I stare at the blue earthenware bowl of musty potpourri sitting under the TV and try to figure out how to even begin explaining.

"Remember that one *Final Fantasy* game where you think you're fighting the final boss, but then it turns out you can't stop the apocalypse and it happens anyway? That's my life. The post-apocalypse. World of ruin." I tug at a loose thread dangling from the arm of the couch. It digs into my finger enough to hurt but doesn't come free.

"What happened?" His eyes are wide. He understands the gravity of the situation.

"Everything," I say.

He sets the controller down and mutes the TV.

"So there are some things we haven't talked about this year," I begin.

He nods.

"Zoe, for one." Even speaking her name hurts, and I'm alarmed when a lump rises in my throat. I wage an internal battle with my feelings and my bodily fluids, barely able to keep either under control.

"Did she hurt you?" he asks softly.

"No," I say. "I mean kind of, but it wasn't her fault. I fucked everything up." My stupid eyes well up, but this time I don't try to stop it.

"How did you fuck it up?" he asks. "Nobody is a better friend than you."

His expression is so open, so honest. He couldn't tell a lie even if he wanted to. There's no one else in the world I trust with what I'm about to tell him, not even my mother, in spite of the fragile new honesty between us. Everyone should be so lucky to have someone as kind and genuine as Will for a friend.

"I fell in love with her," I say. My heart aches with the admission.

"I kind of thought maybe that was what happened," he says. "But I didn't want to assume." There is no judgment in his expression — only sympathy and understanding. He's had his fair share of doomed crushes, even if none of them came to quite such an apocalyptic end.

"As we got closer, she helped me understand that some things about my life with my mom are . . . not normal. Or reasonable. And maybe they didn't have to be that way. But all the quirks I developed thanks to growing up with my mom — they didn't seem to bother Zoe at all. We laughed together. We talked a lot, and she never judged me or my mom. It's just . . . I didn't know what to do with someone who actually saw me, all the ugly and awkward parts, and still liked me, you know? I thought she had to feel the same way I did. I thought she loved me, too."

I give him a stuttering, abridged version of what happened when I tried to kiss her. I even tell him about the glow stars. My cheeks burn with shame, and my chest feels like it's caving in all over again.

"You can't blame yourself for falling for someone. You're human." He says it with such utter conviction.

Those words are the ones that break me. Because he's right.

I *am* human.

Not a robot after all.

Will sits there, waiting for me to respond, oblivious to the fact that he just stripped away the last of the protective armor I've clung to as long as I can remember. There's so much I withheld from him over the years to protect my mom — to protect myself — but not once has it made him less steadfast. Maybe I should have confided in him all along.

I take a deep breath, knowing I have more to tell him but still scared.

"After the catastrophe with Zoe, it only got worse," I say. "You should grab a Dr Pepper, because it's going to take a while to explain the never-ending disaster of my family."

He vaults over the back of the couch and rummages in

the basement fridge his mom keeps well-stocked for our gaming days. "You want one?" he asks, offering me a can.

I shake my head.

"Chocolate milk?"

My mouth quirks upward a little. My comfort drink ever since we were kids. He knows me so well.

He hands me a milk box. I stab the straw through and sip it while telling him about Mom, and Dad, and everything I've learned about my family in the past few days. I tell him how confused I am that no one ever told me I almost had a brother, that his death was what led to the crumbling of my family. I tell him how unfair it is that I never knew, that I've been forced to live in my mom's universe where the loss of Sebastian defines everything. I explain how I finally talked to my dad, and I feel like a total shithook for being so terrible to him all these years, but how could I be blamed when I only knew half the story? I tell Will how much I want to visit Dad, but how scared I am to leave Mom alone.

He leans back on the other side of the couch when I'm done. "Wow," he says. "What if you went to see your dad at the end of the semester?" he asks. "It might help to catch up with him, not to mention that England would be awesome."

"Leaving my mom after all this Sebastian stuff . . . I don't know," I say. "Everything is so fresh. I don't even know what it's going to be like now."

"Getting out for a while might help," he says.

"But what if she stops sleeping? Eating? What if she loses her job or suddenly gets sick and there's no one there to help her?" Every time I try to dismiss a worry, three rise to take its place. I don't just need to get some space from her — I need to know she'll be okay.

"She's a grown-up. She'd figure it out," he says. "Her problems aren't all your problems."

Doubts swirl in my mind. How many problems are my mom's, and how many are just my worries and projections? They're so tangled up — our lives, our genetics . . . our routines. And I'm doing exactly what she does: seeing catastrophes around every corner.

I need to know that she's okay, but maybe there is a better way to do that than the constant checking, the enabling, the worrying.

I want her to know that I love her immeasurably, but that I can't show her that love by accommodating her illness.

"Maybe you're right," I admit. Maybe the only way to sort things out is to get some space. The thought scares me to death. But maybe like Mom, it's time for me to be brave. She somehow got by in all the years before I came along, and it might be easier for me to figure out my own issues if I get some distance from hers.

"Damn right, I am," he says, finishing off his Dr Pepper in a giant gulp before tossing it over his shoulder into the recycling bin.

I can't help a small smile at his brash confidence. I hope he's right that space is the answer. Other than Will, there's very little in my life I wouldn't be grateful to get some distance from right now. The idea of running into Zoe when I return to school tomorrow physically pains me. I don't know how I can face her and relive the humiliation of being rejected.

And as Will hands me a controller and launches some sort of dreadful military first-person shooter that I would never in a thousand years play of my own volition, I'm surprised to find that the distraction, and his company, are exactly what I need.

The absence of Zoe still aches inside me, fierce and bright as the gunfire in our game. Every thought of her is a bullet, and every wound just shy of fatal. But as desolate as I feel without Zoe, it means so much that Will is there for me, and that I can always count on him.

I have never been so grateful not to be alone.

Zoe

The week creeps along with no sign of Sam. She doesn't respond to messages, and I don't see her anywhere, even at school. It's as if she's invisible.

I miss her in ways I didn't know I could miss someone. She is the person I'd become accustomed to sharing things with; she's tangled up in everything. The void left in her wake is more painful than I ever would have imagined possible. She is the only person I have ever let my walls down for, the only person who was really allowed inside. I was always so afraid that people would see that I was defective if I showed them my real, unguarded self. But Sam saw me as I am. And instead of loving me less, she loved me more.

She loved me too much. And it cost us both everything.

In the weeks that follow, I occasionally catch a glimpse of her ponytail and hoodie as she plows through the hallway crowds, head down. She does not want to be seen, I know. I struggle between wanting to reach out to her, both because I miss her and because I feel desperate to help her feel okay about things, and respecting the distance she is clearly signaling she wants. But one day I see Will approaching in the hallway—he's impossible not to spot, since his head is basically at a different latitude from everyone else's—and I stop him.

"Oh, hey, Zoe," he says, swiping at his hair and looking sort of shiftily off to the side. But then his face seems to soften a little and he adds, "How're you doing?"

He knows.

My pulse speeds up at the thought of what Sam told him and the worry that they both hate me.

We move over to a bank of lockers to get out of the way of traffic, the sounds of shoes and shouts echoing around us. "I've been better," I say. I don't want him to tell Sam I'm doing great. That seems hurtful as well as dishonest.

He nods, and his deer-in-the-headlights expression speaks a thousand words. He must feel disloyal to Sam in talking to me and worried about what I might say or ask.

I force a small smile. "It's okay, Will. I just wanted to ask how Sam is."

God, he's decent. I see the confusion on his face, the struggle to do right by Sam, and it makes my heart ache with gladness that she has such a good friend.

"She's okay," he finally says. And he shrugs, which I take to mean he does not feel at liberty to say more.

"Good," I say. And then my stupid emotions rush over me like a tsunami and my eyes tear up. I glance down and nod. "That's good." I blink a few times and look back up at him. I want to ask him to tell her that I'm thinking of her, that I miss her, that it's okay, but I know it's a step too far. The last thing I should do is put pressure on either of them.

I need to go before I full-on cry. So I touch his arm and say, "Thanks, Will," and then I disappear into the crowd ahead of the second bell so I don't make us late.

As November pushes forward in a cold, gray drizzle, I try to push forward, too. But Sam is never far from my thoughts. Jonah is scheduled to come home for a long weekend at Thanksgiving, and when my mother suggests inviting Sam and her mom for Thanksgiving dinner, I can no longer forestall talking to her about what happened.

So I ask my mom if we can schedule that spa and lunch day she promised for my birthday. A day for just the two of us seems like the best time to talk about things that matter. Like Sam. And the DNA test I submitted.

So the Saturday before Thanksgiving, my mom and I are at Papa Haydn's for lunch. We're seated at the windows, where we can watch the crush of shoppers scurrying about on NW Twenty-Third Street. It's not a terrible day for it: despite a wet morning, the afternoon is free of rain, and the sun weaves in and out of the clouds.

Mom and I decide to share a salad and a fish entrée so there's plenty of room for dessert, even though I know she won't do much more than taste it. She's so careful about her health, and I don't know if she knows how much I appreciate that.

When our order is placed, I tell her, "Thank you for taking such good care of yourself."

She tilts her head at me.

"You've fought so hard," I say, trying to contain the emotion that begins to feel larger than I want in public. "Ever since the diagnosis. I just . . ." I shrug. "I'm so glad you're okay, and so grateful that you're always on top of it."

She reaches across the table for my hand. "Oh, sweetheart." She takes a breath. "I want to be here for a long time. For you and Dad and Jonah, and, I hope, for my grandchildren someday."

I nod, welling up a little. "I need you, Mom. We all do." I swipe at my eyes, and I don't know if I'm more weepy because I love her so much and am so afraid of losing her, or if it's more fear of hurting her when I tell her I took the first steps to try to find my biological family.

"You're going to make me cry," she says, and she's right. Her eyes are damp already.

I try to smile at her. "Mom, I have to tell you something."

Her expression changes quickly. "What is it, Zoe? Is something wrong?"

I shake my head. "No, everything's okay. But . . ."

I take a breath, and then I launch into it. All of it. Through the baby shrimp salad and the crusty bread and the stuffed trout and a lot of iced tea, I tell her what happened with Sam. And about the DNA test. And about all my sorrows and anxious feelings about both.

Her reaction when she hears about Sam overwhelms me. She gets it. And even though her heart goes out to Sam, she doesn't think it means I did anything wrong. It's all too easy to see what we want to see, she says, and she's so sorry for both of us, sorry that we both have to go through the pain of losing someone we loved. Her compassion at the fracture of such an important friendship means everything to me.

Amazingly, she is equally understanding about the DNA test.

"I'm glad you're searching for your biological family," she says. She pauses as the plates are cleared and dessert menus are delivered. "I know you've always wondered." She smiles, but she looks like she might cry. "I hope whatever comes of it is good. I can't bear the thought of your being disappointed. I've thought about this a lot, since the cancer. The idea that maybe you could find other family." Her chin wobbles. "Maybe there's someone out there who wants to know you, and who would love you. Maybe even your birth mother, who knows?"

I swallow against the lump in my throat. No one could ever take my mom's place — the very notion is repugnant to me.

"I can't bear the idea of not being here for you." She shakes her head, then takes a sip of water. "But when things were worse, I thought about it. And I thought that maybe if I couldn't beat the cancer, I would make sure you knew it was okay with me if you searched. I thought about her a lot — your birth mother. I mean, what would my life be without this woman? Without my Zoe? And I wished there were some way . . ." She pauses, shrugs. "Some way I could thank her." Her voice breaks at the end.

"I should have talked to you about this at home," I say, wiping my eyes. "I'm sorry. I didn't know how emotional it would be."

"It's okay." She sniffles and tries to pull herself together. "Anyway, I'm glad Sam encouraged you, and I'm so sorry about what happened with her. She's such a dear thing — my heart just breaks for her."

I smile bitterly. "I don't know that she'll ever want to see me again."

"I hope she'll come around. In the meantime, I'm here for you. Whatever happens with the DNA test, whatever you decide . . . I'll be right here, Zo."

"Thank you." There is a brief stab of pain at the reminder that Sam might not be a part of it, but at least I won't be alone. For the ten thousandth time, I thank my lucky stars for my parents. I am so unfathomably fortunate.

"Now." She picks up the menu. "How many desserts do you think we can get away with ordering?"

I smile. "This is a birthday gift, so I guess as many as I want?"

She grins. "So be it." She starts perusing the menu.

"Mom?"

"Hmm?" She glances up at me.

"I wouldn't trade you for anyone."

Emotion washes over her face and she says, "I wouldn't trade you for anyone, either, Zoe. Not anyone else in all the world."

And I know she means it. She *wouldn't* trade me for anyone. The truth of it burns clean in my chest, shooting holes in the Theory of Original Defectiveness until it resembles nothing more than the pile of dust it always was.

The winter holidays are warm and bright, and I'm glad to have Jonah home for them — the whole week from Christmas Eve through New Year's Day. We set up our small synthetic tree with wooden ornaments, whose occasional toppling does no great harm. My mom and I mull cider and pop popcorn and make Grandma Betty's Christmas cookies — six kinds. We give Jonah new bird videos and soft sweaters and some plastic model birds, and he is so happy, my heart feels like it might swell right out of my chest. There is a moment when my parents are taking him back to LLV when he becomes uncooperative, but to our amazement, it is over before it even starts. He's doing better than any of us had imagined possible.

I still think about Sam every day, still hope she'll turn up in my messages or in the hallways at school. But as second semester begins, she seems more gone than ever. I don't even spot her ponytail anywhere. When I get the role I hoped for in the spring musical, I have a new rush of sadness at not being able to share the good news with her. And just when I think I can't miss her any more, my DNA results come in.

For a while, I don't even open the email. I wonder if she'd respond, if I told her — if she'd be true to her word that she'd be here for me. But I know it's not fair to ask. I know she needs the time she's taking, and there's nothing I can do about it. So I open the email and am presented with information that feels like a complete miracle to me — me, the safe haven baby, me, the drop-in with seemingly no history. I discover that my roots are in Scandinavia, Great Britain, and Western Europe, with a few scattered odd bits. These are the places my mysterious people came from — these are the seeds of my past.

And yes, I'll sign up to look for DNA matches, but maybe not quite yet. The idea of what might come from that makes me miss Sam too much. I can't stay stuck in this endless loop of hope and disappointment.

I never wanted to let her go, but the dangling threads of our relationship hurt too much. Like Sam, I have to take control of what I can. And when I consider all she did for me, all she gave me, I am overcome with so much gratitude and love that at the very least I want her to know that.

In a way, it's incredible that we ever connected at all. If I hadn't thought to go to the art room in search of things for the *World Over* set . . . If she hadn't agreed to let me use her painting . . . If she hadn't accidentally sent me that text meant for Will . . .

For that matter, I could have been adopted into a different family, and Sam and I might never have met at all.

We are all the products of detours.

I spend the next couple of weeks on a labor of love: collecting the best moments from Starworld into a single document. For Sam. And then I write my final note to her.

Dear Sam,

I hope you're doing well.

I got my DNA test results. I have learned a lot about where my ancestors came from, and someday, when I'm ready, I'll register to find my biological family. I talked to my

parents about all this, and they are both being incredibly
supportive — even my dad, who has taken to calling me
the Viking since learning of my Scandinavian genes. ☺
I wanted you to know because none of this would have
happened without you. I am more grateful to you than I
can say — for that, and for so many other things.

Attached you will find the moments in Starworld I loved
most — the ones that made me laugh, the ones that taught
me what I most needed to learn, the ones that made my
heart sing. I will always treasure Starworld, and the ways
you made it bespoke for me. Thank you for giving me the
fairy tale I never knew I always needed.

I can't say I understand life's random twists and turns, or
what meaning to ascribe to them, if any, but I will always
be thankful for the detour that brought you to me. You will
always have a place in my heart.

hopes the stars hold brilliant things for you

Love,
Zoe

I read the message over twice, then I click send.

As the words *message sent* appear on the screen, my heart
aches with regret. Regret that it ended as it did. Regret at the
pain I caused someone I love. Regret at the loss of a friendship
more precious than a dragon's lair filled with gold and jewels.

But I know it is time to let go.

I close my computer.

Goodbye, Sam.

Sam

The late March weather in London is a lot like Portland: wet and chilly in a way that sinks into my bones. But that's the only thing that's the same. Sometimes I still can't help gawking at the funny-looking cabs or the historic buildings that line every street, and while back home I prided myself on my ability to get around on the MAX, at first I got lost on the Tube nearly every time my dad sent me on an errand.

After some epic meltdowns and frantic calls to my dad the first few times it happened, now I make a point to stop and look around when I end up in the wrong place. I have my phone, I can navigate home, and chances are that whatever area of town I popped up in is fascinating in a way I never expected.

It's how I ended up in a random alley near Hyde Park pressed against the wall, wide-eyed as a bunch of horses clopped by with cheerful helmeted riders.

It's how I stumbled across Gay's The Word, a bookstore where I found the first sci-fi book I've ever read with a female protagonist who falls in love with another girl. I hugged it to my chest after I finished reading, trying to cling to the spark of hope that one day I might get my own happy ending.

So much more is possible than I ever knew. I'm figuring out how to get lost and found. I'm discovering that life can take me in unexpected directions — like graduating in December, visiting Dad, and then accepting an internship offer at his engineering firm so I can spend my last semester in London before college. I'm finally getting to know Dad again and having the pleasure (or misfortune) of expanding my knowledge of pranks and dirty jokes thanks to Grandpa's terrifying repertoire of both. I'm using every opportunity to destroy them and their friends at poker. Most of all, I got the distance from Mom that we both needed. I'm learning that I have anxiety, even if it's not OCD, but that it's something I can work on. It's part of me and I'm learning to manage it one day at a time.

As for Sebastian, he's slowly morphed from my parents' lie of omission and the catalyst of my mom's decline into something else: my brother.

Now that I know he existed, sometimes I let myself think about what growing up with a brother would have been like. Maybe I would have borrowed his hoodies once he got taller than me. Teased him about his crushes. Taught him to play my favorite games and had him teach me to play his. I wish he'd been there to grow up with me so maybe Mom would have been there, too. So maybe Dad would have stayed. So my family might have been different, better, whole.

And even though he never got to see this world, I wish I could tell him how much he would have been loved.

Instead, I'm navigating my future myself, sometimes well and sometimes ineptly — and learning to be okay with that.

At my internship one Friday afternoon, I manage to come up with an improvement to a testing algorithm we've been bogged down in for weeks. The two junior engineers I work with, Nakul and Ed, are so excited, they bounce around the room like Ping-Pong balls. We celebrate by raiding Ed's Cadbury stash, which he reserves for special occasions such as surviving a date without saying something stupid or when the CEO nods at him in the loo. After we're so stuffed with chocolate our stomachs hurt, Nakul calls my dad in to show him what I've done.

As Nakul walks my dad through the adjustments I've made to the algorithm, I catch my dad's eye. Pride radiates from him so strongly, I can feel it.

"You really came up with this all on your own?" he asks.

I shuffle my feet. "Yeah. It wasn't too hard once I figured out the problem had to do with time, not quantity. The new algorithm takes both into consideration so it can be applied more broadly."

Dad beams. "Well, isn't that just the dog's bollocks." The warmth I feel at his pride manages to temporarily counteract the meat-lockerish temperature of our office. "Sammy, why don't you leave a few minutes early and get us a table before the rush? Buy yourself a pint and the rest of us will finish up here and be along shortly." He hands me a twenty-pound note.

Ed and Nakul high-five at the prospect of starting their Friday night early, and I grin. The engineers are my kind of people. They make math jokes that it takes calculus to understand, and I never miss the punch line. I fit in better than I ever did back home, and working with the engineers gives me room to speak up instead of trying to make myself disappear.

I pack up my things and take the lift down, then head out into the chilly afternoon. It's not raining, for once. The days finally feel like they're getting a bit longer, and it's nice. Somehow the passing of a season makes my presence here feel less like a vacation and more like something real, even if I don't intend to stay forever.

Halfway to the pub, my phone buzzes in my pocket with an email notification. I pull it out and am not surprised to see it's from Mom. We usually talk on the phone every weekend and email a few times during the week, and I find that the distance helps us communicate with more honesty. I smile at the article she sent me a link to — the formal announcement of the new VPs at her company. She told me a few weeks ago that she got her promotion, but somehow this makes it that much more real.

The truth is, she may have finally made vice president, but she's had a lot of victories that make her promotion look minor in comparison. She started going to therapy not long after I left. She returned to her old Stitch & Bitch group, which she talks about a lot. She's even coordinating an effort to knit blankets for a local women's shelter. I'm happy for her even though I still worry. I know she still struggles with routines, based on the times I sometimes receive her emails or texts, and occasionally I hear the familiar sound of window latches or catch her counting under her breath while we're on the phone. But she's working on herself. She often tells me she misses me, but these days it usually sounds more loving than frantic.

And although there are many things I am enjoying here, I miss her, too.

Down the street I pause in front of the pub, feeling a little surge of nervousness. A few clusters of people are already gathered outside, standing around near the entrance and enjoying the "nice" weather. Dad hasn't ever sent me to the pub by myself before, and though I've gotten used to our customary post-work pints on Fridays, it still feels strange to go to a bar when I'm only eighteen.

I step inside and walk up to the counter to order. The place smells like old wood and wet wool under subtle notes of stale beer and frying fish. While I wait for service, I take a moment to be conscious of my feet resting on the worn wooden floor, how I'm rooted to the ground, reminding myself to put my heart where my feet are. It's something Mom told me she's been trying to do lately. It helps her handle anxiety over new experiences, or to come back to the present when she needs to stop thinking about the past or the future.

It's a new thing, that: the notion that a heart belongs where you set down your feet, where you are in a moment. For her, not in the past, in a baby book on the bottom shelf in her office, or some fear-stained version of the future in which something terrible happens to me. For me, not perpetually lost in daydreams, wishing I were somewhere else or trying to disappear.

The bartender I like best finally comes over to take my order. She smiles when she sees me. Today she's wearing a *Planet Quest* T-shirt, and her long hair is in a messy side bun. She seems to be perpetually trying out some new hair color. Today it's fading indigo, like she dipped her hair in the twilight sky. She can't be more than a few years older than me — maybe a student at university. She looks like she studies art, but I've never asked.

"Where is your harem of men today?" she teases.

I smile. "They're on their way."

"Let me guess — a cider for you while you wait? We just got a new one this week from up north. It's dark and dry — I think you'll like it."

"That sounds great," I say, impressed that she remembers what I usually get.

"Right, then! I'm on it like shit," she says, and then her cheeks go bright red. "I mean, I'm on it like flies . . . never mind." She scurries off, laughing nervously.

I laugh too. As it turns out, now that I pay more attention, I'm not always the most awkward one in the room. Awkwardness isn't even the personality flaw I always thought it was. Sometimes it's funny — or in the bartender's case, pretty cute.

With Grandpa as my role model — a hilarious, outspoken man whose curses are colorful as a rainbow and who makes no apologies for his lack of filter — I'm trying out this new thing where I sometimes say things out loud that I used to only let exist in my mind. Even if they're a little weird. Even if profanity sometimes slips out in unexpected ways. Sometimes I embarrass myself. Mostly people smile or laugh, and to my surprise, I kind of like that.

"Your hair is awesome," I tell the bartender when she returns with my drink.

"Thanks!" She smiles brightly, a little less flustered now. "I'm Eliza, by the way."

"Sam," I say, extending my hand over the bar.

She has short nails with chipping dark-blue nail polish, and her handshake is warm and firm.

"Your usual table looks like it's about to free up if you want to grab it." She points to the coveted spot near the windows in front.

I pick up my cider and glance over to where a group of tourists in casual clothes are just standing up to head out.

"I'm on it like shit," I say.

We both laugh.

As Eliza turns to help the next patron, I slip away from the bar and snag the table, taking a sip of the cider she chose for me. It's dark and full-flavored, but not overly sweet. Heaven. I cast a glance back and catch her looking at me. This time I blush.

Is she checking me out? Do I want her to be?

I don't know.

But I'm okay with that.

The truth is, a big part of the reason I'm going to be okay

is Zoe. Through her eyes, I learned to see myself as someone funny, creative, and worthy instead of weird, inept, and robotic. She saw me in a way I was never able to see myself. She helped me figure out who I want to be.

Now I work every day at becoming that person.

I think back to what she sent me last week: her favorite parts of Starworld and an email that almost broke my heart all over again. I'm not ready to look at Starworld yet, but I think one day maybe I will be. The knowledge that she's learning about where she came from, that she couldn't have done it without me . . . it makes me wish I could reach out and let her know how glad I am for her even though the happiness is bittersweet. I still wish things could have been different — that she could have returned my feelings or that I could have somehow avoided fucking things up. I feel worse about how much it must have hurt her when I disappeared.

But even though there are painful memories, there will never be a day I don't remember what it felt like when someone saw me for the first time, in spite of my determination to stay invisible, and wanted me in a way that was uncomplicated and true and kind. There will never be a day I'm not aware that she altered the course of my life simply by being herself and giving me the gift of her friendship.

She taught me so much.

I am *not* invisible.

I am *not* a robot.

So now I try to let myself be seen in small ways — by adding to the lexicon of f-bomb variations, or by sharing my drawings with people once in a while. I doodle gifts for my coworkers and painted a psychedelic moonscape for Dad's flat. And even though all I'm doing for now is fixing other people's math at an internship where my contributions are small, I know someday I'll find a way to engineer rockets that send people to explore the real wonders of the cosmos, not just the galaxies I make up.

These are the ways I pay tribute to Zoe and to Starworld.

To the friend who changed me forever, and to the place that made it possible.

·Epilogue·

October in Portland is true to form: rain, rain, and more rain, a vast swath of gray that frames a wide canvas of gold- and fire-splashed trees. Now, though, it's dark as I hurry across the campus from the Performing Arts Building to my dorm. There is a Halloween party in a while, but first I have a package to open. I've been carrying it around for hours. Sam's lush handwriting is unmistakable, and although I feel fairly steady where she's concerned most of the time, I'm pretty sure I don't want to open this in public.

In my room, I slip off my damp jacket and close my blinds, which takes a minute; my dorm room has a lot of windows. I would have been a lot more excited about Reed if my father had told me that residence halls included ones like this: a renovated 1920s cottage, complete with kitchen and fireplace and sun porch. The hours I spent envying my friends' faraway college plans were a waste; I couldn't love any college more than I love Reed. My classes are challenging, the Theater Department is amazing, and the student population is a study in diversity compared to high school. And free lunches with my dad, plus my curator mom nearby to help decorate my room . . . How lucky can one person get?

I set the box on my desk and reread the return address. Champaign, Illinois.

She did it. She broke away. She's halfway across the country, doing exactly what she dreamed of doing.

I split the taped seal with scissors and pull the flaps open.

At the top of the box, on a mound of packing material, is a colored-pencil drawing done on a large piece of thick card stock. A deep-blue sky studded with sparkling stars fades at the bottom into an ocean. On the left, waves crash onto the beach Sam once made for me in Starworld, with crystals hanging from trees to cast rainbows over the waves. A robot that must be the Fairy Godbot stands beneath the shelter of the branches, looking out over the ocean.

I flip it over to find a message scrawled on the back.

> Zoe,
> I hope you can forgive me for a lot of things, including the delay on the fulfillment of the third quest: the most perfect treasure in all of Starworld. I always knew what it was, but it's important to me that you see it, too.
> Thank you, Zoe. I will always be grateful for your friendship.

unlocks the door in the sky
flies Humphrey through in search of the next adventure
leaves door open
Sam

Something shifts sharply in my chest as I remember how happy her messages used to make me. She gave me laughter when I was hurting. Company when I was lonely. Adventure when I felt trapped. Love when I was riddled with self-doubt.

I never dreamed she would fulfill the third quest. I never thought I'd hear from her again.

I'm glad about so many things. Glad she left Portland. Glad she sounds okay. Glad she doesn't hate me.

Mostly, though, I'm glad I knew her.

I set the card down on my windowsill, peeking through the blinds out over the baseball diamond. A group of boys dressed as various food items gallops toward my building. The hot dog—a tenor from my a cappella group named Miles Parker—attempts a cartwheel and lands on his ass in the wet leaves, making me laugh. It's me he's coming for, and I'm reminded I need to hurry to change for the Halloween party. Fortunately my mustard bottle costume means I won't have to bother with makeup.

I turn and set the box on my bed. It's light; it seems to be filled mostly with packing peanuts. I finally find a flat object inside, wrapped in layers of newspaper. I peel it away, sheet by sheet, filled with anticipation to finally know the answer to the question that has haunted me for nearly a year: What is Starworld's most perfect treasure?

When I pull off the last sheet of paper, an ornate silver oval is revealed, the back of which matches the vanity tray set she gave me for my eighteenth birthday. She held back one of its pieces?

When I turn it over, I find my own image looking back at me.

My breath catches as I realize what she's done.

Oh, Sam.

There is no star so bright, no sky so vast, no galaxy so beautiful, as the gift of love. Of being seen, and known, and loved, even when — *especially* when — all you see when you look in the mirror is imperfection.

But the view of myself through Sam's eyes, the way she saw me inside my walls . . . It is who I would like to be. And, maybe, if that is what Sam sees with her astonishingly keen eye and her beautiful human heart . . . Maybe it is who I already am.

I hold the mirror to my chest, my heart aching.

A light knock comes on the door, which is open. "Zoe? You ready?" Miles peeks in. His smile is quickly replaced with a look of concern. "Are you okay?"

I nod and wipe at my tears. "I just need a minute."

He comes over and gives me a shy smile. He doesn't press for information, and he doesn't try to kiss me. We're at that in-between stage where it's not quite official. He's a slow mover and that is A-okay with me.

"Package from home?" he asks, nodding at the box.

I shake my head, still holding the mirror to my chest. "It's . . ." I search for words. "It's a gift. From a friend." I reach for his hand and give it a squeeze. "I'll just be a minute."

He nods. "No problem. You sure you're okay?"

"Yes." And I am. I am more okay than ever.

He takes a step backwards. "Okay, I'll wait outside. Want me to take that box down to the recycling for you?"

"Sure, thanks." I hand it to him.

He takes it and turns to go. "Hey, is that a new picture of Jonah?" He peers over at the frame on my dresser, propped next to my vanity set. Other framed photos fill the space: one of Cammie, Syd, Erin, and me at graduation, one of just me and Cammie, one of my parents, one of me and Jonah with my parents from when we were little. All reminders of the safe haven that has been my life.

"Yes — isn't it great?" I step over to look at the photo with Miles. It's Jonah in the resource center at LLV, a tambourine in his hands. His eyes are closed and he's smiling, and it reminds me that he's okay, even though he misses us. And knowing he's okay . . . it's everything. "My friends and I did an instrument drive for Little Lambs Village, and the music director sent this picture from a summer concert the residents put on."

"Aw. He looks happy," Miles says.

I nod, my heart tugging in all directions. "Yeah." When I glance up at him, he's smiling at me. My heart tugs in his direction, too.

He holds up the empty box. "Okay. I'll take this down and then I'll wait out there."

"Thanks," I say, closing the door behind him. When he's gone, I hold the mirror up to my face one last time, then set it on the vanity tray where it belongs.

With the fulfillment of the third and final quest, it strikes me that Starworld is a complete story now: it has had a beginning, a middle, and an end.

But when I turn Sam's card over, a line catches my eye: *leaves door open*

When it dawns on me what she means, I race to the door. "Miles! Come back! I need the address on the box."

When I hear him pounding back up the stairs, box in hand, I grab my phone and open my contacts list.

Because an open door is not an end.

It's a detour waiting to be taken.

RESOURCES

As with all narratives, Sam's and Zoe's stories are individual and are in no way meant to represent all experiences with mental illness, pregnancy loss, disability, or adoption. Sam's experience living with her mother is only one dynamic that could exist between a parent with OCD and their child. Zoe's feelings about being a safe haven adoptee and having a disabled family member are only one form such a story might take. To help acknowledge the variety of experiences that might exist around these issues, we've compiled some resources below and encourage our readers to learn more.

Obsessive-Compulsive Disorder (OCD)

As Sam notes in the story, finding information for family members (particularly children) of those who live with obsessive-compulsive disorder can be challenging. Below are some resources that aim to educate friends, family members, and others about how to be better allies for those with OCD. In addition, we strongly recommend reading both fiction and nonfiction by those who live with OCD to better understand the disorder and the wide variety of forms it can take.

Education and Resources

International OCD Foundation: https://iocdf.org

Beyond OCD: http://beyondocd.org

American Psychiatric Association's OCD resource page: https://www.psychiatry.org/patients-families/ocd

Research Papers

"Living with parents with obsessive-compulsive disorder: children's lives and experiences." https://www.ncbi.nlm.nih.gov/pubmed/22903894

"Children of parents with obsessive-compulsive disorder — a 2-year follow-up study." https://www.ncbi.nlm.nih.gov/pubmed/12662254

Recommended Reading

The OCD Stories: http://theocdstories.com

Pregnancy Loss

Sam's mother's struggle with OCD after pregnancy loss is based on real-life research. Many cases of OCD are unrelated to trauma, but trauma can trigger or exacerbate existing anxiety disorders. Post-traumatic stress disorder, anxiety disorders, and depression are all common after the loss of a pregnancy. *In the Company of Angels: A Memorial Book*, which Sam's mother uses to memorialize Sebastian, is a real book and can be purchased online.

Education and Resources

Return to Zero: H.O.P.E.: http://rtzhope.org

Share Pregnancy and Infant Loss Support: http://nationalshare.org

Miscarriage Matters: http://www.mymiscarriagematters.org

Miscarriage Association (UK-based):
https://www.miscarriageassociation.org.uk

Research Papers

"Anxiety disorders following miscarriage."
https://www.ncbi.nlm.nih.gov/pubmed/11465520

"Post-traumatic stress, anxiety and depression following miscarriage or ectopic pregnancy: a prospective cohort study." https://www.ncbi.nlm.nih.gov/pubmed/27807081

Disabilities and Ableism

Regarding disability, perhaps the most important thing we can do is strive to create a more inclusive world — one in which people with disabilities are seen as part of human diversity. As readers, we can seek out narratives by disabled writers in order to see the world through their eyes. As people, we can find ways to challenge ableism and make our communities accessible to everyone.

Education and Resources

For Educators
The Anti-Defamation League (ADL):
https://www.adl.org/education/educator-resources
/lesson-plans/understanding-and-challenging-ableism

For Allies
Stop Ableism:
http://www.stopableism.org/p/what-is-ableism.html

Integrated Community Services (ICS): http://www.connectics.org/latest-news/2016/6/21/what-is-ableism

Recommended Reading

Nijkamp, Marieke, ed. *Unbroken: 13 Stories Starring Disabled Teens.* New York: Farrar, Straus and Giroux, 2018.

Disability in Kidlit: http://disabilityinkidlit.com

Adoption and Adoptees

The range of adoptee experiences is vast, and while there are often common threads, no two adoptees' stories and feelings are identical. An array of resources can be found at the National Council for Adoption website at http://www.adoptioncouncil.org/resources/general.

ACKNOWLEDGMENTS

While *Starworld* initially came to life between its two authors, it never would have become a book without the countless contributions of other people.

As always our agents played a key role in shaping the story and finding it the best possible home. Thank you to John Cusick, Molly Cusick, and Alexandra Machinist for your industry savvy, time, and dedication.

The entire team at Candlewick stepped up to make *Starworld* as magical as possible. Thank you all for believing in the book and giving us so many fantastic opportunities. Special thanks to Pam Consolazio for the gorgeous cover, Sherry Fatla for the thoughtfully designed interior, and Anna Gjesteby Abell and her team for the epic marketing plan. Thanks to Erin DeWitt, Maggie Deslaurier, Matt Seccombe, and Emily Quill for your careful eyes through the copyediting and proofreading process. Most of all, thank you, Kaylan, for being the most thorough and thoughtful editor, never one to shrink away from asking hard questions or working to make a book the best it can be. We were so lucky to have you as an editor and an advocate through the publication process of this book.

Our earliest readers did us a monumental favor by helping us make our first beta-ready draft stronger and more sensitive. Thank you, Katherine Locke and Marieke Nijkamp, for your care and insight, and Rafe Posey, for your thoughtful reads and help wrangling facts, places, and details. A special thank you also goes to Gabe Weiner, story oracle extraordinaire, for your brilliant feedback on an early draft of the novel — and for fielding countless questions about teens, high school, theater, and other subjects. And Mia Drelich always cheerfully responded to pleas for help with speedy answers and brilliant ideas. Much gratitude is owed to plot wizards Kali Wallace and Helen Wiley (who beta read twice!) for detailed critiques of later drafts. And Casi Clarkson, thank you for generously providing notes based on your long career working for the State of Texas Department of Aging and Disability Services.

In addition to the contributions of our beta readers, we are so grateful for the time and input we received from Dr. Barbara van Noppen, assistant professor of clinical psychiatry, assistant chair of education, and codirector of the OCD Treatment and Research Program at the Keck School of Medicine, Department of Psychiatry at the University of Southern California. Your expertise helped add so much nuance to Sam's relationship with her mother, and your care for the people you work with came through in all you shared with us.

Finally, the sensitivity readers we worked with closer to publication made all the difference in helping us do the best work we could in thoughtfully portraying secondary characters with mental illness and disability. Any shortcomings or inaccuracies that still exist in the narrative are entirely our own. Thank you to Jacqueline Reineri (aka Claerie Kavanaugh), Gretchen Schreiber, and Erin Servais for your professionalism and thoroughness. You gave incredibly helpful feedback on tender subjects with grace and dedication.

As usual, a bottomless well of thanks is owed to our families for their support and company in times of both joy and stress. We couldn't do what we do without you.